Love Understood

A Collection of stories

by

James B. Cole

Library of Congress Control Number (LCCN): 2026902028

ISBNs:
eBook: 979-8-90224-073-0
Paperback: 979-8-90224-074-7
Hardback: 979-8-90224-075-4

Published by:
Authors Publishing House
178 Broadway, 3rd Floor, #1343
New York, NY 10001, USA

Main Line: (855) 624-0155
Email: support@authorspublishinghouse.com

Table of Contents

ACKNOWLEDGMENT

This book, which you are about to read is for pure pleasure only and nothing more! The names have not been changed to protect the ones involved, and anyone who may think they are included will be disappointed. However, every individual will have to read this book to learn if you were included or not. Each event included "a happening" that has taken place within the few years of my personal forming and teaching career. As you read the book, page by page, try to understand just how beginning my life and beginning a teaching career starts out in a new (somewhat removed) small community mountain town. Please do not feel sorry for the writer in any way, because the writer had enjoyed living each second, and reliving each second as the volume developed over a period of years. Writing this book was a true experience of reliving events from many years ago.

When my brother was ill, I would schedule my work to have time to spend together. During our visits we talked about many things, and one was for me to get my book published. He knew that I had "filed away" writing articles for years. For his encouragement to complete the book, I am dedicating this book to my brother, Clifford P. Cole, II. Congratulations BUDGIE!

Along the way there are people whom I am happy to recognize for their assistance.

First and foremost, my dear friend, Norma Jean Smither, for her many hours of typing, editing, and publishing the final copy of the book for printing.

I thank my home support, Kathy Cole, wife; Mary Cole Fangman, sister, for editing. Also, thank you to my family for allowing me to collect materials for the purpose of writing and publishing stories about the family.

INTRODUCTION

As the title projects, that **love was understood** in the family because no member of the family expressed love with hugs, kisses, or verbally stating that we loved each other. Even though we each would do things for one another, do jobs together as two or sometimes as a family group and we knew that we all had chores to do as we lived on a large dairy farm. On the farm we had pigs/hogs, sheep, goats, mules, horses, milk cows, turkeys, cats, dogs, guineas, geese and chickens; of which provided much needed food for the family. Yes, we had two years of hard luck back-to-back, and times were really hard due to dry weather and happenings that took place that only Mother Nature was controlling.

We were always clothed nicely, fed well, kept clean – clothes and body; worshipped together and the workdays were never ending from day to day on the farm. We were taught at a very early age to be giving and that you do not express your feelings openly but hold them in and only talk to family members when you really do have a major problem and love was always understood. Along with this lesson we were taught that you do not discuss family business with anyone outside the home regardless of conditions and setting.

As of today, at the age of 69, we were never told by our parents that they loved us. They did not kiss us. Nor have I been told by my siblings that they love me. Likewise, never being told I was loved, nor have I told my siblings that I love them – **love was always understood!** We always worked together, the children went to school together, we worshiped together in Sunday school, we traveled together from the farm in Shelbyville, Kentucky, to Lexington, Kentucky, to visit aunts, uncles, grandparents and other relatives when any need developed.

Now that the reader knows some background about the kind of love our family shared, perhaps this fact alone will assist you in understanding many of the entertaining stories that will be forthcoming!

My family and I will be my personal experiences to write about. These are true stories of my life to my family, community and country.

In the development of these writings a decision was made to incorporate some of our favorite things and some of those would be recipes from long ago that my mother and Grannie Southworth used. Some of the most favorite recipes that have been handed down through the family. One very special recipe would be that of Jam Cake and Caramel Icing that will be shown further back within the publication. The Jam Cake is now in its fifth generation, and each generation has added or changed something from the original recipe. Our mother took out milk and added buttermilk. Once I received the recipe, I added apple sauce that gave the cake a new taste for everyone to enjoy! Plus, I used strawberry jam.

COLE'S JAM CAKE

2 ¼ c. flour

1 tsp. baking soda

½ tsp. salt

1 tsp. cinnamon

½ tsp. ground cloves

½ c. shortening

1 c. sugar

3 eggs

1 c. jam (I use strawberry)

¾ c. buttermilk

1 ½ c. applesauce

chopped nuts (optional)

Carmel Icing:

1 stick butter

1 c. packed brown sugar

½ can evaporated milk

powdered sugar

Mix all dry ingredients. Mix all liquid together. Mix both together.

Bake at 350° 40-50 minutes for a 9 x 12 inch pan, 25 minutes for cupcakes, 45 minutes for a loaf pan. Ice cake with:

Carmel Icing (never fail) Melt butter, brown sugar, evaporated milk and boil for one minute. Remove from heat and allow to cool completely! Once the mixture has had time to cool completely, Start adding powdered sugar, until you have the desired softness. If mixture becomes too thick, add 1 tablespoon of water at a time, Until you have the desired softness.

NOTE: My grandmother took out milk and added buttermilk. My Mother added applesauce and I took out the blackberry jam and added strawberry jam. By adding strawberry jam, the cake has gone to another level of taste and texture. When you use this recipe your challenging moment will be to change something in the recipe to improve the cake.

This is a true story about a family growing up on a working farm. The farm had every kind of animal and birds. We raised tobacco, silage, corn, hay, chickens and a BIG garden. Having all kinds of animals is why I have such a love for animals today.

Our father would only hire farm help when we were housing tobacco, and that was limited. When he did hire help our mother would cook lunch for all the help and then turn around and cook supper for the family.

My sister, Mary, loved working outside, driving the tractor and truck. She could drive and back up a tractor with a wagon attached (loaded or unloaded) better than anyone!

Mary worked on the farm and milked cows until her senior year in high school. She found the courage to tell our father, with the reason being that she did not want to smell like barn. However, she did help us on weekends, holidays and when school was out. I want to share with the reader the understanding of how our father used discipline. Anytime one or all the children misbehaved we would get a whipping with (whatever was available) tree branch, tobacco stick, milker hose, milker strap, or the barber strap he had in the house. When he hit us, the whipping instrument would leave marks on our butts and our legs. We would have whelps and marks on our bodies for days.

Our mother's mother, Elizabeth, better known as Grannie, was the kindest, most loving, and most helpful person I ever knew. She babysat children for years to make her income to pay her bills and live.

Grannie married at the age of 12, married for 40 years and widowed for 40 years. She passed away at 93 years of age.

I do remember this grandfather, Price, as my family was visiting our grandparents on one Sunday afternoon and he would pick me up and sit me on his lap and give me a drink of his beer. I did not like the beer and spit it out all over him. That's probably the reason I do not care for the taste of beer today or the other spirits either.

Our grandfather, Price, went to the funeral home to pay respects for a friend that had died, and grandfather had a heart attack and passed away at the age of 45.

I would come home and walk over to see my grandmother, Elizabeth. She would be watching TV and U.K. would be playing. She sat there with a jar of peanut butter in hand, with a spoon and just eating away while watching the game.

I never knew my grandfather Cole, but my grandmother Cole was a different story. I was very young (under 2) as I remember being lifted up to see her, because she was bedfast. She always smelled like medication (it was liniment of some kind) and the whole bedroom smelled the same. It was not a bedroom; it was a dining room being used as a bedroom since she was bedfast. When we visited, from time to time, our mother, Maurine, would help my Aunt Maude roll grandmother Cole in the bed and helped change sheets and clothing, etc. Our grandmother had 5 sons that would pool money to pay for the house payments and groceries each month. Living in the house were grandmother, Maude, Asa and Charles.

Another child, Edna Cole Finnell was killed in a car/train accident and left a son, Charles behind. Charles Finnell went on to graduate from the University of Kentucky with a degree to teach and coach.

I do remember Grandmother Cole being mean! Our grandmother had 7 children (in birth order): Edna, Asa, Jeff, Solly, Johnny, Clifford and Maude.

REASON, SEASON OR LIFETIME

People come into your life for a reason, a season or a lifetime. When you know which one it is, you will know what to do for that person.

When someone is in your life for a REASON, it is usually to meet a need you have expressed. They have come to assist you through difficulty, to provide you with guidance and support, or to aid you physically, emotionally or spiritually. They may seem like a Godsend, and they usually are. They are there for a reason you need them to be. Then, without any wrongdoing on your part or at an inconvenient time, this person will say or do something to bring the relationship to an end. Sometimes they die. Sometimes they walk away. Sometimes they act up and force you to take action. What we must realize is that the need has been met, our desire fulfilled, and your work is done. The prayer you sent up has been answered and now it is time to move on.

Some people come into your life for a SEASON because your turn has come to share, grow, or learn. They bring you an experience of peace or make you laugh. They may teach you something you have never done. They usually give you an unbelievable amount of joy and you grow and learn. Believe it is real, but only for a season.

LIFETIME relationships teach us lifetime lessons, things we must build upon in order to have a solid emotional foundation.

Your job is to accept the lesson, love the person and put what you have learned to use in all other relationships and areas of your life. It is said that love is blind, but friendship is clairvoyant.

Thank you for being a part of my life, whether you were a reason, a season, or for a lifetime!

Many of these stories were written years ago and just placed in a file and others have been written as of late. Some of the stories within the volume are 50, 40, 30 or 5 years old as these are memories of what has taken place over the years. Some of the stories may make you laugh, cry, or any emotion in between!

OUR MOTHER (MAMA)

Our mother, Maurine Juanita Dorothy (Southworth) Cole, (we called her Mama) was a wonderful woman! "To know her was to love her" is a fitting description of our mother. She was loved by all who knew her. Her family came first in all things and after that was her love for family. There was the summer Bible School that went on for two weeks at a time and if I remember correctly, it went on morning, and afternoon, and we all participated.

She was a beautiful seamstress and with one daughter she spent many hours at the sewing machine. It was a treadle machine, one that had to be operated by using her foot. She didn't need a new pattern for every dress that she made. All one had to do was show her a picture of the way you wanted the dress made and she could cut it out and sew it and the dress would fit perfectly. Our mother would do without so she could do for her children.

There were a lot of hand-me-downs, as we outgrew something it was passed on to the next smaller member of the family. I was thankful when I got my growth spurt one summer because that was the last of hand-me-downs for me.

If you have worn the made-over clothing of your persons or of older brothers and/or sisters, you will understand the phrase, "cutting down or hand-me-down clothes." If you were an older sibling or lived in more modern times, you may not know enough to sympathize with us younger brothers and sisters. We youngsters of a generation ago felt quite often our greatest humiliation when we appeared in public clad in well-recognizable garments in spite of having been cut down to fit us. Worse still we often had to wear cast-off clothing, just as it was, regardless of our size or shape. As I remember being very short in the early years, I had to suffer agonies by wearing pants that had to be rolled up and bagged at the knee to make the lower part of my legs look like Alley Oop's ample ankles. Having an older brother and sister we never had a problem with having ample clothing to wear.

Back in those days if you lived long enough, however, one comes to the day when one can have a suit, overcoat, or a pair of pants all his own. Never again can I feel as big as I did in my first overcoat. It was bought just for me and not already a relic. Some of us may have forgotten how deep our sense of disgrace was when we had to wear out a pair of our sister's slacks.

Our mother, Maurine, was born in a small town, Georgetown, Kentucky, on October 2, 1917. Maurine had a loving family – father, mother, one sister (who died at the age of seven) and three younger brothers. She had to start to work early in life to help make ends meet for the family.

Many times, she would buy material at the store or would have our father get matching bags of feed at the feed store, so she could make a dress or skirt for my sister; perhaps my sister would take up sewing, too. Sometimes she would find a picture of a dress she liked in the Sears Robuck catalogue. When my sister found a dress that suited her, Mama would, in her spare time, have the dress ready for my sister to wear in a couple of days. My sister had her first "store bought" dress when she was in seventh grade. Back then they would wear these large round skirts with a sweater, a scarf around the neck and the shoes were called saddle oxfords that were black and white.

We were fortunate to have our mother with us for so many years. I was at the age of 75 when my mother went to her heavenly home. I was thankful that the grandchildren in the family were old enough to know, love and remember her. My mother was my hero!

I will now provide you with a written character description of my brother and sister as I believe you will pick up individual characters of each as you read the stories that are within.

I will share with you a story about my sister when I was about three years old. My father was driving an old Model A Ford and took my sister to the little country store with him to pick up a few things for the home and while at the store he bought all of us a candy bar. On the way home my sister unwrapped her candy bar in just moments she started to cry, and our father had the job of finding out why. In a few minutes later he learned that she threw her candy bar out the window and kept the paper wrapper. Therefore, he drove back to the store and purchased another candy bar just for her. Oh, her favorite candy bar then was a Snickers bar and still today is her favorite.

As you are starting to see that **love is understood,** starting with my mother because she never expressed love to any of us while growing up. We were never told that we did something good.

Our mother also served as homeroom mother for my brother and sisters' grade when they were going through school. She would stay up late at night as Christmas approached, making homemade candy, cookies and cupcakes for all the students in the grade with my brother and sister. They were in the same grade throughout school. She would always stop and serve my homeroom grade, too, even though she was not voted as homeroom mother by my class membership. I feel this is another example of **love being understood** as she reached out to all the other children.

To be fair, I will tell you a short story about my brother in later teen years. We were living on the farm in Shelbyville, Kentucky, and he was dating. My sister was in college and left her car home for one week to be worked on with minor repairs, such as oil change, etc. During that week my brother, who was in the army, came home on furlough and made the decision to drive her car on his date one night. On the way home that night he had an accident in Shelbyville, as he went to sleep at the wheel and ran into the office of our family dentist's office. Everyone around, when learning what had happened, said, "Well, you were the first patient of the day," joking of course. Our father told us that none of us would say anything to our sister about the accident, so the next weekend when she came home from college, absolutely nothing was said to her, and the family had the repairs made before she returned. But in later years we did tell her what happened, and she somewhat did and did not believe the story.

In growing up all through the years we were never allowed to back talk our parents. Of course, we, in our own way, had to try and each time we learned what exactly our parents meant when they told us no backtalk. In trying to back talk just once we received the worst punishment, that being a slap across the mouth.

Our mother, throughout the years, as birthdays would arrive, she would bake a cake of our choice and flavor. My brother would have a white coconut cake with coconut icing; my sister would have a spice cake with sea foam icing; I would have angel food cake with seven-minute frosting; our father would have yellow cake with caramel icing; and our mother would have whatever cake she felt like making.

One morning after breakfast, I was on the porch putting on my work shoes to go to the barn to clean the milk room. My parents were in the kitchen having an argument of some kind and all at once I saw my father slapping my mother. I lost so much respect that morning for my father. If I told my brother or sister, they would have said something to my mother, and she would have said something to Daddy, and I would have taken the strap. Therefore, knowing what would take place, I decided to keep it to myself!

Home for a weekend visit, I was working with my father, moving something that he needed moved. In the process of moving it, it did not go as planned. He got mad and all upset, so I kept my distance. When he cooled down, he said, "You're just like your mother." That statement made my day!

Our father made sure that we learned to work. However, he never allowed us to play sports, never took us fishing or hunting throughout our lives while growing up on the farm. Even on a rainy day we worked on building a new wagon for the farm or worked repairing a piece of equipment.

OUR FATHER (DADDY)

Our father, Clifford Perkins Cole, I, (we called him Daddy), was born July 7, 1909, and died October 30, 1983. He was 28 years old when he married (Maurine Juanita Dorothy (Southworth) Cole, who was 18 years of age. They were married, on January 12, 1937, at her home in Lexington, Kentucky.

Our great grandparents were Andrew Jackson Cole 1828 – October 1, 1908, and Sarah (Lowe) Cole 1831 – June 28, 1894. His parents were Jefferson Davis Cole, June 29, 1972 – March 12, 1904, and Mary Thomas (Perkins) Cole, December 26, 1870 – October 7, 1951. Maurine's father was Price Southworth, and mother, Elizabeth (Darnell) Southworth, as noted on their Marriage Bond. They lived in Fayette County, Lexington, Kentucky and had three children. Clifford Perkins Cole, II, January 26, 1938; Mary Elizabeth Cole, March 7, 1940; and James Bush Cole, June 28, 1942. I know this sounds somewhat like parent plan hood – one every two years or so. My family's nickname for me was Jamie. Also, classmates called me Jamie until I graduated from high school.

Our father grew up in Lexington, Kentucky, and actually lived on Versailles Road almost on the Woodford County line along with his seven brothers and sisters who were farmers.

Clifford Cole, II, married Bobbie Jean (Glover) Cole, and they had two children, LaCinda (Cindy) Jean Cole and Kimberley Ann Cole, Mary Elizabeth Cole married Julius Ralph Fangman, (8-2-42, 8-10-25) and they have no children. James Cole married Kathryn Juanita (Conrad) Cole, and they had no children.

Today, LaCinda (Cindy) Cole married Monte Ott, and they have two children: Chad Ott and Whitney Ott. Whitney Nicole Ott married Brandon Lee Mink, and they have two children: Braxton Lee and Wyatt Cole; Chad Ott with no children.

Kim (Cole) Jones married Guy Jones, (4-11-62, 10-23-20) and they have three children: Tyler Preston, Hunter and Lauren. Tyler married Nicole Katherine Staricek, and they have one child: Camilla Claire. Hunter married Julie Leigh Crawford, and they have two children: Georgia Reese and Margo Jones.

I want to talk about the household whipping strap that our father used. Our father, when whipping us, would use a barbershop strap. This strap had three layers. The strap was used to sharpen razor blades to shave faces of men clients. When the strap was in use, it would hit you and the next two layers would follow quickly. Our father would grab us by the upper arm and while whipping us he would always ask the same questions, "Are you going to do that anymore?" When I was in the ninth grade, we were required to take Physical Education and dress out for class. Within that process, I noticed that some of the boys had bruises on their upper legs that were just like mine. That brings me to a question: Did all parents whip their children the same back in the 1940's and 1950's?

Our father was a hard person to work around because he would tell you that you had to do something his way and no other way. In other words, it was his way or the highway! He used his voice to control matters at hand to put fear into you. If you did something wrong (and we did plenty growing up) he would yell at you to the top of his voice. He used his voice (tone) to discipline you and made you feel small and worthless. If that did not work, then he would whip us. Even today I do not want anyone to yell at me because it still upsets me in many ways. As we grew up, we would get a whipping from time to time, but our father was always too rough in the discipline activity taking place on our bodies. I'm sure today, with all the child protection laws, that our father would be arrested and jailed for a considerable amount of time as he was very abusive. He must have gotten his mean streak from his mother! At family gatherings I learned that my father would be talking with his brothers and sister about how mean their mother was when they were growing up.

I remember that my brother would get a beating from our father with whatever my father would pick up to do the job with. Sometimes he would use a milker strap that was used to put over the back of the cow to hang the milker on to milk the cow. Sometimes he used a razor strap if the whipping took place at the house. Sometimes he would use a hose that was used for air to make the milker work. Sometimes he would use a big tobacco stick and others whatever he could find to do the job. Of course, my brother would push my father's buttons to the point that he would explode and react. I kept my distance from him, at all times. I tried not to get caught in the middle while the whipping was taking place.

I truly was fearful of our father because, at a very early age, I realized that he could hurt me or someone else because he was so big, strong, and his temper would get out of control. As time and years rolled on, I became more comfortable around him, but I never forgot how he could be if I upset him or made him mad.

Our father taught all of us one fact on how to survive and that is how to work and earn a living because that is all that we ever did, day in, and day out, until we were grown and on our own. I still do the same today after all these years. I've been told that I never stopped working to rest by many of my relatives and friends.

In reality, our father was a person that was very hard to love, but I did love him even though he never expressed love or his feelings to anyone in the family. I did see my father cry one time when he learned that he had lost a brother, Asa, due to an automobile accident in 1952, and I was only ten years old at the time. Again, in the family **love was understood** and not expressed!

At age 69, it is sobering that I may live longer than my father did. I, and my sister will always remember our father as a young man because we never knew him as an old man. Our father died in 1983 following hip replacement surgery in late October. Back then there was no way of knowing what exactly happened to our father. Some said that he had a blood clot from surgery on his hip. We had no test for screening, and few available drugs were helpful for hip replacement surgery. Our father was 74 at the time of his death.

Our father was a very good person when he was out in public or church, or with friends. However, when he was at home, he was a different person. When something went wrong, he would get very loud with the children and upset. I do believe today that he was abusive when he whipped us. When he got mad, he was explosive while turning into some kind of monster.

In helping my father one day to move something, things did not go his way and, as usual, he steps back and starts yelling. When finished yelling, he said, "No use in talking to you because you are just like your mother!" This was the best compliment he could have ever given me. I had to suppress the joy without him knowing what was taking place.

THE FAMILY

During World War II, life was still in God's hands, and life carried on from day to day. On June 28, 1942, a big boy weighing thirteen pounds and twenty-four inches long was born to Clifford Perkins Cole, I, and Maurine Southworth Cole. Yes, I am a war baby and a big one too! The parents of this "small" child finally found a name for him, and it was James Bush Cole, (named after a banker who gave my parents their first loan to purchase our family farm). James was also the name of one of my great, great, great, grandfathers on my mother's and father's side of the family. Bush was a banker (Jimmy Bush) who was a very good friend of the family. Jimmy left me some money which I received at the age of twenty-one years of age. The birth of this baby took place at Good Samaritan Hospital in Lexington, Kentucky, a long time ago on a hot summer Thursday and I held the birth record for many years to follow.

The family, which consisted of my mother, father, brother, sister, and myself, lived in Lexington for several years of my life. Then our parents bought a big farm, and we all moved to Shelbyville, Kentucky, to operate a large dairy farm. During the first several years of my life I had more fun than any one child could ever dream of having or deserved. When I was four years old, my father took me to the dairy barn to help with the milking of the cows and clean-up duties. Of course, I don't think I was much help at that age, but my father said I did a lot of work. As a matter of fact, he said, "I did more work then, than I do now."

I can truly say one thing, there is no greater experience than living, growing up, and working on a farm; because one can learn so much about so many different things that could not be learned by living in the city, or taught through a textbook. As to the size of our farm, it was large enough, yet small enough to be happy and working together while trying to meet the same needs end goals!

The family, as a whole, played a very important role in my life because we have all helped each other, in our many times of need. My parents, I think, are the most wonderful people in the whole wide world because they have given up so much just to help us "kids."

At the age of twelve, I took Christ as my personal Savior. I still can remember what brought me to Christ that night…the preacher was preaching on John 3:16 which states:

"For God so loved the world, that he gave His only son that whosoever believeth in Him should not perish, but have everlasting life."

Somehow after the sermon was over, I found myself, together with my sister, Mary Elizabeth, down in front holding the preacher's hand and telling him that I would put my life in Jesus's hands and that I wanted to follow him for the rest of my life.

After moving to Shelbyville in mid-June, we had to start right into school about six weeks later. By this time, I was in the third grade at Finchville, the school I attended until completing the eighth grade and this was my first graduation. The next few years of our lives were all about the same. That is: going to school, coming home, changing clothes, going to the dairy barn and milking the cows, feeding the calves, chickens, hogs and doing whatever else that had to be done so I could get back to the house for dinner and/or breakfast.

A short time after dinner we would all go to bed because morning would come all too quickly and the same old things would start over again, and again, and again. That is, unless my brother and I would get into a fight; and I really do mean that we did have big fights. As children growing up on a farm, we were very fortunate that none of us ever had a broken bone or any kind of major or minor surgery.

After finishing grade school, I enrolled in Simpsonville High School, which contained ninth through the eleventh grades. While I was going to this school, the county built a new senior high school. I went to the new Shelby County High School in my senior year and was one of the first graduates from that institute.

The second most important thing which happened in my life, at that time, was finishing high school. I think I can truly say that this was an important event in every individual's life because I feel that everyone is seeking a higher education and this graduation was my second one.

During high school I was a member of many different clubs/organizations which the school offered. Among those were: Wild Life, 4-H Club, Choir, Beta (Honor Society), Annual Staff, FFA, Band, Per Club, Per Council, FTA and Drama Club. My brother and sister were in about the same clubs/organizations; however, my sister was a member of 4H.

There are many things which I can do very well. Among those are cooking, canning, singing, teaching, gardening, and farming. Both my relatives and friends agree that I can cook quite well, but when it comes to singing, they have other opinions. The way I feel is that trying is the most important part. After all, it isn't the job you do, but how hard of an effort you put forth to accomplish the job.

When I was a sophomore in high school, my sister, Mary, left for college at the University of Kentucky. I thought that it was very exciting to be going to college. But not until I was a senior in high school, did I decide that I should go to college also. The deciding factor happened when in my senior English class, my teacher, Mrs. Howard, asked the class members to write a term paper on any subject of our choice. I chose Cumberland College as my subject. Since my sister was dating a young man (a twin, local boys) was attending Cumberland College.

In doing my research, I learned about all the interesting courses offered by the college and decided that college was the place for me and that I would like to major in business education. I feel that I have been more than lucky in having attended college, because I know that many students who wish to have gone do not have the opportunity to ever do so.

During the summers following my graduation from high school I was very busy trying to fill out the information on the application for admissions to college, with no help from the High School Guidance Counselor. About the middle or late part of July, I received a letter stating that I was accepted at Cumberland College. I think that this was the fourth most important event that happened in my life to this point.

After the excitement had blown over, I started gathering my clothes and other things for college. As my mother and sister were helping me to get ready for college my father walked in and asked what we were doing. I spoke up and said I was going to college. My father said, "what?!" My mother explained what we were doing. My father replied, "go ahead and flunk out because all you are going to do is party." Then summer was over and soon it was September and time to leave for college and my father was really upset because he wanted me to stay on the farm. My mother and sister drove me to college and helped me move into the dorm. Never any goodbyes said, hugs, kisses, etc., but **love was understood**. I think that my first year at Cumberland was the hardest year I have ever spent away from home, making new friends, time management of self and keeping family in mind. Also, I ran and got elected as one of the six college cheerleaders which really involved me in extracurricular activities, along with running track and cross country.

During my summers, while in college, I worked several jobs, such as construction work, plumbing and heating. Other summers, I managed a Dairy Queen, and I even taught at summer school.

Everyone says that there is no life like college life, and it really doesn't matter where you go to college or its location, but it is an experience you will never forget.

The fifth important step in my life was to graduate from college and begin my teaching career and I did it in three years.

During my first three years of teaching, I enrolled as a student at Eastern Kentucky University where I earned my Master of Arts degree in business education. Of course, I took all my courses each summer to finish within three summer school sessions.

Since college, my first teaching assignment was with the Paintsville Independent School District in Paintsville, Kentucky, where I taught two years and the following subjects: typing, general business, business English, accounting, office practice, shorthand, and sponsored several clubs/organizations. More will follow on these experiences.

My first year of teaching was something to adjust to as I was the youngest staff member and the age of the next staff closest to me was already 45 years of age. The principal operated the school, much as if it were my life in the Bat House town.

I believe that the first rule of good teaching which should be laid down to students in teaching-training institutions should be, "Don't begin to teach until you are ready; that is, willing to teach." Also, be sure to set an example for your students to follow as most do learn very fast for some reason or the other. Teach them to set goals, challenge themselves, and rise to the occasion.

Do you really want to teach? Or was it all someone else's idea? This was the question I once asked myself when I first started teaching as I wanted to become a teacher when I was in the tenth grade. In teaching you can look for adventure, among many other things. The most important thing is that you should understand yourself and diagnose your attitude toward teaching before you start to teach. Above all, don't start with a 'chip' on your shoulder. You must lower yourself, but not your expectations of the students, but always be one step in front of each student. Never lower your expectations for your students as they will rise up to and above what you expect of them most of the time. Before starting to teach, and thinking of one major question, How to Start? Perhaps the formulation of a few resolutions not made to be broken, is a good way to approach the job of teaching. At least, it's time honored!

After Paintsville, my second teaching assignment was with the Falmouth Independent District in Falmouth, Kentucky, and I went through a spring tornado that really destroyed most of the town. We were having classes in school when the tornadoes went over the school building. The next school year we merged with Pendleton County School District where I taught over the next three years: typing, general business, accounting, office practice, shorthand, basic math, speech-drama, and journalism. I served as sponsor of the following clubs/organizations while I was on the hill: FBLA, Pep Club, Senior play cast, publication of the school newspaper, and best of all, serving as senior class sponsor. With all these activities considered, I also served as cheerleading sponsor for the high school with twenty girls on two different teams – junior varsity and senior varsity.

ON CARING AND GIVING

In growing up, our parents taught and demonstrated by example to us that caring and giving was very important to life and to those around us. The best example of giving is when God gave his only son!

God offers you a life of great joy and a surprising route to take you there. Wherever you are at this moment, God invites you to embark on an adventure…I have always tried to practice this lesson learned.

Begin a journey of a lifetime – a Journey of Generosity. "A generous man will prosper; he who refreshes others will himself be refreshed." Proverbs 11:25

When you share the message of generosity, you live the transformation, multiply the joy, and give rise to a revolution.

Generous giving offers you a supportive community to help you pursue your journey, write your own story, and share the message of generosity with others.

Carried from person to person, the call is great for those who have been entrusted with much concern and skills.

Your journey of generosity is an adventure measured not in miles, but in personal transformation and growth. Sometimes smooth sailing, sometimes uncharted waters, but always a course that deepens your faith and relationship with God and individuals.

This message is not new; it is rooted in the timeless story told in scripture and lived out today...*Explore and experience the generous life.*

"...But just as you excel in everything—in faith, in speech, in knowledge, in complete earnestness and in your love for God and one another – see you also excel in this grace of giving..."

One can give, to make a difference for animals every day of the year. Team up with your local shelter or with a group of dedicated friends like you who make regular daily/weekly/monthly visits to help animals. This level of support makes it possible for any group to reach and rescue animals in need. When you decide to donate your time today, you will help someone to continue to be lifesaving for an animal.

Giving back to others is one of the easiest ways you can contribute to society. So why, then, do so few people do so? For some, the idea of giving away hard-earned money is preposterous. For others, there are just not enough hours in the day to give back to others.

When you can learn the importance of giving, your life will change forever. You will soon begin to seek out more and more opportunities and ways to give. Here are just a few reasons why giving is so important:

Giving opens up more possibilities for you.

When you can find it in your heart and life to give something back to others, you will find more and more opportunities opening up for you.

Giving anything of yourself allows more room for you to receive. The possibilities that come to you when you give are endless.

Giving teaches you to be more thankful.

In giving, the greatest lesson often learned is that you have more than you'll ever need. In this respect, giving of yourself teaches you to be more thankful for what you do have, rather than focus on all the things you don't have.

Giving makes room for you to receive more.

Most of all, the act of giving teaches you and opens up space for you to receive from others and God. Giving is like a secret message to the universe that says you are available and open to receiving gifts yourself. Until you can make space to receive those gifts, you will likely find yourself feeling like you are up against a brick wall.

Giving might seem too simple of a concept or idea for you. If so, you might not be prepared to open yourself up in such a manner. When you are ready to receive bigger and better things in life, the simple act of giving will set the ball in motion.

I am a firm believer in supporting the community you're a part of, whether it's your actual neighborhood or your favorite online sites. A well-supported community gives in return and contributing to it ensures that the community will stick around longer than a few months.

There are several ways you can contribute to your community no matter what you do as a freelancer. The trick is doing something you love, offering it for free and distributing it to everyone you can.

Giving back to the community leads to multiple benefits. You're not only giving to the community-you're increasing your professionalism, especially if it's something very valuable.

Giving something to the community doesn't mean you have to spend all your free time on it either. So, what are some things you can contribute yourself?

Really, Why Do I Care?

When you're first starting out as a freelancer, making free things for the community can often seem like a waste of time and resources. I can definitely understand why. You're barely making ends meet to pay your bills and can't possibly fathom spending so much unpaid time on a project. You will soon learn that's okay.

What's really important is that when you get going with plenty of work that you try to take the time to give to your community. I bet you made use of tutorials, free graphics and books when you started, so why not contribute something as well to help a person who is where you were when you started? It's a fantastic feeling to help someone out and I'll go ahead and admit the extra traffic and attention doesn't hurt your business either.

Think about how a client sees your site. If you've got a ton of free resources and articles/materials on our site, as well as a fantastic portfolio, and the other guy just has a portfolio, which looks better in the client's eyes? It's always the one who takes time out for the community. While you shouldn't ever give just to get back, I promise you'll get back more than you put in.

Switch your outlook by focusing on how and what you can give instead of what you will receive. When you learn to give, you elevate yourself to the vantage point of the wealthy. Business opportunities and ideas will appear when you think about how you can help make other people's lives better, easier, happier. Also, as you give, you will be rewarded with the most lavish gifts from everyone whose life you have changed.

The poor think only about what they can receive; the rich think about what they can give. The poor believe that everything is scarce and that they should hoard whatever they have to themselves; the rich believe that life is abundant. The poor think 'it is either this or that; the rich think 'it is this and that.'

Today, I want you to think about your interactions with others in terms of filling up a bucket and pouring its contents onto those people. With that in mind, let's consider two important factors. First of all, what's in your bucket? Jesus points out several things that we should be doing.

First, what's in your bucket? Jesus points out several things that we can choose to pour out on others-namely, material possessions, love, good deeds, money, mercy, and pardon. It's quite an impressive list. Yet, the Lord calls His followers to an even higher standard. He instructs us to give to "takers," love our enemies, do good to those who mistreat us, lend expecting nothing in return, and grant mercy and pardon to those who don't deserve it.

Why would He call us to such extreme action? Because as God's children, we are expected to treat others the way He treats them—for "He Himself is kind to ungrateful and evil men" (Luke 6:35).

The second factor to consider is the size of our bucket. Jesus says that by our standard of measure, it will be measured back to us (Luke 6:38). However, we are also told to expect nothing in return from those we treat with kindness (Luke 6:35). The ultimate reward for our loving and gracious behavior will come, not from them, but from the Most High God.

What are you pouring onto others each day? By showering them with grace, you display the character of your Father and show yourself to be His child. Use a big bucket full of love and kindness, and you'll discover that the Lord uses an even bigger bucket to lavish His goodness upon you.

Scripture of the day: "Give to everyone who asks of you. And from him who takes away your goods, do not ask them back. And just as you want men to do to you, you also do to them likewise." – (Luke 6:30-31) (NKJV)

Particularly scientific although science and technology can be used as tools for caring (following will be some of the clinic, coming through where I do volunteer work). One can care for things—a well-restored vintage automobile, for example, but in medicine and medical practice the caring must be for patients and for the health and well-being of people. To be totally effective, caring must be communicated and come across to a patient/individual or to the public as something genuine and comforting—something that can engender trust. When developed and used effectively-that is, communicated—caring can become a powerful therapeutic tool for a practicing physician and, perhaps surprisingly, an effective political tool for the medical profession or just human life.

Yet there is evidence that caring is not now the powerful force that it has been and can be in medicine. The beloved horse-and-buggy doctor cared, and gave solace, and comfort has lived its day. True, there often was not much else he/she could do, but their caring was appreciated and society thought well of horse-and-buggy doctors. Now physicians can do more with modern science and technology than has ever before been possible, and many are so fascinated by this that they become so preoccupied by the scientific diagnosis and the scientific treatment of a disease that they seem too often to neglect the care and treatment of the very human person who has the disease. The human caring communication, between doctor and patient or between the medical profession and society is apt to receive short shrift or is simply overlooked entirely. Nor has the compartmentalization of medicine into specialties and subspecialties done much to help, since a result has been compartmentalization in patient care and, therefore, less emphasis on the less scientific needs of the whole person who may be affected in many ways by the trouble in one or more of his or her compartmentalized parts. Now, what is left of caring seems to be threatened by new pressures in health care that are beginning to drive significant economic wedges between doctors and patients, wedges that some think will surely erode and perhaps finally altogether destroy a physician's incentive for caring.

There is already evidence of economic and political fallout from these trends which seem to have been accelerating so rapidly in recent years. Many patients have begun to sense that the care of physicians is less than satisfying to them and have sought care (and caring) elsewhere. This clearly has had and is having economic impact on physicians. In the political arena there is mounting evidence of significant progress by other health care professionals to extend their scope of practice in response to what is perceived as a growing demand for their services. There has been surprisingly little interest among practicing physicians or in the medical profession, as a whole, either in identifying the cause or affecting a cure for what already seems to be a serious ailment in modern medicine and modern medical practice.

Perhaps it is not too late, as we've seen our country saved over and over again. There are soon to be many more physicians, and many of them will have more time on their hands, time that it will be to their economic advantage to use for caring and communicating with patients and the public. It is not to be forgotten that the desire to care for people, as well as their ailments, is why most physicians decide to become doctors in the first place. What is needed now is for practicing physicians and the medical profession to resurrect the human and caring aspects of their great calling, bring them to the fore, and make medical science and technology, and the social, economic and political forces that are so evident today, their servants in this cause and not let them be the masters. This can and should now become a personal commitment of every physician and an organizational commitment of the profession. It may be well that the power inherent in the caring function can serve physicians as well now, as it has in the past. After all, the real and ultimate social, economic and political power in this nation still lies in the hands of the people-people who nearly all will somehow have their lives affected by physicians.

As for "why is caring important" in general, I would say because it ensures relationships between people (a crucial element to life), it is the expression of sympathy (so without caring no one would want to help anyone) and it motivates people to do the things they do. (for example: firefighters put out fires because they care for the people it will effect, police officers catch criminal because they care for the well-being of society…).

In closing, I must tell the story of re-gifting. My wife and I are members of this small Bible group, and we give each other anniversary and birthday cards, etc.

This one person gave us, on our wedding anniversary, a box of chocolates and when we opened the box, we learned that apparently, she had the box of chocolates for a great while as they had turned a grayish white. We did the honest thing as we took the box back to the giver and that is when we learned that she had re-gifted the box of chocolates. Rule of Chocolates, be honest in what you give!

THOSE IDOL CHILDREN

Students are amazing because just when you start thinking that they will not come through is exactly when a student does succeed in class.

Students cheat whenever they find the opportunity. A business career won't change their individual conduct. How many times do we hear this or say it ourselves? True, a student who cheats in high school is not likely to stop cheating others, or him/herself once he/she starts his/her career. Why do students cheat? What are we doing about students cheating? After all, the student is with us six hours of the day and during the very impressionable years. Perhaps if we cared about <u>why</u> students cheat, we would become more concerned that they do cheat.

Have you ever stopped to analyze why so many students seem to be involved in cheating in today's schools? I don't believe there is a simple answer for the reason(s) behind the cheating. In fact, out of nineteen seniors that I have now within the school I teach, I know over three-fourth of the students, cheat. The reason for student cheating became quite evident to me. However, the attitudes and the lines of thinking regarding the excuses for cheating indicated a curious, fallacious reasoning in these young minds.

The school had better improve security. Were criminal charges filed? All tests that were compromised should have been redone and all who took those original tests should have taken the new tests. Those who passed the original test without cheating would also pass the new test. Canceling the ceremony was not something I would have done.

The students should have been retested and their parents, too. It is sad that no one reported this to school or to parents. It reflects on the relationship of students to parents and on the school system. People do not connect cheating with stealing. When one cheats, they are stealing from someone else.

Cheating is much more widespread than people think. Parents put so much pressure on their students that cheating seems like the only way to keep them happy. I'll admit, I know a recent high school graduate who cheated in high school more than a few times. It comes down to, does he cheat and have his parents tell him how happy they are, or does he stay honest and face a lecture about how he could be doing better? I can also say, most of the people with a high-grade point average at my school cheated on a regular basis.

As a former high school administrator, I disagree with the way this matter was handled. It would have been very easy to have the students re-take a revised version of the test vs. cancelling a graduation that was a meaningful milestone for the students. The individuals responsible for hacking into the computer system should not have been allowed to participate in the graduation program of any type. A school counselor or someone with great integrity, whom the students hold in high esteem, could have used this as a teachable moment for the students who took advantage of the hackers' work. I wonder if the principal or superintendent would have made the same decision if his/her child was a potential graduate of this class.

Parents and educators of today seem to believe in this Generation "Y" thing, it's okay not to take responsibility for their errors in judgment. In case you do not know what the "Y" generation is, I will tell you. The "Y" generation refers to the young people that wear slacks/pants very low below the butt line and appears as if they will lose their pants and one can see the "Y" of the cheeks. Just pat the students on the back and say, let's hit the re-start button and "do over," just like a computer game. The real, non-PC world isn't like that. If the parents of the students want to go outside the school and have some sort of graduation, fine, school officials did the right thing. I wonder what sort of punishment these parents dished out to their students. I would bet many, just kind of smiled and patted their student on the back saying, "I like the way you think!"

Students are under so much peer pressure. I'm sure if even one student found out about the whistle blower, he/she would be in great fear of beatings before and after school. That information always gets out and sometimes the one who didn't say anything gets blamed, causing a lot of unnecessary fights. The teachers would be very suspicious if a student got an A on the test but had poor daily work on pre-test and assignments. I say re-test all with a revised test. I just can't see the innocent being punished. Sort them out, if at all possible.

What Exactly is Cheating?

Cheating is when a person misleads, deceives, or acts dishonestly on purpose. For students, cheating may happen at school, at home, or while playing a sport. If a baseball team is for students who are eight or younger, it's cheating for a nine-year-old to play on the team and hit home run after home run.

At school, in addition to cheating on a test, a student might cheat by stealing someone else's idea for a science project or by copying a book report off the internet or turning it in as if it's his/her original work. Copying someone else's words or work and saying they're yours is a type of cheating called **plagiarizing** (say: play-jeh-rise-ing).

How Do People Cheat?

Cheating can happen in a lot of different ways. A student is doing it by sneaking answers to a test, but it's also cheating to break the rules of a game or contest or to pretend something is yours when it isn't.

When people cheat, it's not fair to other people, like the students who studied for the test or who the true winners of a game or contest were.

It's tempting to cheat because it makes difficult things seem easy, like getting all the right answers on the test. But it doesn't solve the

problem of not knowing the material and it won't help on the next test—
unless the person cheats again.

Sometimes it may seem like cheaters have it all figured out. They
can watch TV instead of studying for the spelling test. But other people
lose respect for cheaters and think less of them. The cheaters themselves
may feel bad because they know they are not really earning that good
grade. If a student gets caught, they will be in trouble at school, and
maybe at home, too.

Why Do Some Students Dislike School?

If you don't like school, the first step is finding out why. You might
not like school because a bully is bothering you, or because a student
you don't like wants to hang around with you. Or maybe you don't get
along with your teacher. You might feel different or worry that you
don't have enough friends.

Sometimes it's a problem with your classes and schoolwork. Maybe
the work is too easy, and you get bored. Or maybe the work is too hard,
or you don't feel as smart as the other students. Reading may be difficult
for you, but you're expected to do a lot of it. You may be getting farther,
and farther behind, and it may seem like you'll never catch up. Maybe
you're dealing with worries, stress, or problems that make it hard to
concentrate on schoolwork.

Why Students Cheat?

Some students cheat because they're busy or lazy and they want to get good grades without spending the time studying. Other students might feel like they can't pass the test without cheating. Even when there seems to be a "good reason" for cheating, cheating isn't a good idea.

If you were sick or upset about something the night before and couldn't study, it would be better to talk with the teacher about this. If you don't have enough time to study for a test because of swimming practice, you need to talk with your parents about how to balance swimming and school.

A student who thinks cheating is the only way to pass a test needs to talk with the teacher and his or her parents so they can find some solutions together. Talking about these problems and working them out will feel better than cheating.

Truth and Consequences

Many students feel tempted to cheat occasionally. Most resist and do the work instead. Some students cheat once and feel so bad that they never do it again. Others get caught and decide it isn't worth it. Unfortunately, some students start cheating and feel like they can't stop.

Students who cheat may feel worried about getting caught. Whether they are caught cheating or not, these students may feel guilty, or embarrassed, or ashamed – or all three. Even if the cheater feels fine or doesn't get caught, that doesn't mean it's okay. If you see someone cheating, or if someone asks to copy your work, you can tell a teacher or another grown-up.

Students who get caught cheating might be given a "zero" score on the assignment, be sent to the principal's office, and have their parents contacted. Worse than the bad grade may be the feeling of having disappointed other people, like parents and teachers. A parent may worry that you are not an honest person, and a teacher might watch you more closely the next time you're taking a test.

Making a Comeback

There are plenty of reasons why a student shouldn't cheat, but some students have already cheated. If that's you, it's never too late to stop cheating. Cheating can become a habit, but like other bad habits, a student can always decide to act better and make better choices. It might help to talk the problem over with a parent, teacher, or counselor. Choosing to play fair and be honest again can help a student feel relieved and proud.

There's an old saying that cheaters never win and winners never cheat. This may sound confusing because sometimes it seems like cheaters do win – at least for the moment. But students who don't cheat are true winners because, when they win, they do it fair and square.

Finding Help

It's a good idea to talk to someone about your problems with school. Your mom, dad, relative, teacher, or school counselor will be able to help you. It's especially important to tell an adult if the problem is that you're being bullied or someone hurts you physically.

Another good idea is to write down your feelings about school in a journal. You can use a journal or diary or just write in an ordinary notebook. It's a great way to let out emotions that may be stuck inside you. You don't have to share what you've written with others.

If you feel disorganized or like you can't keep up with your schoolwork, your teachers and school counselors want to help. Teachers want and expect you to ask for help learning stuff. If all your subjects seem really hard, a school counselor can help you sort things out. Special help with schoolwork is available if you need it.

Now, what can you change on the "don't like" list? Would remembering to do your homework help you feel more confident if you're called on in class? Can you get help with schoolwork that's hard? Who can you talk to about a worry or problem you're dealing with? Could you find a way to show off your special interests and talents? If you made just one new friend, would you feel less alone? If you helped someone else feel less alone, would you feel even better? Which activities could you try that would help you meet new friends?

Four predominant reasons were given for cheating: competition, pressure from parents, pressure from peers and indifference.

When a student does cheat, I believe it is because the competition is high or pressure by parents/peers all but forces some students to cheat. For a parent/peer who wants his/her child to get on the principal's list when the ability of such a student is below this standard, there is no alternative but to cheat rather than disappoint a parent or face possible punishment.

Indifference as to the rightness or wrongness of cheating was indicated by one of the boys when he said, "I think many students don't take school seriously enough to see anything wrong with cheating." One of the girls put it this way: "there is just a sense of not caring one way or another." Another boy felt about it in this way: "some selected students cheat to brag about it." Most students agreed that students like to brag about loafing through school or no-the-job and from school to work this habit carries over directly. Teachers and/or administrators derive little comfort from such attitudes that indicate no sense of personal integrity.

No one really wants to talk about the indifference in students. Students are indifferent to standards of achievement. About one-fourth, in any school, will disagree with this statement.

Ideally, students seem to care; they seem to want to live in a world characterized by people of integrity - - and where the value of the person is held in esteem!

When I was teaching, I always instructed the students that no one could keep you from cheating if that is what he/she wanted to do. However, I did tell the students if they insisted on cheating from someone to be sure that they did not give the same answers.

On the next major test, as I was grading each, I noticed that one student on the last question wrote: "I do not know the answer to this question." Would you believe on the next test that I was grading, they had the same answer, but with a twist, for the last questions: "I do not know the answer to this question either." This should tell you something or to get you to think something!

TOO MANY TURKEYS

Being very young but remembering this story about our mother and her turkeys is one not to be forgotten! I was around two years of age, and our mother raised about thirty turkeys, and she planned to sell them all to people for Thanksgiving dinners. She started out in early spring with the turkeys, and they were growing great. As fall approached, the turkeys were at a good size and just several months away from Thanksgiving. To my mother's surprise, the turkeys got out of the enclosed area that they were in, one day, and just at that time, the grasshoppers were plentiful. Mama always said that turkeys were dumb, and you could not do a thing with them. The turkeys proved her right once they finished eating all the grasshoppers in sight.

Mama got all the turkeys back into the enclosed area and all was good, but during the night, once they started drinking water, the craw (this is a bag on the turkeys' neck that holds food until they can process it) on each turkey would swell up and not having ample room, the craw would explode. The next morning Mama was sick to her stomach, but she said she was going to try something because she did not want to lose all the turkeys, so she sewed up the craw on each turkey's neck with needle and feed sack string.

She worked on each turkey one by one until she finished all thirty turkeys and applied medication to help them each heal from the open wound and stitches. After playing doctor for about a week, all the turkeys were back eating and putting on weight. Finally, Thanksgiving week arrived, and Mama killed and dressed all the turkeys for people who wanted a turkey for Thanksgiving. Oh, we even had one of the turkeys on our Thanksgiving table, too! The lesson learned there - - our mother never again raised turkey.

HERE KITTY

Mama let an old orange peregrine fuzzy cat take up with us at the house one spring. The cat became very much part of the family. Several months passed and one night the cat had kittens under the house, but it was several weeks before we would ever see them. Of course, we fed her because she was feeding the kittens, and one day, about noon, the mama cat presented the kittens. The mama cat had three kittens, and each had a personality that matched the names that we eventually gave each of them. All three kittens were males and the color, orange, just as the mother was, and one kitten had long fuzzy hair like the mother and we named this one, Fuzzy. The second kitten was very thin, long, and, somehow, we named it Skinny, and the third kitten was just full of life and ran all the time with loads of energy and we named this one, Frisky.

As summer approached, we played with the little ones every day and they grew to be large cats, much larger than the mother. They all three loved to play with us and if we got a tree branch and left a leaf on it, they would run over each other trying to get the leaf, **as love to these cats was understood.**

RULES DEALING WITH STRAY CATS

Here are some simple rules when dealing with cats and having time.

1. Stray cats will not be fed.
2. Stray cats will not be fed anything except dry cat food.

3. Stray cats will not be fed anything except dry cat food moistened with a little milk.

4. Stray cats will be fed nothing except dry cat food moistened with warm milk, yummy treats and leftover fish scraps.

5. Stray cats will not be encouraged to make this house their permanent residence.

6. Stray cats will not be petted, played with or picked up and cuddled unnecessarily.

7. Stray cats that are petted, played with, picked up and cuddled will absolutely not be given a name.

8. Stray cats with or without a name will not be allowed inside the house at any time.

9. Stray cats will not be allowed inside the house except at certain times.

10. Stray cats will not be allowed inside the house except on days ending in "y."

11. Stray cats allowed inside will not be permitted to jump on or sharpen their claws on the furniture.

12. Stray cats will not be permitted to jump up on or sharpen claws on the really good furniture.

13. Stray cats will be permitted on all furniture but must sharpen claws on new $440.99 sisal-rope cat-scratching post with three perches.

14. Stray cats will answer the call of nature outdoors in the sand.

15. Stray cats will answer the call of nature in the three-piece, high-impact plastic tray filled with Fresh 'n 'Sweet kitty litter.

16. Stray cats will answer the call of nature in the hooded litter pan with a three-panel privacy screen and plenty of head room.

17. Stray cats will sleep outside.

18. Stray cats will sleep in the garage.

19. Stray cats will sleep in the house.

20. Stray cats will sleep in a cardboard box lined with an old blanket.

21. Stray cats will sleep in the special Kitty-Komfort-Bed with non-allergenic lamb's wool pillow.

22. Stray cats will not be allowed to sleep in our bed.

23. Stray cats will not be allowed to sleep in our bed, except at the foot.

24. Stray cats will not be allowed to sleep in our bed under the covers.

25. Stray cats will not be allowed to sleep in our bed under covers except at the foot.

26. Stray cats will not play on the desk.

27. Stray cats will not play on the desk near the computer.

28. Stray cats are forbidden to walk on the computer keyboard on the desk when humans are using it.

THE CHRISTMAS TENT

On the farm is where this story starts as children growing up in the 40's and early 50's. When I was about nine years of age at Christmas time our parents gave the children an outdoor tent and we were told that we could not put the tent up until we were out of school in late spring. Children included my brother who was a middle teenage, my sister who was approaching the teens and me, the youngest of the three.

In Mid-May, when school was out and after dinner one bright and cool full moon night, our parents decided that it was time for us to put up the tent. As you looked up at the sky you could see thousands and thousands of bright shining stars and the glow of the Milky Way striking through the sky along with all the sky characters--big and little dippers, the kit, etc. Our parents were on the front porch resting after the evening meal and a hard day of farm work, the three of us children got the tent out and started to assemble it from the instructions provided. We placed the tent on the ground in the center of the following: the smoke house where my father cured pork – bacon, hams, shoulders and had sausages handing ready to cook, grapes (these were concord grapes and our mother made jam, jellies, and juice that we would use during the long winters for food), chicken house (where we keep our laying hens to produce eggs), peach tree, beside a fence (with a gate going into the chicken lot, where the chickens ran and ate grass and bugs, with running water) and with a peach tree (this tree produced the largest, best tasting and juices peaches of any known) in front of the tent. We felt that we were well hidden from everything – even the dark that was quickly approaching with a full moon overhead.

Now that we had the tent all in place and ready for camping out for the night, my brother asked my sister and me to go to the garage, get an old lantern, put some fuel in it and come back quickly. All three of us got into the tent and my brother struck the match to light the lantern and to our surprise, everything went up in hot flames. Of course, the sky lit up in red, the meat house was on fire, the grapes were cooking, the chicken house was red hot, the peach tree was overcome with hot flames and gone forever; along with the tent. What tent? The grass was on fire! We knew that at that moment, it was about to become one of the worst long hot summers of all time!

About this time, our mother was thinking that the house was on fire and came running through the house to check things out; our father ran around the house to find out what was going on. By this time, the three of us had gotten buckets and gone into the chicken lot, where we had running water, for water to put the fire out. Remember, we never saw the tent again!

We knew that we were in big trouble, and a whipping of our lives was about to take place. After the fire was out our parents took us into the house on the screen-in porch in the back of the house. Our father got his favorite strap and started to work on my brother. When finished with him, our father handed the strap to my mother, and she proceed to use the strap on my sister. When Mama finished with my sister, Mama handed the strap back to my father and he proceeded to use the strap on me. Once my father was finished with me, Daddy reaches for my brother and gives him another round of strapping. Thinking that would be ample, but to my surprise, we all got another round of the strap with the famous words, "are you going to do that again?" and, of course, we gladly said, "No!" By the way, the strap was about 2-3 feet long and it had three layers and three holes in it, each about 1-5 inches in length. After all of this, my brother got a third round of the strap as he was the oldest and should have known better! At least this is what I heard my father say to my brother.

The events of that night have been well remembered even today. When we went to bed that night I told my brother that I would never, never, never, listen to him again as long as I live because every time I listen to him, I always ended up getting into trouble and getting another strapping. Quite frankly, at the age of nine, I had enough of being talked into doing something wrong and then punished for my actions later! Yes, he is my brother, and I love him, but he is extremely hard to love! **But love is understood.**

Oh, my sister and I learned later the next day that we put gasoline in the lantern and that's why it exploded so quickly. I wonder all these years later why we did not get cooked in the tent fire. I was talking to my sister, by email in February 2012, about the Christmas tent and she remembered the experience and she quickly informed me how well she remembered the tent, what happened afterwards that took place that night and, also, that she never wanted to experience another episode like that one. I must agree!

CATTLE SHOWS

One of the big activities that we were engaged in growing up through the years, was showing Registered Brown Swiss cattle in 4-H (the 4 H stands for Head, Heart, Hands and Healthy: and FFA stands for Future Farmers of America).

We each started out showing in 4-H but as we got older my brother, Cliff and I, graduated into FFA once in the 9th grade enrolling in agricultural at the high school. Back 60 years girls were not allowed to be enrolled in agricultural classes and that is why my sister, Mary, continued showing cattle in the 4-H program.

Brown Swiss cows are a breed of dairy cattle. They are the second-greatest milk producers in the world, and their milk makes excellent cheese. The Brown Swiss was bred in the harsh climate of the Swiss Alps and was imported to the United States.

Originating in the Swiss Alps, Brown Swiss adapt well to high altitudes and hot or cold climates, while producing large volumes of milk, ideal for cheese-making of any kind. Their unique ability to yield high components with an ideal fat-to-protein ration sets them apart from other dairy breeds.

Correct feet and legs, well-attached udders, and dairy strength contribute to their exceptional productive life, allowing them to thrive in any modern dairy set-up. Style, balance and fancy frames also make

Brown Swiss easy winners at county, state, national and international shows.

The Brown Swiss Cattle breed originated in the mountain tops of northeast Switzerland before historic records began, around 4000 B.C., according to some historians.

We had a string of show cattle and after all these years I do not remember individual names that we had for every cow that we showed. I do remember several highlights about some of the show cattle that we showed.

My brother had the grand champion cow named Molly for years at the Shelby County Fair and the Kentucky State Fair, and in the wintertime when the cows were up in the dairy barn, due to bad weather, Cliff, would lay down on Molly and go to sleep on top of her back. The most amazing fact about the story of Molly the cow is that she would have twin calves every year. She was a big producer - - production of milk and reproduction. At 9 years of age and 365 days in milk, a Brown Swiss cow can produce 65,430 pounds of milk, 3557 pounds of fat and 2031 pounds of protein.

My sister, Mary, was showing a dry cow named Whitie, meaning not milking, but soon to have a baby calf, all summer long at all of the local shows she showed great, but when she arrived at the Kentucky State Fair the cow gave birth to a calf about 4 hours before she was to show the cow in competition. We were told if the cow did not clean herself of the afterbirth that she could not be shown. So, we had a friend come over and take the afterbirth from the cow and made good of the situation. Well, things worked out for her to show the cow, and won her class, but as soon as the class was over, the cow broke away from my sister and ran through the cattle barn, looking for her calf at the state fair with hundreds of people around, until the cow returned to her newborn calf. As everything settled down, no one was hurt, and no livestock was injured.

Once I enrolled in an Ag class at the High School, my brother and I showed against each other in every class. Of course, we never missed showing something in all the classes. One year he would win the class or show and the next class or show I would win the honors.

Our father would help in the show barn, and with others helping us get the cattle ready to show - - bathing, grooming, giving them drinking water (extra water made the cows look full and the judges like that), and we would take the cows to the show ring and show them. Sometimes we would have additional help as we showed cattle in every class we were unable to return to the barn and get another one to show. Therefore, our helpers would have the next one ready to show outside of the show ring and we would trade them the one that we just showed with the one ready to show.

The 4-H program always showed on a different day than the FFA and we were always helping our sister with everything in showing her cattle. Do not be fooled because the Brown Swiss breed is a lazy breed and not too much will bother them as they are very easy to work with and to show even though they are one of the largest cows in the six livestock breeds.

When you are showing cattle, the morning starts extremely early as you need to feed and water the animals, clean out our stalls (this went on all day and night) and provide new bedding, everyone needed a bath (cows and humans) so they would look the best when they were being shown. Most could have too much hair, so we had to clip head, half of the ears, tail, udder, (if milking age), in general trim any part of the body to make them more appealing to the judges. (More on training, grooming, and showing cattle later).

In getting ready to show cattle one starts early in the summer by keeping the cattle up in daylight to make sure they have a good color about the hide. During that time, we would break the cattle to lead, stand and allow us to put our hands all over them – practice daily. When you showed the cattle, you would have a leather halter to put on the head to lead them into, around and out of the show ring.

At home we had milking machines to milk the cows, but when we were showing cattle away from home, we always had to milk the cows by hand and that took a while longer as milking by hand is somewhat slow. The last two years that the family showed cattle, the Kentucky

State Fair installed a milking polar for everyone to use, but in doing so, the fair board got to keep the milk.

Showing Your Dairy Animal

Few other activities in the 4-H or FFA daily project have more potential for educational and personal development of youth as do the 4-H or FFA dairy shows. These shows play a major role in helping youth become self-directed, productive, and contributing to adult citizens by developing valuable life skills. These skills are more than physical skills – they are a combination of acting, thinking, and feeling.

Showing an animal helps a young person in the maturing process – developing responsibility and sportsmanship. Shows help youth learn to function as adults in society and to accept responsibilities, gain an ability to communicate, ask questions, solve problems, make decisions, and how to work with other people. The experiences of owning and working with animals, being responsible for their care, health and growth, and exhibiting them in a competitive environment are tremendous assets in the character-building process.

This publication was developed to provide 4-H or FFA members with guidelines in preparing dairy animals for showing. Providing these guidelines in a booklet form makes the information more accessible and useful.

Having a Good Animal

To do your best at the 4-H or FFA dairy shows, you need to start with the correct type of animal. If you start with a poor calf, you can easily become discouraged. If you have more than one animal to select from, you need to select the best. When buying a calf, purchase the best you can afford.

Birth dates are important when buying or breeding for show calves. The beginning dates for the various classes are March 1, June 1, September 1, and December 1. Any heifer born in March, June, September, or December; therefore, usually has an advantage over animals born later in the 3-month period. Short-aged animals are usually at a disadvantage until maturity.

It is most important to select heifers with good conformation. If you are not familiar with determining which animals are a good type, consult with someone who has knowledge in this area. The following tips will help you in selecting an animal to show:

- The animal needs to be long, stretchy, and of good size for her age and breed.
- It should have sharp, clean withers; a straight, strong back; a long, wide rump; and feet and legs with correct set.
- The heifer needs to show promise of outstanding udder development and have well-placed teats that hang plumb.
- It should have a good spring of rib and be deep in the chest and rear flank.

Your animal needs to be the offspring of a proven bull with high PTA milk and type and out of a cow possessing good type with above-average production.

A good animal does not guarantee success in the show ring; but without a good animal, it is difficult to consistently do well.

Grooming the Animal

Fitting an animal for a blanket when the weather is cool is more difficult than when the weather is warm. The hair of the animal stands up to aid the animal in reducing the stress of cool weather. For your animal to look its best at the show, blanket it for about 6 weeks.

Before you blanket the animal, give her a good bath. Select a warm day, or move the animal inside out of the wind. Wet her with water and lather her well, scrubbing with a brush. Avoid getting water in her ears; rinse well and let her dry.

Burlap bags sewn together make a good blanket; commercial fabrics also are available for blankets. Be sure the blanket is large enough for the animal. It should be tied in four places – around the brisket, under the heart girth, and around the rear legs. Blanket patterns are available at your county Extension office.

It is best to make long straps that can be tied in a bow so they can be untied easily and adjusted as needed. **Do not** tie the blanket too tight. If the straps are too tight, the animal will be uncomfortable when she lies down or else the straps will be pulled loose. Keep the blanket on, at all times, except when brushing. Brush the animal vigorously each day to remove hair.

An alternative to blanketing an animal is body clipping, which, if done properly, can achieve the same results as with a blanket. Clip when the animal's hair is excessively long and blanketing is not feasible. Clip at least 2 to 4 weeks before the dairy show. This amount of time allows the hair to grow to a length that will lie against the skin instead of standing up. Take care when clipping during extremely cold weather. Small animals may need to be blanketed or housed to protect them from cold stress. You should also remember to protect clipped animals when transporting them in cold weather.

Feeding Your Animal

The nutritional needs of your show animals are of major importance. If an animal's nutrient needs are not met, it will not grow at an acceptable rate and, therefore, will be smaller than other animals in the show class. Feed your animal a balanced ration throughout the year.

A good ration is built around high-quality forage. Feed heifers all the good-quality hay they will eat. If you are feeding by hand, give hay at least two times a day. Remember that good hay helps in rumen development, which shows up on the animal as a deep body with a good spring of rib. Most exhibitors prefer good, green, leafy grass hay; however, if you have a choice of legume hay and poor grass hay, feed the lugume hay. Sudan grass or millet, cut in the boot stage, makes excellent hay for show animals. If you don't have good hay on your farm, it is worth the effort to find an adequate supply of quality forage. Show calves must have good hay, or they will not develop properly and will be shallow-bodied.

Feed hay in a rack, preferably out of the rain. If you do not have a hay rack, much of the hay will be wasted.

Most all the forage grown in some states must be supplemented with grain to provide a balanced ration for your animals. Feed your animal so she will be thrifty and dairy – like at show time – not too thin and not too fat.

You can best control your heifer's body condition by the amount of grain fed. If your animal is in good condition, she will need very little grain. On the other hand, if she is thin and in poor condition, she may need 6 or 8 pounds of grain per day. Some heifers gain much more rapidly than others.

Good, fitting rations are light and not too high in protein. A good home-mixed fitting ration that contains about 14 percent crude protein can be a proper diet for any show stock.

Before you take your animal to the show, teach her to eat and drink from the same pails you will use at the show. Your animal must have plenty of clean water available at all times.

Brushing and Cleaning the Animal

Brush your show animals at least once a day. You can brush the animal with a soft brush and then rub it with your hands to remove loose hair. New hair comes in short, soft, and silky. Daily brushing can make your animal take on a new look.

After you brush and observe your heifer for a few days, you may see the need to increase the thickness of your blanket. The purpose of the blanket or body clipping and the brush is to remove the long hair.

Most showmanship classes include fitting as one of the selection criteria. You want your animal to have a soft, silky hair coat, which is accomplished by blanketing or boy clipping the animal and brushing often. It was on show day to identify those animals on a daily brushing schedule. They have finer texture and more gloss to their hair coats than do the animals not brushed regularly; extra brushing pays off on show day.

Trimming Feet of a Show Animal

Properly trimmed feet are important. If the toes are long and unshapely, trim them early in the conditioning period. Trim at least 2 weeks before the first show. Heifers with long toes tend to walk on the backs of their heels, detracting from the appearance of the legs.

The feet of calves and heifers are much easier to trim than a cow's feet, because they are easier to restrain and the hoof is softer. Your heifer can easily be thrown with a couple of half-hitches in a long cotton rope. The toes can be trimmed with hoof nippers.

Trimming feet of mature cows is a job for someone with experience. One method is to use a sharp, 1-inch wood chisel as the animal stands on a 2-inch-thick board. Experienced trimmers attempt to remove excess toe and sole growth to get the cow forward on her toes and to reduce heel compression. A balanced hoof is important. It is important to avoid making the hoof bleed. If this does happen, the animal may limp for a few days. This is why you need to trim at least 2 weeks before show date.

Clipping a Show Animal

Clipping is one of the most important things you can do to fit your animal. Clipping improves the animal's style and overall appearance. All dairy animals are basically clipped the same way; however, study each animal before clipping and determine if you can improve her weak points by clipping her a certain way.

All 4-H'er's and FFA'er's showing dairy animals should learn to clip their animals. You will need to have an experienced person teach you by example and then coach you as you try it. It is a good idea to practice on animals you do not plan to show. Until you have mastered the art of clipping, clip slowly. Hair can always be taken off but clipping too much cannot be corrected. It is rare that an animal needs to be body clipped entirely. Clip such animals at least 60 days before the show to allow a new coat to grow back.

Most animals do not appreciate clipping. It may be necessary to use a nose lead to pull their heads to a post to prevent them from hitting you when swinging their heads. Placing the animal in a grooming chute makes the animal easier to handle, and clipping goes faster. Blueprints for building grooming chutes are available from your county Extension office.

Clip the head, neck, ears, tail, and udder (cows and springing heifers only). Other parts of the animal can be clipped on an "as-needed" basis. Clip the front and rear legs so as to have the appearance of greater flatness of bone and to remove stains. Trim top lines to improve straightness. Clip the withers to a sharp point to improve angularity. Body clipping is acceptable. Especially when the body hair is excessively long. Do not clip the belly and udder of heifers that have not calved and are not springing.

Most people start clipping at the head. Clip the entire head and neck as short as possible. This is accomplished by clipping against the hair. Leave the whiskers on the nose because this makes the muzzle appear wider. Clip the inside and outside of the ears. Blend the neck and shoulders by clipping in the direction the hair runs. Start at the point of shoulder and clip upward to the top of the shoulder blade. Use the clippers to make the point of withers as sharp as possible.

Clipping the tail and tail head area is easier, and some people prefer to start here. Clip the tail from a point about 4 inches above the hairs on the switch. Clip against the hair on the tail until you reach the tail head. Blend the longer hair and close-clipped area at the point where the tail lies over the pin bones. You can blend the clipper lines by clipping with thei hair. Don't clip all the hair off the top line. If the top line is not level, clip the high areas and blend these into the lower sections of the top line.

Every clipping rule recommended for a heifer can be applied to a milking animal. Animals that have freshened will need additional clipping. Clip the udder as close as possible and then clip along the milk veins to make them more noticeable. Clip the belly area, between the milk veins. Blend all clipper marks, using the natural body lines to help hide them. It is easier to clip a full udder, and you are less apt to cut the skin with the clippers when the udder is full.

Training Show Animals to Lead

It is best to begin with a rope halter when breaking an animal to lead. Tie the animal in a well-bedded place, and do not lead much in the first couple of days. This allows the animal to get accustomed to the halter and to learn you are not going to hurt her. It is best to tie the animal to a wall with a smooth surface so the animal will learn to respect the halter without injuring itself.

You can begin to teach your show animal to lead by leading it to water twice daily. Within a few days you may begin to take it out for short periods of time. A few minutes each day is better than long session several days apart.

After the animal is broken to lead, train it to walk and post properly. Use a dairy show halter with a chain for this exercise. Train the animal to walk slowly and with short steps with its head carried high. Always lead your animal in a clockwise manner; this puts you on the outside of the circle.

The preferred method of leading is walking forward at a normal pace. You should walk opposite the head on the left side, holding the lead strap with the right hand close to the halter and the strap neatly, but naturally (preferably not coiled), gathered in one or both hands. Holding close to the halter, or with one hand inside the halter, ensures a more secure control of the animal.

As the judge studies your animal, the preferred method of leading is walking slowly backward, facing the animal and holding the lead strap in the left hand with the extra lead neatly but naturally gathered in one or both hands. At all other times, walk facing forward at a quicker pace. When given the signal to pull into line, move quickly to that position in the ring.

Lead at a comfortable pace with the animal's head held high enough for impressive style, attractive carriage, and graceful walk. Never allow a large gap to occur between your animal and the one ahead of you. Do not crowd the exhibitor ahead of you nor lead in front of an animal so it cannot be seen by the judge.

When posing and showing a dairy animal, stay on the animal's left side and stand faced at an angle to her in a position far enough away to see the stance of her feet and top line. Pose the animal with her feet squarely placed. The find leg nearest the judge is to be posed slightly behind the other when showing heifers. For cows and springing heifers, the hind leg nearest the judge should be far enough ahead of the opposite rear leg to allow the judge to see the fore and rear udder.

Train each animal so you (exhibitor) can move it quickly and easily into the correct pose. The position of the rear legs should be reversed when the judge walks around to view the animal from the other side. Do not "over show" an animal. When the judge is observing the animal, get the feet posed reasonably well, and let her stand. Do not delay the show, in an attempt to pose the feet perfectly. Face the animal uphill, if possible, with her front feet on a slight incline.

Always move quickly into line when given the signal by a judge. Never crowd the exhibitor next to you nor leave enough space for another animal when you lead into a side-by-side position. Animals may be backed out of a line when a judge requests that her placing be changed. Move the animal back by exerting pressure on the shoulder point with the thumb and finger of the right hand while pushing back with the halter. You may also lead the animal forward and around the end of the line or back through a break in the line. Do not lead the animal between the judge and an animal being observed by the judge. To move the animal ahead, pull gently on the lead strap. Do most of the showing with the halter lead strap and avoid stepping on the animal's feet to move them.

Placing an animal's feet in the correct standing pose requires much practice for the lead person and the animal. One way to learn proper feet placement is to study photographs in breed publications.

Washing Your Show Animals

After your animals arrive at the show site, wash them thoroughly. Liquid detergents for kitchen or laundry use are suitable for washing. Use a stiff brush and work all the dirt next to the hide.

When washing around the head, hold the ears closed to prevent water from getting in. If water gets in an ear, it may cause the ear to droop for several days. Wipe the ears clean with a cloth dampened with rubbing alcohol to remove the ear was and dirt.

Don't forget to wash between the rear legs and udder, an area easily missed. Thoroughly wash the switch; you can remove tangles by using hair conditioner after washing.

Your animals may have to be spot washed just before the show. Be careful to allow enough time for the animal to dry completely before show time.

Other Hints to Help Show Your Animal

Showmanship is one area in which youth may excel, regardless of the correctness of the conformation of the calf or cow. Placing in showmanship competition is based strictly on the appearance of the exhibitor and how well the animal is shown in the ring. This is why so much emphasis is placed on these classes in some shows. Anyone who has the money can buy an animal of superior conformation; but to win in showmanship, an exhibitor **must** work hard to train an animal and to learn proper showmanship techniques.

- It is generally agreed that white shirt and pants are the preferred dress for showmanship contests. Everything else being equal, the person dressed in all white is placed ahead of those who are not.

- It is important that the exhibitor learn to watch the animal, and the Judge, at all times. Do not be distracted by people and things outside the ring. And, keep your animal, under complete control, at all times.

- Quickly recognize the conformation faults of the animal you are leading. Keeping this in mind, show to overcome them. You may be asked to exchange with another exhibitor and show a different animal.

Frequently, a Judge will ask questions about the exhibitor's animal to find out just how much work the exhibitor has done and how much he or she knows. Questions could include those about feeding practices, age of the animal, the animal's name, sire, and dam, and production, if the show animal is in milk.

If you are showing milking cows, it is important to have the right amount of milk in the udder to best show its conformation. This is often called bagging. Cows producing a normal flow of milk should be milked about 12 hours in advance of showing. Try to determine when each cow class will be shown, and milk accordingly. You may wish to allow more time for cows that are in the latter part of their lactations. Do not over bag your cows, since it may cause the teats to strut, draw attention to a weak front udder attachment, or cause your cow to be nervous and hard to handle.

Checklist to Show Your Animal

Plans and details are important if you have success at the show. The following list provides guidelines for preparing for a show:

- Be sure you are familiar with the feeding and management arrangements at the show.
- Be sure you arrive on time.
- Make sure you have the registration certificate on each animal you plan to show.
- Be sure health requirements are met.

- DHI Production records are needed if you are showing cows, especially if they are entering the production contest.
- Bring needed items, for example, brushes, forks, brooms, and cleaning equipment.
- Have a tie-halter with a snap and double-tie rope for each animal.
- Have a show halter ready for show day.
- Have a uniform ready for show day; white is preferred.
- Be sure you know the arrangements for transporting your animal to the show.

The exhibitor who pays attention to the many details about showing is usually the most successful one. Showing is hard work, but the rewards are numerous. Showing a dairy animal provides exciting opportunities for the whole family. The companionship and interests shared with your "showing" colleagues are positive influences for continued personal growth.

Self/Int

THE SMOKE HOUSE

Outside there was a smoke house where meats were smoked and preserved for the coming year with brown sugar and salt for the family to eat. There would be hams, sides of bacon and possibly sausages and other meats, too. The smoke house was made of grain boards (very thick and several layers of wood) and the door was made of the same material with a tin roof top.

There was a coal house in one corner of the back yard, an outhouse in another corner with three holes: a papa bear, a mama bear and a baby bear size. We also had another outhouse in the barn yard and every summer we would dig a hole in front of the old outhouse, pull the outhouse forward about 5 feet placing it over the new hole and using the soil taken out of the new hole and putting it in the old outside hole. That is how, in the olden days, one would do this to keep your outhouses fresh. Oh, the barn yard outhouse was only a one-seater.

Back, some several yards, was the chicken house. There was a water pump (well or sometimes called a cistern) just outside the kitchen door at the end of the porch on the other side of the driveway. A cistern was there, to catch the rainwater that was directed by gutters from the house and porch roof to the cistern. This cistern was in the corner of the porch, and the water was used for washing clothes. It was soft water and very nice for washing hair or bathing. The cistern was often used to keep butter, milk and other foods cool by putting them in a bucket and lowering it to just above the water level. We had several summers that were very dry (no rain fall) and we had to buy city water and have it pumped into the well/cistern.

There was a trap door in the porch floor, which led to the cellar below the house, along with an outside entrance, too. It was always called a cellar and not a basement. The floor in the cellar was hard packed ground. There was an outside door to the cellar, but it was fun to raise the trap door and go down the stairs when it was raining or in cold and snowy weather. The house was built on flat ground and as you went toward the front of the house in the cellar, it was dark, and you were not able to stand erect. This area was where canned goods were kept in a cupboard on wooden shelves. It didn't freeze and jars of food kept very well.

There were lots of fruit and vegetables that were canned and stored there. At least an acre of this five-acre area garden was plowed every spring and planted in every vegetable available. There was a big field of corn. For the pole beans, many poles would be placed in the ground and tied together at the top tee-pee style. The bean vines would grow up the poles, blossoms developed, and the long Kentucky Green Beans would mature. It was so much easier to pick them up standing up, than to have to stoop down to pick the bush beans. There was lots of okra, tomatoes, squash, onions, carrots, cabbage, broccoli, corn, cucumber, parsnips, potatoes, eggplant, etc. and things like asparagus, rhubarb and garlic that came up every year.

SUMMER PICNICS ON THE FARM

How well, I can recall all those summer picnics that we had on the farm growing up. Our relatives from my mother's side of the family and those members of my father's side of the family too, would all show up for a special weekend during July annually until I left for college.

In getting ready for the picnic my father would pull three of the largest wagons up into the backyard under several large maple trees for shade and we would always have each one filled with food. Likewise, my mother started cooking the first of the week in efforts to get ample food fixed and then on Friday, many of the women would show up and help with the cooking. One could name the food and look around for it and you would find it.

Two of the wagons for the picnic were loaded with country hams, fried chicken, roasts, and all kinds of vegetables fixed every way possible. One vegetable item that always made a big hit was fresh corn on the cob as everyone ate as much as they wanted with fresh homemade butter from the farm.

The third wagon was for desserts. We would always have every kind of pie, cakes, cookies, watermelon, homemade ice cream, and sometimes we had some unusual things, but they were excellent, too. Sometimes we would have three or four of the same kind of cakes, or pies. We would start to eat around 2:00 p.m. and just continue to eat until dark and then most everyone would have a bedtime snack. Of course, we would have iced tea, lemonade, water, soft drinks of all kinds and even fresh milk that was milked that morning.

During the afternoon we would set around talking, visiting, and catching up on what had been going on in each family. Many members of the family would play ball, croquet, ride horses and ponies, and play games of many types. Some of the women would bring clothing with them from home and they would get together and try things on and if something fit, they would take it home with them—recycling, before they knew what it was called.

Several of the relatives would go to the barn in the evening and mornings to help us milk the cows, feed the calves, gather the eggs, and do whatever else had to be done at that time.

Most of the time everyone would stay the weekend and sleep wherever one could secure a bed, car, or perhaps just sleeping on the floor. In staying over the weekend, some stayed one night and others two nights, this gave everyone the opportunity to get up to date on what had been happening in all the different families.

Before everyone started home, our mother would make sure that every family on both sides of the family had a good supply of jam, jellies, apple butter, apple cause, eggs, milk, butter, bread, corn on the cob, potatoes, other fresh vegetables from the garden, and any other canned goods that they may use at home.

ROTTEN EGGS

Before you learn about the many egg fights that were fought on the farm you should have an understanding about the type of eggs that we used.

We got our little eggs from what were called bantams. What are bantams? They are called the flower garden of the poultry world. Bantams are miniature chickens, usually one-fourth to one-fifth the size of standard chicken varieties. Because of their many different types and assortments of color patterns, raising bantams is rapidly becoming one of present day most popular hobbies. Little is known of the origin of bantams although they are believed to have come from the Orient. Some bantams have feathers on their legs and some even have feathers on their feet. The males mature to about 26 ounces and the females mature to about 21 ounces. Also, today, we have hens who laid white or brown eggs.

As for the size of the egg that a little hen would lay, and to see the real size that your index finger and your thumb and touch the ends together and that will give you the approximate size of the egg.

As we were feeding hay out of the hay loft, we would find a nest of eggs every now and then that the little bantam hens would lay. Depending on who found the eggs, this is what we would do: we would take the eggs and shake them real hard one at a time until we finished shaking all eggs found. This would help the little eggs to rot, and we would hide them out somewhere that no one else could find them until we had an egg fight.

Every now and then my brother would find eggs that I had hid and I would find eggs that he had hid and each of us would hide them from the other brother. Of course, when our father went to town that was when we always had our egg fights. My brother could throw straight, and I got hit a lot, but I could not throw too straight, and I missed a lot. We would throw the eggs in the hay loft, dairy barn, the shed of the barn and even outside of the barn many times as the weather permitted.

Our father would return from his trip to town, and he never asked questions such as: have you boys been fighting with eggs? Or do I smell rotten eggs? We would never have given him a straight answer to his questions because we knew that we would be punished for fighting with eggs, period, and even more so, using rotten eggs. In case you have never smelled a rotten egg, it has a stench of that of a skunk, without a doubt. These egg fights would take place mostly in the summer when school was out and it was nice and hot which allowed the rotten egg smell to linger longer.

THE WHITE THANKSGIVING GOOSE

The chicken yard was talked about previously, but not to the extent that it will be described in this story about the white goose that would chase all of us when we traveled through the chicken yard. This goose was "mean to the bone" and would always chase you, bite you, or do something to you as you would go through the chicken yard to the dairy barn. If the white goose happened to bite you it would give you a black/purplish bruise for several weeks. If you have never had a goose bite you, in your lifetime, you are in for a real hurting experience.

With our chickens, we had some white geese, as the lot on our farm was a sufficient size place with a small pond for many animals to live. Not knowing what had taken place, until my mother requested that we prepare the big white goose for Thanksgiving dinner. We got the goose to the house, but it weighed 40 pounds plus. It had more pounds than any other goose that we had in the chicken yard.

As our mother was dressing the goose and cleaning it to its final stages, she noticed that the goose had small bumps all over its body. She tried pulling the bumps off, but to no success. Then she got a small paring knife and started to cut the bumps out. Little did she know that the goose had been shot over a period of time, and she learned that the bumps were full of BBs! Just estimate how many times my brother had shot that white goose and our mother found over 100 BBs in it. Our mother always said that she missed a few BBs and left them in under the skin of the goose.

It actually took our mother several hours to finish removing all the BBs from the white goose. This is when we all learned that my brother had been taking his little BB gun with him and shooting the white goose as he traveled through the chicken yard to keep the white goose off him. Then, we figured out, that was why the white goose got to be so mean and would chase and bite you any time that any of us would travel through the chicken yard.

Well, Thanksgiving arrived and that white goose was very delicious to all that ate him, and we still talk today about that goose many years later and why my brother had the courage to shoot the goose with BBs to start with. That question has never been answered today and all those years later.

BUDDIE

He was almost invisible, floating along the creek and pond on the farm under the shade of the trees overhanging the creek's edge. His little black nose was bobbing up and down in the water as he swam, taking in air and noisily blowing out water each time he surfaced. If it had not been for the noise he was making, he might never have been found.

That's what our parents were told when they went to pick up the little blond puppy at the home of a coworker down the road. Jeannie, home for the summer from college, was working as an intern at the clinic in town. At work that day, she had heard the story of a puppy pulled from the creek just before he would have been swept over the fence that spilled over into the large pond. The puppy needed a home, and Jeannie had a history of finding homes for homeless dogs. Especially one looking to be Lassie!

That night Jeannie repeated the story of the puppy's rescue to the rest of the family. The coworker and her husband had just finished an afternoon of boating on the old pond and were in the process of pulling their boat out of the water when they heard the puppy desperately trying to breathe as he floated toward the dam. The water was only a couple of feet deep in this part of the pond, so the husband quickly waded in, snagged the puppy with one hand, and held him close to his chest as he returned to the bank of the pond.

The wife gasped as she saw the puppy. There was a noose around its neck, and the end of the rope was tied to a small section of concrete block. This dog was supposed to be dead. Someone had tried to kill the puppy by tossing him into the creek with a concrete block tied to his neck. But the block must have hit the rock near the water's surface and broken into pieces. That's what saved the puppy's life. With a piece still attached to the rope, it was heavy enough to keep the little puppy from swimming, but not heavy enough to pull him under.

After Jeannie finished telling the family about this dog's short history, she announced that rather than look for a home for the puppy, we were going to keep him in our family. After having heard about this puppy's harrowing experience, no one in the family disagreed. I then said we should name him Buddie since he was pulled from the creek. All the children agreed, but Jeannie, with her mother's backing, said, "His name will be Buddie." I made another logical plea for Moses, but to no avail. The puppy would be named Buddie. Now we have another story behind the name of the dog. Our oldest brother was having trouble saying some of his words and he wanted to name the dog Budgie but had trouble saying the word correctly. As he said the word it would always come out as Buddie. My brother ended up getting his family Nickname of Budgie.

I guess I should introduce myself. My name is Daddy; our parents have three children. You already know Mary's name. Our sons are named Clifford and James. We have our daughter named Mary. We live on a large farm just outside of Shelbyville, a small community near Finchville, Kentucky. At the time of this event, all our children were attending primary grade school and during the summers would help work on the farm. Although we have had many large breed dogs on the farm in the past, at this time we just had the boys' little play dog, "Snow Ball." Of course, realizing that Buddie would become a very large dog we would start training him to work cattle, sheep and other animals on the farm.

A friend of mine who raises Collies came over to take a look at Buddie and immediately said he knew why Buddie's original owner had tried to kill him. When I asked what he meant, he explained that Buddie was not a purebred Collie because of the size of his head. He explained that Buddie's head was too large to be a pure pedigree. He thought that Buddie's entire body was going to be larger than a traditional Collie. I thought about Buddie floating down the creek barely able to lift his nose out of the water to breathe. His large head had caused his rejection but also saved his life. A normal puppy would not have been able to stick his nose high enough out of the water to breathe. A smaller puppy would have been pulled under by the remnants of the concrete block. It made me think about how sometimes what we see as a flaw in people can actually be advantageous to them. It was at that moment that I had this overwhelming feeling that I was going to learn a lot from Buddie.

The rest of the summer went by fast, and soon it was time for the kids to head back to school for the fall semester. As the school bus arrived every afternoon Buddie would be waiting at the end of the road for the children to get off the bus and would run and walk with them to the house. Somehow Buddie always knew the time of the day that the bus would come by the house as he never missed a day waiting on the children. Since I don't get home for lunch some days, it would be a long, lonely day for Buddie without the children.

Buddie had developed a tight bond over the summer with the children. Buddie was already considerably larger than we felt that he would grow, but Buddie always looked up (figuratively) to all the children as his big brothers and sister. Buddie felt that he was a beautiful Collie and thought he was just as large as any dog. Buddie thought he was king of the woods as he ran among the tall oaks and saw other creatures flee out of his path. Buddie didn't realize that it was one of our horses that was running behind him that gave him the authority he was so proud to have.

Our house overlooks the creek, and the old pond, so we could have the opportunity to view all the wildlife common to the wooded area from our porch. Although deer and turkeys dominate from a number standpoint, we also see foxes, raccoons, beavers, possums, and skunks. In the air, we have a wide variety of birds including many species of ducks as well as Canada geese and some cranes. However, when we are outside with Buddie we're always on the lookout for bald eagles and coyotes.

I wasn't worried about the coyotes anymore since Buddie had chased one off our property. Of course, learning thought the coyote was afraid of him. I just had to make sure that Buddie never left the house alone. Our greatest fear was of bald eagles. We have one that glided by twice a day at mid-morning and mid-afternoon. I first became aware of the threat of bald eagles after reading about the problems local hog farmers were having with the national bird. We have some free-range farmers in the area that raise pigs in large outdoor pens where the pigs roam free. The farmers couldn't figure out whom or what was taking their pigs, because the baby pigs would just disappear. There were no traces of blood left behind and there were no tracks in the mud around the pens.

After losing a number of pigs, one farmer decided to stake out his pen from a position under a big maple tree about a hundred yards from the pigs. Unlike the movie stakeouts that involve a van loaded with electronic equipment, this farmer only had a water bottle and a set of binoculars with him. He wasn't there long before the mystery was solved. All but one of the piglets was with the sows and this lone baby was destined to be the target. The farmer watched as a big eagle circled overhead. Then suddenly the eagle swooped down, snatched the piglet with its long claws, and carried it off into the air toward the farmer. The farmer said that everything happened so fast that it was hard to believe it was real. The desperate squeals of the baby silenced the rest of the wildlife in the area. As the eagle flew by, the squealing stopped, and the farmer raised his binoculars to see blood dripping from the pig's belly where the eagle's claws were piercing it. A few moments later, everything was back to normal; the songbirds were singing; the other pigs were snorting and grunting. Nature had taken its course, and the farmer had fewer hams to eat that winter.

I'm all for nature taking its course, but not when it threatens the life of mankind. After hearing about the pigs, I made some changes and restricted the amount of time that Buddie was outside alone. I decided to keep them inside while I was at work, so I installed a dog door between the kennel and the garage and another door between the garage and laundry room. He could move back and forth as he pleased between the three areas. When I would let him outside to run freely, knowing the eagle had already made its last flight by the farm for the day.

As the winter season approached, outside time was in the dark. Buddie didn't seem to mind running by the light of the moon. I would let him out about six each evening, with the overhead door of the garage left halfway open so he could get back into the house whenever he desired. He would come home each evening between nine and ten. We would sit together on the sofa in the living room and watch the local news and Jay Leno. Watching the *Tonight Show* together had become a ritual. I would sit in the middle of the sofa with Buddie on my left snuggled up against my thigh. Buddie would be lying down on the cushions with his head resting on my thigh. If I was in the kitchen or bathroom when Jay Leno started talking, Buddie would start barking until I took my designated position in front of the TV. We would watch the entire show and stay on the sofa until Conan came on. Conan's voice was the signal to go to bed. We would all go upstairs to my bedroom (Buddie would prefer I call it "our" bedroom). Buddie would sleep on the pillow next to me, and I would sleep right in the middle of the bed. That left half of the bed for each of us.

In the morning, Buddie would lie in bed until the last second before I went downstairs to leave. As I left the bedroom, he followed me down to the laundry room where I checked the water pail before I left for work. When I returned in the evening, the cycle started all over again.

It was amazing how Buddie respected all humans around. If Buddie finished his food before the family was finished eating, he would just bark once to let us know that he was finished eating. Without missing a beat as he chewed his steak, Buddie would use his large head to head-butt the small pieces of steak left on the plate. It was probably the most carefully executed maneuver a person would ever see. In a forceful, but smooth motion, Buddie would swing his head so that his big nose went under the body of the plate and propelled into the air and then gathered up the other parts of the steak.

Once a week I grilled a large steak on the deck grill. As soon as I lit the grill, Buddie would lie down in the middle of the deck. He would never beg. He knew I would make several trips in and out of the house while I cooked the steak. He knew that when the steak was done, I would go into the house and eat my share of it. He knew that the next time I came out I would have two plates with their share of the steak cut up into little pieces for him to eat as I removed the others from the grill.

We continued to grill steaks throughout the winter, with the exception of the holiday weeks because all the family was home for Thanksgiving and Christmas.

As the spring semester was winding down, everyone decided they would stay home that summer. It was starting to get pretty lonely on the farm, but I realized that I would have to adjust to living alone. The children all planned to go on to school. As I adjusted to this lifestyle, it was good to come home to Buddie. He was like grandchildren to me, and he treated me like a grandfather, always giving me love and respect. Our routines continued with Buddie running in the woods each night and always getting home in time for Leno.

In my job, I have learned over the years that whenever you change a procedure or routine, you need to monitor the new process for unexpected results. One day in June, I learned that I needed to apply this knowledge to any changes in routine with my personal life. It was a beautiful sunny day, and for the first time in months, I was not scheduled for a luncheon meeting at work. I only live twenty minutes from the office, so I decided to go home for a quick lunch. This was the first time I went home for lunch in the year that Buddie had been in the family. When I opened the door to the house, Buddie came bursting out greeting me. He knew I was early, and it was not time for him to run, so he came back into the house with me. As I started to take food out of the refrigerator, I could see he thought I was making something for him. I didn't want to disappoint him while I ate in front of him, so I let him outside to run while I was home. I watched him run around to the back of the house before I returned to the kitchen. I could see him from the window, dashing down to the creek where they could run around in about a half-acre of grass between the creek and the woods.

I took another minute or two to make my sandwich and was ready to go out on the deck, but thought I better check on Buddie one more time. I went over to the window and saw Buddie standing at the edge of the lawn by the creek. I looked again but did not see Buddie this time. This was strange because he always stayed close to the house. I couldn't figure out what was going on because he never stands still; he's always running when he is down by the creek. Now, however, he was just standing there like a statue looking up stream. I looked to my right to see what had caught his attention and froze. My heart started beating rapidly, and I went into what I call my fear mode. The eagle was on a glide path leading straight to Buddie.

The last time I was in fear mode was during a car accident. My car had spun out on ice and was slowly spinning in circles as it glided toward a ditch. During these times, my adrenaline starts to flow, and time seems to slow down, but it's not the time that's lowing but rather the fact that you're thinking fast. During those times, you were able to think about all your options and take appropriate action but today was different. The world had slowed down, my adrenaline was flowing, and I had thought about options, but there was only one. I didn't have enough time to get outside and yell at Buddie. My only option was to stand in front of the window and watch. Many thoughts were going through my mind; this is what it feels like for a parent to watch his child being run over by a car. I should have considered that the eagle could have changed its schedule when I changed my routine. All I could do was watch the final moments of Buddie's life. I remembered the drops of blood dripping from the little pig's belly and thought about blood dripping from Buddie.

He just stood there staring at the eagle, as if he were daring the eagle to fly into his territory. He was Buddie; he was invincible. In Buddie's world, every creature in the woods feared him. Buddie believed that nothing could harm him. As the eagle drew closer, it began to flap its wings to adjust its altitude to the perfect height to enable it to reach down with its strong claws and grab helpless Buddie.

This day as I watched the eagle stretch its legs out and begin to open its claws, I took one last look at Buddie and said, "Jesus, help him."

That's when it happened. As my heart was racing, I saw a black bur come bounding out of the woods. I thought to myself, "There is hope; there is a deer."

Buddie exploded himself to catch the deer, expecting to play on the lawn, but as he hit the grass and took sight of the deer and the eagle, Buddie was transformed. He has always been fast, but Buddie covered the fifty feet between him and the deer in two seconds or less. The eagle didn't see the deer; it was focused on Buddie, and Buddie wasn't fleeing. This was probably the first time this eagle was being stared down by its prey.

As Buddie flew across the lawn, I expected him to go straight for the eagle, which would be only a couple feet off the ground as Buddie reached the deer to play. I was wrong; Buddie had another set of priorities. Instead of going airborne, Buddie lowered his head into the grass, so his nose slid under the deer, then sent his friend flying with the hardest head-butt Buddie had ever received. The deer flew at least twice as far as normal and did not land on his feet. His landing was a soft one, though, as he rolled through the long grass along the creek's side.

Buddie was not finished. In the same motion that sent the deer into the safety of the long grass, Buddie's body went straight up and, while in the air, spun around to face the attacker straight on. As he turned, I saw his face. I had never seen Buddie show his teeth, but even from where I was, I could see every tooth exposed and the fierce look on Buddie's face. Although it was silent in the house, I could practically hear Buddie's snarls and growls.

The eagle, in total shock, veered off over the water and flew downstream. Buddie, now back on his paws, chased after the eagle for a short distance barking, "I am Buddie; don't mess with me!"

Buddie took a sitting position on top of the creek bank as I ran from the house to the creek. Buddie maintained his position, stoically on top of the creek bank, keeping an eye on the deer that was now playing in the shallow water. I sat down next to Buddie, and he laid his head on my thigh like he did every night. As I rubbed his neck, I could feel that he was still tense. I told him what a good job he had done, taking care of his friend, at which point he lifted his head and looked into my eyes. He didn't have to speak because I saw it in his eyes: "I am my brother's keeper."

After this close call, I made a new rule for myself that required me to always stay with the Buddie when he was outside during daylight hours. The rest of the summer went by without any further events. The seasons were moving quickly as we kept to our routines through fall and winter. Although we followed the same routines, I did make some modifications to give me more flexibility. I purchased a DVR that allowed me to record the local news, Leno, and Conan. If I needed more time before I sat on the sofa with Buddie, I would just replay the local news. As long as Buddie heard the voices of the local broadcasters, he was in no hurry to get positioned on the cushions. If I was tired and wanted to go to bed early, I would play reruns and fast forward through the news and Leno to get to Conan.

The next spring, Buddie was almost two years old. What started out as a typical Monday evening turned into anything but typical. I went to get Buddie into the house. I waited to see Buddie because he was always, no more than a minute in doing so. For some reason, Buddie was home earlier than usual; it was only eight o'clock. After five minutes passed, I became concerned. I walked outside and called for Buddie. It was quiet, no barking, nothing. This wasn't right. Since the experience with the eagle, Buddie kept close to the house. I returned to the house, grabbed a jacket, and a flashlight to go looking for Buddie. I headed toward the creek, and I called and called for Buddie but no reply at all. Now I was really concerned, and I thought something would lead me to Buddie. I went back to the house and up to my bedroom. I thought it was the best place to wait a while, but later I went down to the creek again.

I took my rifle from the closet, made sure it was loaded, and then headed for the creek. I heard the rapids in the creek as I walked across the lawn. I remembered the many nights that Buddie and I had fallen asleep while listening to the peaceful sound of the rapids that flowed through our open bedroom window. This peaceful memory was short lived, because as I stepped into the woods, I felt like a child. It was scary. The tall trees cut out most of the moon's light. My flashlight could only illuminate a small path in front of me. I realized I didn't know anything about coyotes. Did they make any noise before they attacked? Then I remembered that I was there for Buddie, and suddenly all the fear left me. This feeling reminded me of when my children were younger. Something that would fill me with fear when I was alone would actually instill boldness and courage in me if I had to protect my children. I had to find Buddie.

I searched and followed every path in the woods. I went over each area at least twice and still no Buddie. After two hours, I returned to the house. I crawled into bed and closed my eyes. I laid there with my eyes closed and prayed. I couldn't sleep; I just kept praying. In the middle of the night, I opened my eyes and looked over at the window. I knew something bad had happened and that Snowball knew what it was.

As morning approached, I got dressed and planned my day. This time of the year the sun doesn't rise until I've been at work for an hour, so I planned to go in at my normal time, revise my schedule to free up the morning, and then head back home to search for Buddie in the daylight.

As I drove to work, I thought about how my life had become a country song. The pickup I was driving was a company vehicle, and the company was talking about eliminating the vehicle program for managers, which meant I would lose the pickup. Now Buddie was missing. I was living alone as everyone at home was in school, and now I was losing my truck and my dog. I tried to think of a son that would apply to this situation, but instead I just cried all the way to work.

The hour in the office sped by, and before long, I was back on the road heading home. I took the same route as earlier, but now the sun was up, and I didn't like what I was seeing as I drove down the narrow country road that leads to my house. My heart was starting to beat fast, and my hands were clenched around the steering wheel. As I looked up about a half mile ahead of me, I saw crows circling above the road. In the movies, you always see vultures circling over a carcass. In Kentucky, the sight of crows flying in a small circle means something dead is below them.

I hadn't seen anything on the road when I drove to work. If there was something there, it had to be in the ditch. The crows had started to descent, but as I approached, they flew off. I parked along the side of the road and got out to take a look around. I was hoping to find a small animal, but the first thing I saw was red blood on the gravel road. As I walked across to the other side of the road to take a closer look, I saw broken glass on the road further up the hill, most likely from a headlight. I walked to the edge of the road and looked down into the ditch. There was Buddie, lying in the ditch. His eyes were closed, which seemed odd, because every other animal I have come across that has been killed on the road always had its eyes open. He looked like he was sleeping. I didn't see any blood on him, so I knelt beside him to see if I could wake him up, but Buddie was going to sleep for eternity. Buddie was dead. I touched his stiff cold body. I still couldn't see an injury that would have left so much blood on the road, and then I rolled him over to see the wound. My firsts thought was that he died instantly. He was essentially cut in half with only the skin on the other side of his chest holding him together. He most likely died on the road and was then moved to the ditch. Whoever moved him had treated him with respect. It must have been one of the neighbors.

As I knelt, I started to think about all the times I had spent with Buddie; now I had to bury him. Buddie weighed 110 pounds, but he was now in two fifty-five-pound pieces held together by a little skin. I didn't want him to break apart completely, so I carefully put my arms under each section of his body. I struggled at first but was able to lift him up and balance the two pieces as I carried him over to the pickup. I gently laid him in the pickup box and closed the tailgate. We were only a quarter of a mile from home. As I drove, I decided to bury him right away. I went into the house and grabbed the blanket off the sofa. We sat together on this same blanket almost every night for the last two years. I went outside and wrapped Buddie in the blanket. I had seen him on this blanket so much, it was only right to bury him in it. The blanket held the two parts together as I carried him to the edge of the woods. As I held him, I remembered the first day he came to our home and into our lives. I remembered that Jeannie said Buddie's rescuer had held Buddie close to his chest as he carried Buddie out of the creek. I pulled Buddie tight to my chest and hugged him and hugged him again. Life was not going to be the same without Buddie. I laid him on the ground and retrieved a shovel from the garden shed. I dug the hole right along the main path leading into the woods. It was near the spot where Buddie saved the deer from the eagle. In some weird way, I felt that Buddie could still watch over the family when we were experiencing harm in some way.

As I gently laid Buddie in the hole, I started sobbing. With each shovel of earth, I put over him I thought about how my life was going to change. Buddie had been the best friend I had ever had. He was always there for me and never questioned anything I did. Then I realized that this was going to affect the rest of the family more than me. The two of us had been together 24/7 for the last two years. I realized Buddie no longer had a big little brother to take care of him. I finished burying Buddie and went to care for the other animals. On the way back up to the house, I called the rest of the family to let them know what had happened.

Needless to say, the family did not handle it well. I realized, after the fact, that I should have let the family help me bury Buddie. If I had, they would know where Buddie was, instead of constantly looking for him. A few months after Buddie died, some neighbors up the road acquired an adult Collie. The first time I saw this new neighbor he ran full speed toward me. I kept calling him back, but he would not listen, he just ran faster. The Collie didn't know what this little dog wanted and started to walk toward me. Buddie would have run to greet others.

July is one of the few warm months and it was on one of those hot days in the middle of the month that a young man knocked on my door. Before he introduced himself, he announced, "I am the one who hit and killed your dog." I just stood there looking at him. I had talked to a number of the neighbors to see if they had heard about anyone having an accident with a dog, but no one had. I didn't think I would ever know the details of Buddie's death, but now his killer was at my door. I had been standing there just staring at him for so long, the young man felt uncomfortable and finally said, "I'm really sorry," and started to walk away. I stopped him and asked him to come into the house. We sat in the living room, and I asked him his name, which turned out to be John Henry. I asked if it was Jon or John, to which he replied "John, but I go by Jon." I asked where he lived and found out that he was from Taylorsville. He said that on the night of the accident, he and his friends were just driving the country roads, avoiding the highways because they were drinking. He said although they had gotten rid of all the liquor in the car, they didn't report the accident because they were all under the age of twenty-one.

I asked him exactly what had happened. He said he was driving too fast on the gravel road, and when he came up over the hill, he saw a dog in the middle of the road. "Did you say a blond dog?" I asked. He was silent for a moment and then started to cry. After a moment, he began talking in broken speech between sobs. He explained that he had hit the brakes and was sliding toward the dog when suddenly a big dog ran in front of his car and knocked the little dog into the ditch. Jon said he thought the big dog was going fast enough to get out of the way, but the front corner of the car hit the dog in the middle of his body.

Everyone stayed in the car for a while because they were afraid to get out. Jon said he just couldn't believe what had happened. He knew the big dog was dead, and he was trying to understand why a dog would give his life to save another dog. He thought about how hard it would be for a person to give his or her life for someone else, but this dog just did it with no hesitation. After talking a bit and making sure each other was okay, the boys got out of the car and walked to the front of the vehicle to find the right headlight destroyed and some minor body damage in the area around the headlight. They looked for the dog and did not see him right away. Then they found him on the side of the road about twenty-five feet in front of the car. Jon said that he and one of his friends carried the dog off the road and laid him in the ditch. I asked Jon if he did anything else to the body. Jon was quiet for a moment and then said, "I closed his eyes."

I told him I had noticed that Buddie's eyes were closed, and I said, "Buddie would have appreciated that."

He asked in a surprised voice, "The dog's name was Buddie?"

I said, "Yes, the big dog was named Buddie." Jon started to cry again, and I thought to myself, "this kid is really emotional."

Finally, Jon told me that he had really been struggling with what to do with his life since graduation from high school. He didn't have enough money for college, and he didn't want to go into the Army or some other service because he didn't want to end up in Iraq. He had been bouncing around from one fast food job to another up until the accident. He told me how seeing Buddie had changed the way he looked at life. "If a dog can be fearless and courageous enough to save another dog, then I should be brave enough to try and help other people. So, anyway, I enlisted in The Marines, and I start training next month. That's why I came here today.

"I couldn't leave for training knowing that whoever owned the dog, Buddie, didn't know how the dog had died. So, I came out here and started knocking on doors, and your neighbor told me you had lost a dog."

"So," I asked, "why does the name, Buddie, have so much significance?"

He said, "Because I've been praying a lot, asking God if I'm doing the right thing by joining the Marines. Now I know I am. Your dog's name was Buddie, so I know I'm doing the right thing."

Again, I asked, "But why Buddie, why does Buddie mean it's right for you to join the Marines?"

I thought he was going to cry again, but instead, Jon looked me in the eyes and with the strongest voice he had used all day, he said, "I know that God wants me in the Marines because the recruiter that signed me up was very inspirational."

"Wow," I said. I thought about how Buddie was affecting people even after his death. I remembered how important it was to Jeannie and that he be named Buddie instead of Moses. I thought about how Buddie would normally have been down at the creek, not on the road as they were that night. What was a kid from Taylorsville doing driving down an old stagecoach road in rural Finchville, Kentucky, on a Monday night?

I looked over and saw Jon smiling for the first time since he arrived. He was looking down at Snowball (our new white dog), who was still licking Jon's hand. I said, "Snowball has really taken to you; it normally takes him a lot longer to get to know a new person." Snowball was a most unusual dog in that he had a double curl on his tail and that made two full circles.

Jon said that Snowball acted the same way in the ditch that night of the accident, "My friend and I had just placed Buddie in the ditch, and I looked at his eyes and decided to close them. As I ran my hand over Buddie's face to close his eyes, Snowball came up and started licking my hand." I told Jon that Snowball sensed his concern for Buddie and that Snowball was showing his appreciation by licking his hand. I told Jon that Snowball would always remember his scent and that Jon would always be Snowball's friend.

The room then went silent. I'm sure that Jon, like me, was reflecting on what we had just discovered by putting our stories together. After a moment, Jon stood up and said he needed to get back to Taylorsville, so Snowball and I walked him to the door. I gave Jon my card and asked him to write or email me when he could and thanked him for telling me about Buddie. He thanked me for understanding and said he was glad he came out to see me. After a firm handshake, he left.

I watched Jon, walk to his car, and then I looked down at Snowball and thought about all the things God had put in motion over two years ago, things that inspired a young man and saved the life of a dog. I watched Jon drive off and then looked at Snowball again and said, "God must have something big planned for you!"

An ending note on the dog named Snowball. Snowball ended up being a great dog as he learned to travel through the countryside and fathered many puppies over the years and he would always come home to build up his strength and would return to the "wild" to father more puppies. As a story follows on "Snow Ball, III, his grandson.

RECALLING THE GOOD OLD DAYS ON THE SCHOOL PLAYGROUND

Every well-equipped school playground had its swings and seesaws and every other device to make children happy. All these things are up to date in form and balance, as much as a part of the modern school and playground as the equipment was of our own devising.

Swings were of numerous kinds. Very primitive ones were grave vines, right where they had grown. Many a boy lost a year's growth through the excitement of swinging his girl on a grapevine swing. No grapevine was ever quite balanced enough to give one a chance to show off, that is, in going far out over something, without also endangering life and limb. Not always were the vines any too well anchored in the treetops; they had a way of falling and spoiling our play time.

My sister and I were swinging on one of the grapevines when we were little tads the day she fell and bit through her upper lip and still got a switching anyway when she got home that afternoon after school. I did not hurt myself then, but the apple limb that Mama used to punish me for running away from home and causing a tragedy, hurt my feelings properly as much as the bite hurt my sister. Of course, standard swings were made of rope usually attached to a horizontal or near-horizontal limb of the tree. That was real fun, until the rope broke and caused a sprained ankle or bruised body. We could stand up and pump, until we sometimes turned entirely over the limb and came down ingloriously.

When we took turns about at the swing, we had to let the cat die after going up high; some rascally boys prolonged the cat's life until there was no pleasure afterward. Our seesaws were easy to get started. The most primitive one of all was a plank from the lumber pile thrust between the rails of the worm fence. Fashionable farmhouses nearly always had plank, such as those now found primarily around stock farms. With two or three bodies on each end and with efforts being made to jolt the fence broke, causing a spill and some sprained ankles. The seesaw plant itself had a way of finally going to pieces, with the usually unpleasant results.

Closely related to swings and seesaws were flying Jennies, which even the poorest could have. There were no prancing steeds as on the modern merry-go-round. We cut a small tree off some four or five feet from the ground, timed all the limbs off, balanced it properly, and then bored an auger hold through it, to fit on part of the stump, which had been trimmed accordingly.

MEMORIES OF GROWING UP IN LEANER TIMES

Life has certainly changed in Kentucky since the 1940's and 50's. Looking back on my childhood days I can remember so many good things, but there were also many things not so good.

I remember my Mama and what a helpless woman she was. She depended on Daddy for every decision and never handled any money; there wasn't much anyway. Daddy bought what cattle feed, groceries that were needed and made sure that all the bills were paid.

The farm I grew up on was located in Shelby County, Kentucky, near Finchville, Kentucky; the land had some roll to it but not much and the soil was excellent for crops. My Mama, sister and I raised the garden, Daddy had the land ready for planting and Mama did most of the canning and freezing in preparing food for the winter months. Of course, when the tobacco crop was raised and sold, there was some money, but it usually went to pay down the mortgage on the farm. Daddy would take a wagon pulled by two horses up the hollow and over the hill and down another hollow sometimes to the store. In the store, in one corner was flour, sugar, a big barrel of salt and another one with crackers, coffee, brown beans, and, in fact, most of the small things were there for the picking. For our corn meal, on Friday we would have a corn shelling time. The shelled corn had to be ready for the grist mill on Saturday morning.

All the time I was growing up Mama never complained much or seemed to want much. If she asked Daddy for something, maybe she would get it and maybe she wouldn't. Daddy would spend his money on livestock and equipment, mostly always farm related.

I remember when we got our first television in 1957. It was Mama's birthday in October and Daddy said it was a gift for her. Up until this time all we ever listened to was the radio -- music, Amos and Andy Show, Jack Benny, and a few others.

We have always had cows to milk and butter to make and ample of both for sale to the public. I remember many mornings going to the barn and a cow would be having a calf. All of our cows had names, as to keep up with breeding and milk production would be recorded.

Our mother would be making butter and buttermilk, and she would get the children to help turn the churn as we always had so much energy. During the process of churning the mixture, we would get into a fight over who was going to churn, and our mother would make us stop, and as the buttermilk was almost made, we would get into another fight over who was going to get to drink some of the buttermilk, when finished being made.

I remember on Thanksgiving night in 1950, we had the biggest snowstorm of all time, in many years. There were drifts several feet high. You couldn't see to get around to do your farm work as the snow was over the fence. The snow stayed on for more than a month.

All in all, we haven't had it as hard as our Mama did. I have survived many things. I have some very good memories of my childhood days and then there were the bad memories. We have not had very many serious things happen in our married lives. Our family has had respect for one another and shown love (not expressing it), but **our love is understood.**

The old family life was hard work, and not much play in growing up. Although after a hard day's work, with supper over, and with the dishes all done, we would go to the front porch to rest, tell stories, and listen to the radio. After dark we all went to bed early. We had to get up in the early hours to fire up the old wood stove and bake bread. In the summer we had to make enough bread to last all day because it got so hot later in the day. In the winter, we made bread three times a day to utilize the heat from the stove for heating the house.

We did have several very dry summers and short crop years all at the same time and our mother always managed to have ample food on the table, three times a day, with snacks, etc., along the way. When we had a shortage of sugar, I will never understand how our mother came up with desserts and sweet items for us to eat, but I do know that she used a lot of honey and molasses. One dessert that all family members loved was her "Poor Man's" dessert. Mama would make pie dough, pull it out, pour in a jar of fruit preserves of some kind, roll it up and bake it. Then she would make a lemon sauce to put on top of it, and it was very good!

Well, all in all, our family has had a good life, no bad sicknesses or any bad trouble with the children or grandchildren. I am a proud son and pleased with all our family accomplishments in my 69 years. I hope I can have many more good years.

CLOSE CALL

I lived in a big house on one of the busiest roads in our little, small town, in Finchville, Kentucky, on Route 55.

The house was white with black shutters, two stories with an attic and a basement, and fifty or more years old and with lots of big maple trees around it.

My family knew that many repairs needed to be done to it because it was so old, but we didn't know about one major problem. That problem ended up being life threatening.

Eleven years ago, when I was six, it was a normal night of wheezing and gasping of air for my brother. He struggled with asthma when he was young, so his throat was sore often. This night was one of those nights.

"Mama," I screamed across the house from my bed.

"Mama," I shouted again.

She always took a while to get up and make it to our room. But this night did not hear the old wooden bed creak. I thought to myself, "I can't go get the water myself. I'm too scared. Indians could be lurking under my bed just waiting for a little six-year-old boy to place his feet down on the floor." Then they could snatch the young boy up and never return with him. There could even be a monster in the closet waiting for the little boy to take his covers off his little body so he could have a nice little midnight snack.

It was not easy being six. The thought that I needed a drink of water was now almost nonexistent. But the thought of Indians or monsters made me want my Mama. I yelled one more time.

"Mama! Mama! Mama!

Be right there, honey," Mama finally replied.

I heard the old bed creak. This was a great relief because I knew that the Indians had not gotten her and my Daddy. This also meant I would get a drink of water. My parents' room was just down the hall with one quick turn to the right. I knew it would not be long. She was making her way through the hallway. I could see her by now. I was so relieved until I saw her stop and fall to her knees outside my bedroom. She had fallen on the old dark cowhide that we used for carpet.

"Daddy, I'm sick. Could you get James a glass of water?"

Once again, I heard the creak of the old wooden bed frame of their bed.

Thump, and Daddy was up out of bed.

The thump sounded like when my Mama fell, but it was quite a bit louder. I then looked into the hall and saw my Daddy next to my Mama. I knew something was wrong now. "Kids we need to get out of the house," my dad yelled not long after she fell.

"What is wrong, Dad?" my sister asked.

"Something is wrong with the air in the house. Now come on, we need to get out of the house NOW!"

I slowly got out of bed along with my brother, still with the thought of Indians under my bed in the back of my mind. Once I put my legs down and nothing happened it was alright. I now concentrated on hurrying to get out of the house. I quickly slipped some pants on and walked to the hallway.

My sister and brother were all ready to go when I came out. We waited for my parents to get their robes. My Mama and dad then crawled out of their bedroom.

"Why are you crawling?" my sister asked.

"Your Mama and I have to crawl to stay away from the bad air," my Daddy tried to explain to us as we were moving towards the front door.

My brother, sister and I still did not understand. But we did not ask any other questions because we knew Daddy knew what he was talking about.

"Okay kids. Let's go," Daddy said.

We made our way downstairs to the front door where the phone was. My parents were now standing up once they got downstairs.

I'm going to call my mom and dad. We can stay over there." My Daddy explained to us and our Mama.

I did not listen to the conversation that Daddy had with my grandparents because my Mama was putting coats on all three of us children.

"Okay. They know we are coming. Let's go," my Daddy told us.

After we were out of the house, we all felt much better. We made it safely to my grandparents' house. My brother, sister and I went straight to bed. It was so late by the time we got to my grandparents that morning arrived in no time. That day someone came to look at the house to see what exactly went wrong. My Daddy thought it was carbon monoxide from the furnace, and he was right. The furnace repairman said we would have died in an hour if we had stayed in the house.

This goes to show that the Lord works in mysterious ways. A simple glass of water is desired by a six-year-old boy, saved five lives. I am glad I had a sore throat that night.

TURN BACK THE HANDS ON YOUR CLOCK

If we could only turn back the hands on our clocks or the pages of time, wouldn't it be wonderful and lots of fun?

If you could turn the pages back, who would we talk to first?

When I was about twelve years old, I read H.G. Wells' classic novel, ***The Time Machine*** and made a book report for English class. Since that time, I have been somewhat fascinated by the concept of time travel in the book and in the movie in later years. In reading many different theories about the time machine over the years and watching the movie several times over has become one of my favorites. The time tunnel transported heroes back to great moments in history, resulting in some rather exciting adventures.

The idea of time travel, through time to the future, never appealed to me much or even to travel back in time. Much different than others I have never had a desire to see into the future because it's bad enough to live it as one goes through time, day by day. I rather doubt if most would really want to know what the future may bring. It probably wouldn't fit our preconceived notions, and we probably wouldn't like it very well.

Mostly, I will admit that the possibility of witnessing some of the great events of the past intrigues me, but a lifetime experience has taught me to at least try to look at most situations in the proper perspective and sort out those things that are truly important to each of us.

If one could turn back the pages or the hands of time, my destination would not be likely be anything grand. Instead, I would like to spend a day with my grandparents as I knew them then and my parents as they were when they were still young and full of dreams and the job of living.

What I wouldn't give to sit for a while on the front porch with my paternal grandparents for a single afternoon. I would like to just talk with Grandpa Price Southworth for a time and watch as he sat there in the swing, chewing his tobacco, and whittling on an ax handle or some similar project. He gave me my first drinks of beer at age 2 and I spit it out. That is possibly why I don't care for beer today. Thanks, Grandpa! Grandpa didn't spend a lot of time in idle conversation that I remembered, but what he said was generally profound and worth listening to. He had a unique understanding of time and life and felt that he should pass along the lessons of life experiences to his grandchildren. He grew up harder than most of us could imagine in an unsympathetic world. He was turned loose to "root hog or die" when he was a little over five years old in a time where there was no welfare safety net or concerned social workers. Through it all, he earned an education not available in the most expensive of schools. That education was learned in the "school of hard knocks." He learned to read and write and figure, but equally important, he learned the value of honor, truth, hard work, paying one's bills, and veering the ground he stood upon.

I would like to spend another late spring morning with Grandpa, hoeing corn alongside him, in a long garden where the rows seemed endless and my own future stretched out ahead of me just as the corn and bean rows did. I have always hated hoeing corn or thought I did back then. In my mind today, I can still see the rise and fall of his hoe as he seemingly glided from one end of the field to the other with a minimum of effort. There's no disgrace in honest labor no matter how menial it might seem as he would tell us.

I didn't realize at the time the impact this message would have on my own life. So much of it soaked in even though youth and impatience made for no such allowances. I remember today that his words were your most prized possession as he would always caution. Grandpa Price (passed at 40) would say, "Never give it lightly and always take care to keep it. A liar is not welcome in any court."

How I wish that I could go back, if only for a little while to say, "Thank you." How wonderful it would be just to be back on that porch, listening intently this time as the old man and my Granny passes on their many oral history lessons. If I had listened more closely back then, I could have saved myself endless hours of research now about historical and family questions. More importantly I could have heard history, as it was lived by those having firsthand knowledge of it. Somehow it just didn't seem as important back then. It's amazing how clear hindsight can make things understood after living several years and attending a few of those classes in that school experience and "hard knocks" we were talking about earlier.

Many things we take for granted, and think will always be around, are sometimes those things that slip away most easily. There is considerable truth to the old adage, "You don't know what you've got until you lost it."

I remember often being seated on the front porch listening to Grandpa's stories when the kitchen door would pop open and Granny would come out carrying a pitcher of cold milk and slices of her homemade apply pies or cookies. In the years since her passing I have never tasted another pie or cookie that could even begin to compare in flavor to those that she baked in the old wood burning cookstove. Some of her recipes have been included within this publication.

I would enjoy, immensely visiting, with my maternal grandmother on her front porch. I can still remember the joy on her face with wisdom lines and her little dog when she saw me coming up to the house for a visit or to help cut the grass or to work in her garden in later years.

Like my grandmother from the other side of the family, she too, had been put out into the world to make her own way when she was only a very young child and she married when she was just 13. Her survival to reach the old age of 93 was a tribute to the human spirit. Rough as her life had been she was still a walking encyclopedia of family history and feuds. Her memory of events such as the sinking of the Titanic,

World War I, and the Great Depression were impressive. Though she had been dead for only about 20 years at this time; I still miss hearing her sing the great old ballads of long ago, and eating Mac 'N Cheese as she watched U.K. basketball on T.V. and one other food she loved was peanut butter. She would eat it out of the jar with a spoon – what else would you want, why not!

No trip back in time would be complete for me without pausing with my Mama and Daddy for Christmas Eve in the late 40's and early 50's. At that point in time, their lust for living was nowhere more evident than in their enjoyment of the yuletide season. Both are old and gone today, and their health was not great in later years as any of us can relate. It would be worth nearly any price to see them young once more and free of arthritis, hip replacement surgery, and heart problems and the ravages of time.

Sadly, time stands still for no man and marches backward only in our memories.

A HAIRCUT, SHAVE AND SHAMPOO

My brother and I would go with my father every time we needed a haircut. The barber shop was in town (Shelbyville), but today the building has been replaced with other structures.

Barber shops were not plentiful, back some 60 plus years ago. But it used to be otherwise, ready money, for those things were not to be found. Also, we did not see too many shaves given while we were in the barber shop.

When we were little, our mother would put an apron over our laps and sheared us, maybe not very artistically, but sufficiently, at least. At first, we felt rather big, for very little children but that soon wore off. Boys wore long hair until they were nearly big enough to start school, and I remember one boy in school, with his hair braided. After a fellow gets big enough to have suggestions of a voice change, he resented being shown by the home folks.

In general, we would each get a haircut in later years at the barber shop, one by one, the neck was left unshaven when the hair was cut. Some people then and now feared that shaving rather than clipping would make the neck hair grow course and abundant, as if the hair could tell whether it was cut with a razor or shears. Nearly every year or so there would be a craze for clipped or shaved heads. Most of the boys who submitted to this ordeal wanted to hide out for a week or two afterwards. Once, and only once, I had my hair clipped. The results were not very pleasing.

Then the craze for the flat top came about the time I was entering high school, and I wore the same haircut until I got to college.

Back then no barber ever gave a customer a shampoo. There was something about haircutting that was so imminently masculine that women were not welcome when the community barber was doing his work. It was well enough for grown women to cut the hair of a little boy, but that was as far as propriety could go. What would those old-fashioned ones say now if they could see our barber shops and beauty parlors?

Our father would challenge the barber who cut our hair, as we all three used the same one, in that he would double it or nothing. If our father was the loser he would pay twice the amount of the haircuts, but if he won the haircuts would not cost us a penny. To this day, I do not remember our father having to pay for our haircuts. After several years the barber would not take the challenge to bet against our father.

During the time that we were having our haircuts many of the old-timers (who live in town and nearby) would visit the shop while they rested in front of the chairs used by customers and tell stories and talk about members of the family and community.

THE BROODER HOUSE

A large brooder house was in the chicken yard along beside the chicken house that was 25 feet by 25 feet with a door and three windows that could be opened, whenever it would get too hot inside of the brooder house. Inside it had a very large heater that was 5 feet by 5 feet (it would produce ample heat for all the chicks) and all the baby chicks would get under it for heat and to keep warm, but it had a control for keeping the temperature at a nice level for the baby chicks.

This is a house with a heating machine in it. It has a clear plastic panel that allows easy viewing of the interior where the chicks stay to keep warm. The brooder was always a good place to raise baby chicks, turkeys, ducks and geese. Other individuals in the community used the same type of brooders to raise quail and other wild birds. Every January our parents would purchase around 300 baby chicks (250 rosters and 50 pullets) and put them in the brooder house to grow.

Months would pass and it would be May, and the chicks would turn into young adult chickens. Our parents would always make sure that within the group of chicks we had anywhere from 50 to 75 pullets (young female chickens) and these were for the purpose of laying of eggs in the future. All the other 200 to 225 chicks were rosters (young male chickens) and they were for the purpose of food for the family.

As May arrived and school was out for the summer this was always our first job. Killing the rosters, dress them (take off all the feathers, clean and cut them up into parts) and they were put into our large freezer, and they were our chicken meat to eat for the coming year.

I remember, one year, my brother always had the job of taking off the head of each and one time we were waiting and waiting and waiting for chickens. Our father went to learn what had happened and found him on the ground passed out. After bringing him back to himself we learned that he saw too much blood, at one time, and that made him pass out. We would always keep a few to eat during the summer and not use the ones in the freezer.

On a Sunday in midsummer, we were having the preacher of our church and family for dinner after church and our mother had me and my sister to go and kill two rosters on Saturday, as they were the last two that we had. We did just that and everything was going well and on Sunday, just as we were starting to eat dinner, would you believe that both roosters started to crow for the first time. Our mother looked at us both and said, "I thought we killed the last two roosters?" Well, we had to own up to the fact that we killed two rather large young hens, as roosters for the most part are larger than hens. Needless to say, we both were in big trouble when the preacher and family left for the day.

The truth was that we had made pets out of the two roosters and did not wish to give them up, but eventually, we had to give them up for the table for Sunday dinner several weekends later.

Here in the flat land of Central Kentucky, one doesn't have to range very far back in time, to recall the day when chickens and eggs were important financial mainstays of the average farm family. Whenever our neighbor would need a pound of coffee, a bag of salt, a poke of flour, a quarter's worth of sugar, or a nickel's worth of soda. They either casketed up a few dozen eggs they had been saving up, or had the children go out and run down an old hen or a fryer or two, which were taken to the country store to swap for these commodities.

In the good old days, poultry-raising was a haphazard operation based not so much on science as a change for folklore. As a consequence, chickens -- largely left to fend for themselves -- were wild as ruffed grouses and catching them involved foot-raising, tree climbing, and other forms of strenuous exercise.

To make the catching job easier, the housewife, if she happened to have some around for "medicinal purposes," mixed a dallop of moonshine with cornmeal bran and dumped it in the chicken trough. After eating this mixture, the poultry selected for trade became a bit dizzy and could be picked up without any trouble at all. They could also have their feet tied and be carried to the store with a minimum of squawking and flopping of the wings.

According to an old belief extant at that time, the moon made the eggs hatch better and faster, and the rusty nail protected both hen and eggs from weasels, skunks and blacksnakes that raided chicken houses often. To produce pullets (to become laying hens), round eggs were selected for incubation. If young roosters were wanted for the skillet when the circuit rider came by, a few sharp pointed eggs were included in the 'settin'. By these shapes, round or sharp pointed, the hen setter supposedly determined the sex of the chicks, or "doodlers" as they were sometimes called.

To make chickens grow fat in a hurry and old hens lay more eggs, some poultry raisers, fermented a mash or coarse cornmeal, (chop) malt and water.

On this mixture of feed, the birds often got drunk as badgers and were "easy pickings" for roving foxes and two-legged chicken thieves, but they got fatter in a week on this fare then in a month or more out scratching for bugs and other morsels from the wild.

Among the more credulous chicken keepers of the past, there was an old belief that during Dog Days, aged roosters surreptitiously laid and incubated eggs. These eggs were marble size and hatched out not baby chicks, but rusty coated lizards.

This belief was absurd, of course, but a lot of big fence lizards have been seen between the logs and on the board roofs of old henhouses, and many years ago individuals believed in rooster eggs.

I always had a love for animals, all kinds were made into pets, as many as possible. I recall one time I collected Batham eggs. A Batham lays one of the smallest eyes of any chicken. This chicken has five toes with feathers on its legs and feathers on the body that feels much like fur. One summer I collected their eggs and set them to hatch some babies. Well, over a hundred hatched. Therefore, I put them in the brooder house to raise to adulthood. As they were growing my mother found out about the chicks. She told me that I was to save all of the females and kill the males for eating purposes. As I followed through for several Saturdays to complete the order, I learned through this experience that I would never raise Batham chickens again because of my love for animals. It gave me additional work to do that was not needed. Oh, I put the females in with our laying hens with hopes that in the future, they will be egg layers, too.

THE RUNAWAY CAT

Turpentine is the key word in this story because from time to time we would have a stray cat to come visit and my brother and I would set a trap to catch the cat. Sometimes it would take a while and others we may get the cat overnight.

The reason for catching the stray cat was because it would get into things, tear up feed bags, fight with our home cats, eat chicken eggs and chickens sometimes, and would just generally damage things around the farm.

After catching the stray cat, we would get it out of the cage (sometimes the cat would bite us or we would get big scratches) and I would hold it very tight and my brother would lift up the tail of the cat and rub its butt with a used corn cob (without corn on it), making the area raw. Then he would apply turpentine on the raw area. At this point, there was no holding the cat because it would take off like a fired rocket and we would never see the stray cat again.

At this point, you should be laughing if you have insight to see this entire event taking place. Of course, we did this every time we had a stray cat. I feel that the word got out after we did several cats, we never did have any other strays to appear.

A SICK KID

The story is about a medication called "Fletcher's Castoria" when I was a kid – would rather take it and enjoy the nostalgic taste than use pills that are not very gentle. I am glad that it's still on the market today.

Before you read the story about what happened just take a second to read about the medication.

Warnings – Fletcher's Castoria – This is what the directions say about the medication:

- Ask a doctor before use if you have stomach pain, nausea, or vomiting. A sudden change in bowel habits that lasts over 2 weeks.

- Stop using it and ask a doctor if you have rectal bleeding or fail to have a bowel movement after use. These may be signs of a serious condition. You need to use a laxative for more than 1 week.

- If pregnant or breast-feeding, ask a health professional before use.

- Keep out of reach of children. In case of accidental overdose, get medical help or contact a Poison Control Center right away.

If you want to get the best price for **Fletchers Castoria Pain & Fever,** it's always good to compare and shop around for the most affordable **Fletchers Castoria Pain & Fever** on Medicines and Remedies. You have a choice from among several brands on the market.

Use **<u>supsale.com</u>** for all your shopping needs, search, sort, save and buy more wisely.

Active Ingredients: Each teaspoonful contains: Senna Concentrate (33.3 mg/ml)   **Inactive Ingredients:** Citric Acid, Flavor, Glycerin, Methylparaben, Propylparaben, Water (Purified), Sodium Benzoate, Sucrose (Sugar)

This is what took place with the medication—being at a very young age, all three of us kids were very sick at the same time with something, and our mother gave us this good tasting, sweet, and smooth medication for whatever we had—that I do not remember in later years. However, once we each started to feel better, my brother, being the oldest and first to feel better, got up out of bed and started looking for that good tasting medicine.

This is the story that our mother told on my brother and what happened. He climbed on everything around and finally started climbing around in the bathroom and climbed up on the bathtub to reach into the medicine cabinet.

Once he found the medicine cabinet he looked and looked and finally reached up and got the bottle of **Fletcher's Castoria**, and to the surprise of everyone, managed to drink the entire bottle of **Fletcher's Castoria** medicine just because it tasted good!

Our mother took over at this point by giving him other medications to offset the laxative from working him too much, if you get what I am talking about. After it was all over with he is still living today and just maybe he learned something from the experience, but he would not tell you if he did.

KIDS HAD MORE FUN IN THE GOLDEN OLD DAYS

In today's fast-paced world it seems to many of us that our youth are not enjoying their children as much as we did in the days of yesterday. Of course, each generation remembers its youth as a time of great fun and excitement.

When I was a kid in the 40s, years ago, April 1 had a three-fold meaning for us: (1) it was the first day of the year that my parents "might" let us go barefooted, (2) it was the day for April fool jokes, and (3) it was my grandmother Cole's birthday.

My grandmother Cole was a well-educated woman, but some 60 years ago, going barefooted headed the list. If April 1 was a warm day, off came the shoes and socks. April usually was a month of off and on days as they are currently. When May arrived most of the days were barefoot days, except for time spent at school and church. I remember all of this from a boy's viewpoint. I didn't observe girls enough to remember their barefooted habits.

Sixty years ago, the schoolteachers had authority to spank or whip pupils who misbehaved. If a pupil got a spanking or whipping at school, it was automatic that the pupil would get another whipping once they arrived home that day. Kids minded their parents or got their bottoms spanked or their legs switched. Kids had chores to do daily. They did the chores and still had ample time to play. It was a world of no radio, television, limited comic books, no little league sports, no computers, cell phones, and no fast-food restaurants.

Kids made their own fun. Going barefooted was a part of that fun. The soles of our feet, tender in spring, were tough when school reopened in the fall. We learned by trial and error where to walk and where not to walk. A place not to walk barefooted was in the chicken yard, the dairy barn, hog lot or the barn lot. If you've never been in a barn yet you should visit one soon.

Going barefooted resulted in a nightly take of washing dirty feet before going to bed. It was more than a task. It was an ordeal for a tired, sleepy kid to have to wash his/her feet, but it was the lesser of the two evils. The other was getting a spanking for getting the sheets dirty.

Once in a while you would get a bee sting from going barefooted and it really hurt but the next day no one remembered what happened the day before.

A boy's valuable possession was a tobacco stick, usually made of oak, about four feet long with a girth of one square inch. This was used in playing, tin can hockey. A tin coffee can, with lid on, was placed in the center of a yard or small field. Sides were chosen and the game started. The tobacco stick was used to knock the coffee can across a goal line. This game was also called "shinny" because our shins often took a beating.

The tobacco stick was also used to bat flying bats at night. In using a flashlight to make light the bats would fly into the light to catch bugs, and we would swing our stick to hit them.

Our fun changed with the changing of seasons. In the spring we made our own kites and flew them. We shot marbles, spun tops and played scrub baseball. A popular game was dinks. Stores sold clay marbles about the size of moth balls. These were called dinks and cost about five cents per hundred. A small circle or square was drawn on level barren ground. Each player anted the same number of dinks. Players took turns shooting a large marble called a taw. A player kept the dinks he/she knocked from the ring or square; this was called: "playing for keeps," which was frowned on by some adults.

Spinning tops was more than just the art of being able to make a top twirl around at high speed. It was a game of trying to splinter your opponents' tops. A new top had to be worked on before it was ready for battle. The blunt metal tip of the top was extracted. A nail was driven where the tip had been. The nail was filed to its finest point possible. It was now game ready. Players then spun their tops. The object was to hurl your top downward into a spin in such a manner that the fine nail point would strike another spinning top and make a dent in its wood or even groove out a tiny chunk of top. All tops back then were made of wood. Plastic tops were first used in the early 70s.

Scrub baseball was played by as many players as wanted to play. There were no sides. No score was kept. Four batters were chosen. All others took positions on the field, with the order of progression established before play began. If a fly ball was caught, the batter was out and the person catching the fly exchanged places with the batter. When a batter struck out or grounded out, the catcher became one of the four bests. The person making the out then went to the end of the line of progression.

We seldom pitched horseshoes. The old men, as we called them, took over the game and they were really good. To most of us horseshoe was a dull game.

By midsummer it was swimming, June bugs, and fishing. Preparation for swimming began about the last of May with inoculations against typhoid fever. Three shots were taken, one each week in alternate arms. It was sort of a status symbol to let everyone know your arms were sore from the inoculations. Sixty years ago (long before the wonder drugs like penicillin) typhoid fever, like pneumonia and diphtheria, was most often a one-way street to the cemetery.

There were no swimming pools, (only in town but we could not run to town to swim) only swimming holes at the creek, with crude wooden platforms and leaning trees with one-wire swings for swinging out over the creek and dropping off into the water. Most of the swimmers were not actually swimmers, they waded and wallowed in shallow water and wore everyday clothing. Few wore bathing suits for the occasion.

As I told you previously, June bug season was a delight. The June bug has strong legs with barbs on them. They are easily found, eating corn, tomatoes, grapes, and any other type of fruit one could find. A strand of light sewing thread was tied on the back leg of the June bug where the leg meets the body. The other end of the thread could be held while the June bug flew in a futile attempt to escape. When a June bug was tied to the other end of the thread, the two bugs would fly in a circle when pitched into the air. The thread could be tied to a clothesline, and the bugs would fly around and around and wind the thread around the clothesline. Three or four bugs could be tied at each end of the thread and placed on a cloth rug and there would be a tug-of-war. Or a June bug could be put in a slingshot and shot high into the air. Sometimes they seemed dazed after such a fast and high trip.

During the hot summer we soaked corncobs in cold water and had corncob fights. We played cards while sitting on the grass in the shade. We had toad frog hopping contests. I would catch toads, poke a few BBs down their throats and watch them do off-balance hops.

August was supposedly a dangerous month for going barefooted. August was pure Dog Days. It was our belief that August was the worst month for dogs to go mad (rabies). Walking barefooted in dew-wet grass was a big no-no! Our bare feet might come in contact with saliva that had dropped from the mouth of a mad dog. When the grass was dry, there was no danger. Some of us wore tennis shoes in the mornings and took them off in the afternoons when the grass was dry.

In the fall we played football, leapfrog, and went hunting for hickory and walnuts, which were found in abundance along country roads and in unfenced groves.

An enjoyable and daring part of out-of-door fun was hiding behind the barn or smokehouse, and smoking dried corn silk, ground coffee, grapevine, the dried bloom of a week called "Life Everlasting," and cubebs could be bought at the drug store for about ten cents for a package of ten. They were made to be smoked as a treatment for catarrh, an inflammation of the mucous membranes in the nose and throat.

In winter when no snow was on the ground, we played checkers, dominoes, Rood (10 kinds), popped corn, and pulled taffy candy. Our checker playing wasn't very good. The best thing about winter, except for Thanksgiving and Christmas, was that kids took a bath only once a week – on Saturday night, standing by a stove or in front of an open grate fireplace and sponging off with water from a large wash bowl or tub, that held about three quarts of water, after which long, winter underwear was put on and worn for a week. Winter, overall, was a long, slow season. Mostly it was a time of waiting for spring when we could start the fun cycle over again.

SPRINGTIME ON THE FARM

When you live and work on a farm young Kentuckians greet spring warm weather by shedding shoes. The return of the birds, the lengthening of the days, and the new flowers and buds are no more signs of spring than are children's many activities. At our home in the country on the farm, we did not have many tops or kites, with the exception of a few homemade ones; our spring signs were of another kinds.

When the fish began to swim upstream, we went fishing but not too much in those days, with cane poles when they were handy, but more often with long, slender, not-too-straight limbs that we had cut with our own knives from the trees along the creek, mostly willows because they were strong. As I stated before, I do not recall doing much fishing; it sems to me that fishing was for grown-ups. Before I was big enough to cut my own pole, Daddy would cut one for me, having previously baited his pole and set it to catch the first eager biter. I always felt slighted in this event, for I wanted to catch the big fish for myself, so I could boast about it just one time.

Not long after the first fishing weather, sap begins to rise in the hickories. That means that the bark will not be easy to slip off when young inventors get ready to try their skills. The first thing to be made, ordinarily, was a whistle. To make a good one required some skills, we used to laugh at the poor little fellows who were too clumsy with their knives even to make a whistle. After this invention is properly attended to, any average boy wants a hickory-bark whip, which is really a work of art when properly made in those days of long ago. Until it gets dry and stiff, it quite properly resembles the blacksnake whip used by grown-ups and confers a certain distinction on its owner and maker.

Just around the corner from hickory-bark whips and whistles is another hickory product, just as typical as that. That is the leaf hat, but hickory has to share this honor with the papaw. But hickory leaves are better in the long run, for they are tougher and, therefore, can be worked into more shapes with the right number of pins made from dead weeds. But leaf hats, after all, are pretty girlish, though I must confess to having made several in my early days.

Spring brings playhouse time, though fall is good for that, too. I refer to playhouses made out in the woods, where moss grows green and where all sorts of things can be found to decorate a house with and to even build a rock fireplace for night use. Spring moss is green though, and fall, when we had to wear shoes, our feet were so tough that we felt that we would spend the winter barefooted and suffer no injury. But several months of wearing home-knit yarn stockings soften up the toughest feet. Hence, when we pull off our winter apparel and try being natural again, we own a pair of the tenderest feet that ever were known to mankind.

We always had acorn hulls that were not noticed, the fall before, seem like big rough rocks; and gravel can take on more elements of torture than anything I have even known except a stubble field. But by degrees even tender feet can become accustomed to a harsh ground again and get by just about everything but broken glass and rusty nails.

Spring is here then to stay until the frosts of the fall, long prophesied by katydids, come again and compel us to shut up our aching feet in hard leather shoes for the winter.

DEATH ON THE HILL

School was out and my brother and sister had just graduated from high school. I had just finished my sophomore year of high school. Why they were in the same class is another story later.

The summer started out very hot and as farmers we were always putting up hay for the livestock, in order to have enough feed for the approaching winter. At this time, the family was renting a farm on the other side of the county, and we were in the process of putting up hay from that farm. We had been in the hay field for several days and looked forward to getting finished and getting the equipment home. On our last day my brother and I loaded up the truck with hay, roped it all down and started home through town.

About a mile from home as we were going over a hill on the highway I noticed, looking back through the marrow on the truck, that hay was falling off the truck and we tied the hay down with ropes before leaving the farm where we loaded it. We stopped the truck and that is when we learned that some boys in town had jumped onto the back of the truck and laid down on the top of the hay. Somehow, or, someone on the truck, cut the rope and caused the hay to start falling off. To our surprise we learned that a boy had fallen off the truck and hit his head on the side of the blacktop and was killed.

I ran home and had my mother call the police because we had no cell phones in those days, plus we had a party line. All in all, the police investigated and wrote the report; we went home with the rest of the load of hay and drove back with a tractor and wagon and reloaded the hay that had fallen off the truck to clear the road.

As the summer went on, just as hot, our parents received notice from the sheriff that we were being sued for the death of the boy that was killed. This notice really upset everyone in the family and friends around us.

Later we learned that these boys had been jumping on various trucks going through town and when one would stop at a stop light they would jump on—city boys finding something to do with all the spare time that they had.

My father, brother, and I had talked with lawyers through interviews of what actually took place. Some of the questions that I recall quickly was: "Did you give permission to the boys to ride the truck?" the boys were saying "yes," and we were saying "no." The interviews were going back and forth, over and over, again and again.

As the trial date was arriving quickly, we had some luck to come to us in a good way. Our father had a good friend that lived in town who was a "jobber." Mr. Ben Raymond sold cattle, for a commission, for farmers having a surplus of young heifers and to farmers needing young heifers with calves to milk herds. He also worked one of the boys riding the truck to cut his grass, trim bushes, etc., around his home. They were talking one day and the boy shared with Mr. Raymond that they got on the truck in town without permission to do so.

Mr. Raymond called our father, and my father and Mr. Raymond went into town to talk with lawyers on both sides, and the court case was dropped at that time!

After all of this was over, we learned that the group of boys had been jumping wagons and trucks for the last three summers, to this point, and they would ride the load out of town as far as it would go. Once they got off the load of hay they would hitchhike back to town and do it all over again, time after time.

Looking back from present day, I know that we were better off having lots of work to do on the farm and not having free time, on our hands, to allow us to get into trouble growing up.

"BIRTH AND DEATH" is the beginning and the end of earthly life, and no human being who has within him even a faint longing for the Truth can disregard the two important questions – how does life enter the physical body, and what becomes of it after death?"

Physical death must lose its terror when we know that for the forward-striving human being it is simply a crossing from one sphere or creation to another.

People React Emotionally and Physically

When coping with a death, you may go through all kinds of emotions. You may be sad, worried, or scared. You might be shocked, unprepared, or confused. You might be feeling angry, cheated, relieved, guilty, exhausted, or just plain empty. Your emotions might be stronger or deeper than usual, or mixed together in ways you've never experienced before, as I'm sure, the family losing a son in the hay accident.

Some people find they have trouble concentrating, studying, sleeping, or eating when they're coping with a death. While others lose interest in activities they used to enjoy. Some people lose themselves in playing computer games or eating or drinking to excess. Some people feel numb, as if nothing has happened. All of these are normal ways to react to a death.

What is Grief?

When we have emotional, physical, and spiritual reactions in response to a death or loss, it's known as grief or grieving. People who are grieving might: (1) feel strong emotions, such as sadness and anger, (2) have physical reactions, such as not sleeping or even waves of nausea; and (3) have spiritual reactions to a death – for example, some people find themselves questioning their beliefs and feeling disappointed in their religion while others find that they feel more strongly than ever about their faith.

The grieving process takes time and healing usually happens gradually. The intensity of grief may be related to how sudden or predictable the loss was and how you felt about the person who died.

Some people write about grief happening in stages, but usually it feels more like "waves" or cycles of grief that come and go depending on what you are doing and if there are triggers for remembering the person who has died. Death is the end of life, a permanent cessation of all vital functions. Dying refers to the body's preparation for death, which may be very short in the case of accidental death, or can last weeks or months or even years.

KILLING HOGS

We always raised hogs, more than what we needed, but every year at Thanksgiving we would kill eight hogs or so, for home use, (pork meat for the next year) and from Thursday through Sunday, we would work up the meat, cutting it in pieces and parts such as hams, slabs of bacon, shoulders, jowl, and cut up the fat to make lard for cooking purposes, etc. Our mother would take the head of the hog and cook it to tender and then she would make souse and Hogs-Head Pudding or Head Cheese and we would eat these products for breakfast. Here is how you make it:

HOGS HEAD PUDDING OR HEAD CHEESE

Boil the forehead, ears and feet, and nice scraps trimmed from the hams of the Fresh hog, until the meat will almost drop from the bones. Then separate the Meat from the bones, put in large chopping bowl, and season with pepper, salt, Sage and summer savory. Chop it rather coarsely; put it back in the same kettle It was boiled in, with just enough of the liquor in which it was boiled to prevent burning; warm it thoroughly, mixing it well together. Now pour it into a strong Muslin bag, press the bag between two flat surfaces, with a heavy weight on top; When cold and solid it can be cut in slices. Good cold or warmed up in vinegar.

One statement that our father said that I will remember for life and that was "that a hog is good from its rotor to its tutor."

The first day we would kill the hogs, and allow the meat to cook out overnight, the next day we would start to cut up the meat and cutting away the fat and unwanted skin. The third day we would start to cook the fat (called rendering) until parts would become crispy and all of the water was cooked out of the fat (then it becomes lard) and during the next coming year our mother would use the lard to cook with – fry chicken, fried pork chops, fried pies, make pie crust, break, etc., because back then we did not have factory made cooking oils.

The third day was always a special day because when the first batch of lard was done, we would take part of the lard to our house, and my mother would use it to cook fresh cake doughnuts (to make these you will have further information back in the document). If you have never eaten a fresh cooked cake doughnut right out of the oil, you have missed out on one of the pleasures of life in eating! She would put white icing on some, cinnamon and sugar on some and she even made yeast doughnuts while she was at it. These doughnuts were enjoyed by everyone around and she always made so many that we had leftovers the next day.

On the fourth day we would start to apply brown sugar/salt cure to the meat and put all of it into the smokehouse and we would continue to apply the cure to the next for several weeks until you could tell that the cure was taking to the meat. Of course, the weather would help sometimes if it did not get too cold. If the weather became too cold the cure mix would not go into the meat, and the meat would spoil. The perfect time to cure meat would be when the temperature was around 25 degrees and with some moisture in the air and the cure on the meat would sweat, and the cure would go into the meat just the way you wanted it.

We would allow the meat to take in just the right amount of cure mix and then we would brush it off and hang the hams, shoulders, etc., until late spring. In late spring we would take the meat wash off of the cure mix and then sprinkle the meat with borax and cayenne pepper, hand up the meat and all it to go through what is called "June sweat." You apply borax and cayenne pepper to make the outside skin tough and to keep skips out (skips are bugs that boar into the meat, live and meat on the meat and you get nothing but trouble.

Along about August we would start eating the meat as baked ham, fried shoulder, of course, we were already eating bacon and sausages: Here is how you make country sausage:

COUNTRY SAUSAGES

(to 10 pounds of pork)

3-4 soup spoons of salt

3-4 soup spoons of sage

2 tablespoons black pepper

½ -1 ½ tablespoons red pepper

Mix well

I do remember that when we would run out of bacon and sausages (breakfast food) in growing up, our mother would fix fried chicken or steak for breakfast – yummy good!

She would always make coffee cakes, doughnuts, pancakes, just to name a few for breakfast, and we had fresh milk from our cows to wash these good things down.

Looking at our property from the main road, the dairy barn was to the right of the house and when the wind was blowing in the direction of the barn from the house, while we were milking the cows, we could always tell what was for breakfast before we got to the house to eat.

Our mother was a firm believer that her children should eat healthy to grow up big and strong. This included drinking a quart of milk per day and eating three good meals daily. Our parents always stressed the importance of a good breakfast, and our mother called it the most important meal of the day. Our mother was always a stickler for good health practices. She taught us kids that "cleanliness is next to godliness" and demanded that we brush our teeth regularly. There were no fruit flavored vitamins for kids in those days to take, but our mother was a big believer in cod liver oil. That stuff had to be the most foul-tasting concoction, outside of castor oil, that ever went in our mouths. It was supposed to be food for you thoroughly, or so everybody said. I expected some improvements when Mama switched from cod liver oil in the liquid form to cod liver oil pills once they came on the market. The pills were gel caps or fish eggs of sorts and tasted pretty bad in their own way, but Mama was never satisfied for us to just swallow the evil things. She insisted that we bite into the pills, saying that you had to do so to get the full benefit of the vitamins and minerals supposed to be inside them.

When company came, which was often, sometimes my grandmother would come for a visit too, My grandmother made her wonderful sausage gravy in the old cast iron skillet and baked mountains of large fluffy, "cathead" biscuits in the oven of the old stove. The smoke from the wood smelled almost as good as the biscuits baking early in the morning. In those days eggs were considered a healthy choice, and most breakfast tables wouldn't have been complete without them. Sometimes our mother's breakfast included country ham, smoked bacon, homemade sausage, or all three. The breakfast I remember most at my grandmother's house featured heaping platters of juicy pork chops or golden fried chicken. Again, cholesterol was unheard of back then, and folks were more concerned about food that tasted good. Guests that ate breakfast at Grandmother's house never forgot the experience and still talk about it 60 years later.

A real country ham can be made only with time and experienced skills!

When one thinks of country ham, maybe one envisions a hand-hewn smokehouse: puffing aromatic clouds against a crisp winter sky, or the firm, burnished meat handling from the rafters in summer. If you are familiar with country ham at all, one sniff can jolt recollections in greatest detail – who can forget the stinging aroma of burning leaves, salt, and sometimes mold, tainted by a subtle sour odor? Old timers will tell you that it's similar to the smell of old socks, but somehow, the curious blend of scents is rich, warm and inviting.

The ham grows stronger with age in taste and smell, and it's usually the most seasoned of ham lovers who seek the mouth-puckering twang of a ham at least a year old. One is sure to want to savor the ham in the most traditional Southern breakfast as well – ham slicked from the center and fried, then served with scrambled eggs, grits, homemade biscuits, and of course, redeye gravy.

Today, you'll still find that well-loved morning menu at most Southern-style restaurants, but today you'll also find country ham in all kinds of winning recipes at the prestigious Culinary Olympics, and international competition held every four years in Frankfort, Germany, or in favored dishes of national know chefs.

You can even get cooked and boned country ham squeezed into uniformly shaped loaves, ready for slicing. A good country ham is one of the most demanding items of society with less time and storage space, but a strong craving for a taste of the past for any given special season.

Even though the first Virginia ham appeared over 350 years ago, the curing process, even among commercial producers, has not succumbed to technological take-over. "There are only three things that make country ham," and these three include: time, temperature and humidity. Therefore, the art of curing hams has been preserved in its purest form, with a minimum of ways to decrease production time.

Just less than 50 years ago, curing ham was a standard farm chore for many living in Maryland, Virginia, Kentucky, Tennessee, North

Carolina, and Georgia, where the year-round weather conditions meet requirements for curing ham.

We even know people who have a country ham business; of course, government's strict regulations for food safety, commercial operations have adjusted in their buildings to meet recent requirements. However, the curing process is still the same today.

Who cures the best country ham? This question has been going on for years to get an answer. If politics, barbecue and country ham prevail in the South, so will a difference of opinion. A "real" country ham can only be determined by where you grew up.

The rich tradition of 350 years and scores of hand-me-down stories are as strong as lure to county ham as the unique flavor. Just make a visit to the closest place where country hams are cured and you'll probably find an old timer willing to share some stories about a subject close to his heart and palate.

It may surprise you to find, too, that most commercial businesses in the industry are just as steeped in tradition as the product we make. Owners are typically third-generation ham producers, and the workers often would have 35 to 50 years of service in the family business.

Many of the companies started as a side-line for the first owner. Most of the old-timers will also tell you that once upon a time, having a country ham in the smokehouse was like having money in the bank; it was as good as currency for purchasing goods and/or services 50 years ago. After four generations of ham curing for customers, the family is still serving it to visitors at breakfast, lunch and dinner in the South.

So, all through the South, at any given time of the day, it's a safe bet that somewhere, someone is savoring a taste of country ham. Somewhere, smokehouses hold the preservation of an art. Everywhere, the story of country ham is passing from one generation to another.

Our Mama and grandmother's breakfasts were a tough act to follow, but our mother was equal to the challenge as our grandmother did a very good job teaching our mother what and how to cook. Our mother made the best homemade biscuits of any around and we did not have store bought biscuits in those days.

Mama's breakfast table probably offered a bit more variety than most people. We always kept chickens and hogs, so there was no shortage of eggs, sausage, and ham (fresh or cured). At times we enjoyed fresh fish (salmon) occasionally for lunch. We also had our fill of rabbit and squirrel, and Mama always made gravy to go with these. Our homemade products included: butter, honey, sorghum, grape jelly, blackberry jelly or jam, raspberry jelly, plum preserves, maple syrup, apple butter, apple sauce, peach preserves, strawberry preserves, jam or jelly, or apply jelly. No restaurant in the community offered a wider selection, and we had plenty of cold milk to wash everything down.

Mama fried big, thick pork chops for breakfast sometimes just as our grandmother did, but my personal favorite was always fried chicken.

There were few things I enjoyed more than munching on a hot drumstick and dunking my biscuits in hot chicken gravy. Such feats were generally reserved for the weekends or summer mornings when the children had time to enjoy them.

I will always remember getting up many mornings to milk the cows before breakfast and we could tell that we were having fried chicken for breakfast. The approved or common methods of assassinating the victims were wringing their necks or chopping off their heads with an ax or knife. I was always too "chicken-hearted" for the wringing of the neck, but I used a knife to do the job. Since we raised our own chickens, it was practical to thin out the young roosters and keep the pullets for laying hens. Things didn't always work out according to plans, however.

One weekend our mother and I were talking in the back yard and about that time one of my uncles had brought his family for a weekend visit and Mama said quickly go and kill two more chickens we will need them for Sunday dinner. In life and work, sometimes you do get lucky!

When Thanksgiving rolled around annually, we always knew it was time to butcher hogs. Thanksgiving back in the 40's and 50's was very cold weather (freezing) not warm as it is today in 2025.

We never thought of butchering less than 10 to 12 hogs at one time. When processing the hogs we would lay them on wagons to cool out (body heat) as they were cut into parts: hams, shoulders, bacon, jowl, etc., to allow body heat to cool overnight. The next day we would start trimming everything and there were fat trimmings that was used to make lard.

My brother was responsible for cooking the lard. When the lard was done, this activity took place, it was poured through a strainer lined with a white cloth to catch the finer crumbs. It would take several days for the lard to get hard. Once this was achieved the lard would be stored in the basement of the house to use. When we strained the hot lard and we would get fresh crackling to eat, they were really good. Meanwhile, the hams, shoulders, etc., would take trimmings which would go into the making of sausage. The other meats would go into the smoke house to be cured in time.

Our mother would take odd pieces of cloth from sewing and make bags to stuff sausage in. Once the sausages and all were seasoned and mixed well, we would roll the sausage into long strips and drop these into the homemade sausage bags. Then the sausages were stored in the smoke house for several months until they were ready for the freezer. Next, we would take the sausage to the house and wrap each in white freezer paper and put in the freezer and take it out when needed.

Milking time: This process from cow to the table requires work. A cool glass of milk and a hot buttered biscuit or corn bread is so good! In the early 1930's each farm and many town residents had their own cow or cows, milking them by hand, then processing the raw milk into various components for use in the home and perhaps for selling if they had ample supply. Cows were fulfilling the family and community needs. With milk, butter, cream, buttermilk, etc., the family was set for several meals coming up. Before the automatic milking equipment, cows were milked morning and night, and within the four seasons, too. We had electric milkers, but we milked our show cows (Brown Swiss) by hand due to taking cows away from the farm to show in competition. After the milk was taken (home use) to the house, the raw milk was separated into various needs: sweet milk, butter, cream, buttermilk, and none of the children wanted to churn. The cows that were milked by hand took (show cattle) anywhere from 10 to 20 minutes, but normally with the new machines it only took about tree minutes to milk a cow. We had a herd of milking cows to about 100, not including dry stock, calves, heifers, hogs, chicken, goats, horses and mules, etc., had to be cared for.

On the farm we raised all our own meat: pork, beef and chickens. In January our parents would purchase 200 baby chicks: 50 females and 150 males. When school was out, usually the first part of June, the family would work together to process the 150 male chickens. Processing meant to: kill, scald, pluck, clean out the inside of each, then cut up the chicken into parts, package and freeze. This was our eating chickens for the year to follow. By brother would catch, hang, off with the heads, and bring the birds to us. Our mother and I would scald the birds, my sister and father would pluck the birds, and then my mother and I would clean out the birds, but up and bag for the freezer.

No one would have guessed that our father would have a hobby of German Sheperd dogs. It was not only a hobby but income for the family. Our father had one male dog (Romie) and three bitches. These three females were used for the purpose of producing puppies for profit. These females were: Snow, she was as white as snow; Princess, she was a regular looking German Sheperd dog; and Ginger, she had a brown cast all over.

The big male, Romie, was a true color of a German Sheperd dog. Daddy would let him come into the kitchen while we were having breakfast. Romie knew his place in the house as he would go under a white table that our mother kept the radio on. Outside Romie was tied to a very large maple tree in the back yard. Romie would charge anyone that came in to see Daddy.

As for the puppies, each female would have anywhere from four to eight puppies and we would play with them until they were eight weeks old and then they went to the army to be trained to become service dogs.

My brother was in the army and my sister was at the University of Kentucky and I would soon be leaving for college. With all of the movement taking place in the family, our father had to put the farm, livestock and equipment up for sale. Naturally, all members of the family were concerned about Romie because he was so big, strong and vicious.

Finally, Daddy found a new home with Transylvania University in Lexington, Kentucky.   Romie would be walking with the night watchman on campus and would be their guard dog.

Once the puppies and the adults were sold, our mother would complete registration paperwork on each.

Having goats had a purpose as we milked the goats twice daily for my grandmother Southworth as she had an ulcerated stomach and her doctor told her to drink goat's milk. We took the milk to her every other day to Lexington. After four years of goat's milk, she made the decision to have surgery to remove her ulcers for good.

SLED RIDING

To sleigh ride in the wintertime and when the snow is on the ground is always lots of fun with a light layer of ice on the surface. We were living in Lexington, Kentucky, off Parks Mill Road on our small farm and one winter's night snow fell with ice in it. The next day we went sledding in the field and the color of the sled was bright red. I still have my sled today and I use it as a coffee table in our den.

Allow me to set this experience up for the reader: just outside the yard was a stone fence and a driveway running the length of the fence, our father left an old horse drawn wagon parked on the other side of the driveway. We got our sleds out and my brother and sister doubled up on one sled to ride down the hill. Back then a horse drawn wagon had a tongue that you would hook a team of mules/horses up to it, in order to pull the wagon. The wagon also had that same tongue running all the way back under the wagon to the other end of the wagon.

As my brother and sister took off down the hill they somehow went under the middle of the wagon, and to their surprise, the cross tongue caught my brother (my sister was on top of my brother riding) and pulled them off and the sled went on down over the hill to the bottom and ended up in the creek. What a ride!

REMEMBERING THE OLD COOKING STOVE

How well I remember our mother having milk on the back of the old black stove making buttermilk, butter, cottage cheese as we were very young and growing up through the years. Back then our father would take these products to town and sell butter, cottage cheese and eggs to customers in town.

Today our entire lives are governed by time and something quick. Everyday everything seems to get faster. We can fly from New York to London almost as quickly as we can drive from Cincinnati to Atlanta. We can speak to friends in the Philippines almost as fast as we can talk to our in-laws just across the road. We can prepare a complete dinner in less than ten minutes.

Yes, we are controlled by time and, to be honest, we seem to be able to accomplish a great deal more because of this. But, as with everything else, we lose part of our lives as we take advantage of improvements. I'm not sure if all the trade-offs are good ones.

I admit that I take advantage of every labor-saving device that I can. I am one of those individuals who will throw a frozen dinner into the microwave and sit impatiently for the timer to buzz. When the meal is consumed, I only need to pick up everything and throw plates, napkins, and leftovers into the chicken bucket as we give our chickens scraps from the house. Just think of all the time that I have saved.

It is after some of these speedy meals that I quite often begin to think about kitchens and meals in my distant past. They were occasions rather than things that just had to be done. Meals were then events to be enjoyed rather than periods of lost time to be endured.

The central elements in those "then" kitchens were, strangely enough, the stoves. Oh, I'm not thinking of the new hi-level, multi-purpose mysteries which now grace out cooking rooms; I'm referring to those black, cast-iron coal burners that sat in the corner.

These stoves were especially welcomed on cold winter days. The warmth from the 'cook stove's' coal fire just seemed to last longer. These seemed to be feeling of well-being in the room as we sat basking in the glow.

These coal stoves were magnificent creations. There was room for 4 pans of steaming goodies. The oven had room to prepare several tasty treats at one time. On one side of the stove was a reservoir to heat several gallons of water at one time. At the eye level, jutting out over the cooking surface was the "warming closet," where leftovers were kept warm for those later night snacks.

Without a doubt, though, my fondest stove memories are of early mornings and late evenings. Nothing ever felt better than putting on a stove-warmed pair of jeans before going out into the cold Kentucky morning. Too, before in-house plumbing, I would take an evening bath in a large washtub behind the stove. For some reason that night's sleep was quite comfortable.

Yes, many memories held by those of us who grew up in the light of a coal stove are fond ones. We remember those meals which were prepared for us on the rough, black surface. We remember that glow on Mama's and Grandmother's faces when serving the meals; often those glows came from standing over the hot meal for hours on end. If we really think about it, those meals just seemed to taste better than the "quickie" meals that are ever present today.

In the early 1940's was a wonderful time to grown up. No matter where I have lived or how far from home I have traveled, I still remember those bathing Saturday nights of home long ago.

The memories of the old wash tub still linger strong in my mind. We sure got plenty of use out of that wash tub, before it became discarded into days of yesteryear.

Now that I have grown older, thinking back on those Saturday nights where all three of us kids would take a bath (using the same water) to clean up for the coming week was quite an experience. Back then when you considered that you carried the water, heated it up on the stove, and had your bath, it took a great deal of time. The stove couldn't get too close to the wall, so the wash tub was set between the stove and the wall. The stove made a pretty good hiding place to bathe.

THE OUTHOUSE

When the family lived in Lexington, Kentucky, on Parkers Mill Road (in the country) we had only running water in the house where we lived, and all other conveniences were found outside of the house in the backyard. We always had two kinds of paper in the outhouse to allow our visitors a choice: regular toilet paper or a Sears catalogue. Our outhouse was well planned as it had papa bear, mama bear and baby bear size seats.

In the back yard we had a well with water pump on top that worked really well, a chicken house, smoke house and an outhouse with three seats. Sometimes in the olden days these were called tribe "Johns," "reading room," and other names.

Our sister would always wait to do her business (number one or two, if you know what I mean) way after dark and our parents would make me, or my brother, go with her as she had a fear of the dark. Of course, one would take a flashlight to light the path and would wait outside of the outhouse while she was inside taking care of business.

Our father had hogs on the farm in Lexington, Kentucky, in the house on the back porch our mother kept a 'slop bucket' (where she put all scraps, threw away vegetables, etc.), and our father would take this out to feed the hogs once a day. But one day he was a little late in doing so. Meanwhile, our sister started to play around near the bucket, and somehow, she managed to fall into the slop bucket and all that you could see were her arms and legs sticking out of the bucket.

Of course, our mother had to get her up out of the bucket and wash and clean up and get rid of the slop bucket, too. In looking back at this situation many years later we all still laugh just as much as now as we did back those many years ago.

Observing wind movement when visiting the outhouse is very important. Another general rule which requires attention is that the wind usually appears to veer, shift, or go around the sun (righthanded, or from left to right), and that when it does not do so, more wind or bad weather may be expected instead of improvement.

BRIDLE, SADDLE, AND HORSES

Those many years ago, a bridle, saddle, and a horse were considered a handsome start for a young person for a beginner in riding.

We have so changed our standards of values that only the middle-aged individuals will know that today's society is about because we have all outlived the past. There was a time, a rather long time ago, when every youngster was given a horse, a bridle and a saddle and we were no different growing up as we each had all of these.

Once you were given the horse, bridle and saddle this was your start in the world of riding, once you learned how to ride like a "knight of old." Society regarded it as a handsome start for a young person, and it was just that. With strong arms and legs and a strong horse, one could make way into the world. In starting to ride a horse you feel that the wild frontier was calling to all the restless, younger generation.

Once you mastered the art and skill of riding a horse, one could start working cattle and other livestock to help make the farm products pay and make a profit. Every child growing up expected a horse, and few families of the middle class could not afford one.

How delightful was the older custom of setting up the newly married couple in their first housekeeping. The bride's parents usually gave a cow and some chickens; both families gave featherbeds, pillows, quilts, and sometimes furniture. The dowry as such, had long ago vanished today, but the family pride saw to it that each new couple had an even break getting started.

Some of us lived just when this ancient custom was just passing. Since I was the youngest boy, I barely got in on this type of tradition.

Many fathers that I knew then, as a boy, would talk with pride in the declining years in some such fashion about when they started out, they did not have any money and were very poor when they got married.

About the only thing that has not changed, in some 60 plus years, is the human affection for children has in no way changed. Young boys and girls go forth to conquer the world today, not on a horse properly bridled and saddled, but equipped with a car and well or poorly with an education that must be their means of finding their way in an age when free land or anything else no longer exists.

THE CLOTHESLINE

Many years ago, when our mother did the washing of clothes with an old Maytag machine that was called a ringer-washer, and a scrub board was a lot of hard work (present day everyone has an electric washer and dryer) and these are a big step up from back in the 1940's and 50's. Each week before you could use the clothesline someone would have to go out and wipe all the lines to make sure they were clean before hanging your fresh washed clothes on the line to dry.

In the summertime we would catch June bugs, tie a string to one leg on a June bug (more will be given in another chapter) and then tie the other end of the string to the clothesline so we could keep the June bugs longer.

All the clothes washed had to be hung on wire lines outside which was called a "clothesline", and it stretched about 50 feet across the back yard from the garage to the smoke house, and we had four lines to hang clothing on. Mama would wash the towels and sheets first, then shirts and underclothing, work clothes and finish up with rugs.

Our mother, one winter night, forgot to collect the clothing before dark and after eating our evening meal she remembered to go and get the washed clothing in. As she was gathering the frozen clothing from the line, she put her arm around a body within the clothing. Collecting her composure, she released the body and continued to collect the clothes from the line. Once she reached the end of the line she ran to the house and told our father about the experience. Our father got his gun and went outside to assess the situation and found nothing. Returning to the house they discussed that apparently someone was trying to steal clothing; however, in our mother's favor was that the clothing was frozen handing in the winter temperature.

Our mother learned something that dark winter's night that she would never wait until night fall to go out and collect clothing for the drying line.

Clotheslines should never be allowed to remain abroad when out of use. When done with the lines, they should be carefully wiped. If wet, hang up in the open air to dry, after which they should be stored away in a bag. Before they are used again, they should also be wiped to prevent them from soiling or marking the linen.

WASHDAY

Monday was family washday in our family! The laundry room was at the end of the porch down in the basement was being readied for the ordeal. The fire had been started under the big black cauldron to heat the water that was being drawn from the cistern at the corner of the porch. Rainwater from the roof flowed down the gutters to the center drain and carried the water into the cistern. Benches under the window held the washtubs which also had to be filled with water. This water was drawn by bucketful and caried to the laundry room. As the water was heated some of it was put in the first tub for the white things, sheets, pillowcases, towels, shirts, etc., which would be scrubbed on the washboard, using bar soap. These had to be boiled in the big black cauldron and then removed with a big wood stick or paddle to the rinse water, then there was the bluing water and starch for the shirt collars, pillowcases, table clothes, dresses and whatever else needed that treatment. Wire clotheslines were strung across the back yard and after being wiped clean with a damp cloth, we were ready to hang the clothes which had been hand wrung and ready for drying.

Long poles were used to prop the lines up so that the clothes did not drag on the ground. Wood clothes pins were used to fasten the clothes to the line. We had a black washer woman, Pearl Howard. She always helped every Monday with the wash. Mama had three children, in the course of six years. The tub was carried to the back porch for this procedure and when baths were finished the water was dumped over the edge of the porch to go down the drain and on to the back of the house. This was where I was wadding, barefoot, in the water one day when out came a bucket full of hot, hot water from the big black cauldron out the upper window. Pearl didn't know that I was out there, of course, and she regretted that to her dying day.

I guess I was quite a country boy because I loved climbing trees, running, jumping and when I was running and jumping one day I caught the bridge of my nose on a clothesline. It knocked me out and as I came to blood was running down my face. Mama was there right away administering first aid and calling for Daddy to come and see what had happened. I was fortunate that it had done no damage to my eyes. I still carry the scar across the bridge of my nose, but after wearing glasses it was never noticed.

Pearl was probably paid a dollar for her mornings work. If there was a big wash maybe $1.25. She was tall and slender as was our mother and I know that many of Mother's dresses and clothing were given to her. She also helped in the kitchen with cooking when we had a lot of company. The dining room table would be full, and a makeshift table set up on the back porch for the kids. I don't remember her doing any cleaning and I don't know how she knew that she would be needed because we didn't have a phone and she lived in a little area called Little Georgetown where all the black families lived. They had their own school, church and grocery store, but they did come into town for some things. She also worked for other people around the area.

Pearl worked for us when we lived in Lexington, Kentucky, and when our parents purchased the large farm in Shelbyville, Kentucky, Pearl and her husband, Howard, went with us to help move in, care for the farm, cattle, and assist with the work as the children were small at that time.

For this process in the laundry the following are the necessary directions: the ironing blanket should be of a very thick short, called swanskin. Spread a coarse cloth upon the ironing board to lie under it, which makes the surface of the blanket softer and more yielding and elastic to the iron. The old method of heating irons is to place them on a hanger in front of the fireplace, but an ironing stove is much to be preferred. It is not very expensive, and it is very economical in the consumption of fuel, and it keeps the iron much better than the old method. To clean hot irons before using them, first do so upon a piece of sandpaper; then upon a piece of cloth or old bed tick kept for this purpose, and, before putting them on the linen, wipe the faces clean. With an ironing stove they require hardly any effort to make clean. Then to be sure that they are not too hot, that they will not scorch or smear the clothes, take up something coarse and iron it before meddling with the fine things.

Another problem would be that of mildew. Stubborn mildew on material often resists ordinary washing. Use this solution to get rid of it. Do not use it on dark or colored items however, as lemon juice can bleach fabric. Mix two parts salt and one part lemon juice. Wash the fabric in warm soapy water, and then mix salt and lemon juice, enough to cover the mildewed area, and apply it. Place the article of clothing in full sun, rinsing it after several hours. If the stain persists, repeat.

THE GREEN TEACHER

In finishing college early (mid-term), I knew I would have a hard time finding a teaching position. I went home for the weekend and had a phone call from a superintendent that wanted to interview me on Saturday. I was hired and started to work on the following Monday. I moved to a small mountain town in Kentucky named Paintsville. Meanwhile, the superintendent found me a place to live with an older couple on the end of Second Street and on the opposite end was the school. They had a son who was a doctor in town.

Believing that the first rule of good teaching should be to lay out your expectations to students in teacher-training institutions and that being: "Don't begin to teach until you are really ready; that is, willing to teach and work at teaching!" Do you really want to teach? Or was it all someone else's idea or dream? This is the question that one must ask oneself when first starting to teach. In teaching one can look for adventure, among many other things! The most important thing is that you should understand yourself and diagnose your attitude toward teaching before you start to teach. Above all, don't start with a "chip" on your shoulder. One must lower yourself to the level of your students (or work on the level of the students), staying one step or two in front of each student, at all times. Before starting to teach try thinking about one major question: "How to start?" Perhaps the formulation of a few resolutions, not made to be broken, is a good way, as any, to get started.

At least, it's time-honored when one reviews these resolutions: I shall know my subject matter. No one cannot teach what they do not know or maintain self-respect by bluffing. I shall always see each of my students as individuals. I shall learn their names and habits as soon as possible. I shall never forget that the student is more important than any subject matter, or students' lack of ability. I shall always carry an attitude of good faith toward students. Not suspicion! I shall dress as well as I can for the teaching profession. I shall attempt to make teaching as pleasant as possible for myself by being genuinely interested in the students. I shall make a wholehearted attempt to be a successful teacher. At the end of three years, if I find that I do not like teaching, or I do not measure up, or I find that teaching is just not for me, I will not teach any longer.

My own apology is that I sincerely believe that if one makes a real effort to follow these resolutions, one will develop into one of the teachers who really experiences fun and enjoyment out of teaching and life; moreover, one is not so likely to have prematurely gray hair and a washboard brown. It is the hurried, harassed, nagging teachers who inspire our comic strip artists to explore and develop creativity. When one starts teaching, as a teacher, one should forget all racial, religious, political, and social prejudices one may be fostering. Forget any claims one believes one may have to be superior just because you are a teacher. Forget one's personal feelings. One should take the work seriously but forget oneself. Forget romance, for the time being, as school hours will push one for more hours than one can supply. Forget one's own student escapades which, in retrospect, may lead one to mistaken lenience. Forget all comic strip presentations of "egghead" schoolteachers. Eggheads are becoming popular — even powerful. Forget the stories head about juvenile delinquents in the classroom. Forget all articles one reads about imbecile taxpayers who would deny teachers every human pleasure. Forget tales about "dumb" and tyrannical superintendents. Forget all troubles and differences of opinion which you may have as time goes by. Teaching is an ordeal for those who hold grudges, and griping teachers are a withering blight to their friends and associates. If asked off hand, what should the well-dressed teacher wear, what would you recommend? Well, the chances are ten to one that you would answer, "a good dark dress/suite with a spotless white top/collar," a practical dress/suite with bright accessories," or something of the sort. What a world this would be for students if all teachers wore black suits/dresses to school! One of the decided advantages of being a teacher is that you can wear pretty/handsome, soft colored dresses/suites which do a great deal to give life to your spirits. Most classrooms are drab enough without having teachers in them who insist upon wearing widows' weeds. As for women teachers – one should always wear a girdle. In trying to remember those challenging minutes at the chalkboard during class presentations is a mystery today. She should always be meticulous about all her clothing. She/he (the teacher) should never have his/her school suits/dresses extreme. They must not be too short, too tight, nor too figure revealing. You don't want the boys to whistle when your name is mentioned! As for the men – men are dressed as conservatively as bankers in some schools, whereas, in others "California casual" is the style. In any school, that scrubbed, clean shaven look is appreciated. Functional jewelry (watch, tie-clip, and cufflinks are way out now; but class/wedding rings are the standard decorative jewelry for the young ladies. For both sexes in the classroom, the concerns of fine feathers are for the birds! As the first year of teaching started off – like any other beginning teacher I was ready to go, full of powder, and on time -- for the first week was on its way, and over before I was really halfway through the week.

Cheer up, the first week is always the hardest; that is, if you refuse to gripe about your classroom, awful students, and unfair schedules. Facing the facts here and now will be of help at a late date. As I entered the classroom for the first time with all the students looking at me to see if I would kill them or not, I said to myself, "for years I have had to adapt to other people, now they are faced with the situation of adapting to me, my wishes and requests were before me!"

The chances are that I have trouble with classroom management, and little wonder that I did! The beginning of every class period, no doubt, found me at the desk, surrounded at the left, right, and in front by students who, on the way to class, had thought of some questions to ask me (the new teacher). Helpless before their concentrated attack, I was all too conscious of the fact that many supplies, materials, and handouts must be distributed, with the lighting and ventilation of the classroom regulated, and the attendance taken. As the classes got off to a chaotic start, it was a battle to establish order, to say nothing of maintaining order. As most educations have stated that a new teacher is like the students, -- you have not learned how to give orders and to keep yourself free for actual control of the classroom. This only comes with much experience. Like most other teachers I first made a seating chart for every class. Then I first tried alphabetically seating the students, then student personal choice, then teacher appointed seating arrangements with the purpose of correcting minor and major discipline problems. A new teacher learns one thing from teaching about making penalty for infringement of working rules. Never tell the student just what the penalty will be for not doing an assignment. Leave the punishment as a surprise. The day following, after assignments were made, collection of homework papers is another routine task that may cause unnecessary confusion in a classroom. Just how to stop this – I don't know, but I have learned that if you try different methods of collecting papers daily, weekly, etc., it puts some fun and surprise in homework assignment collection. As a young teacher I have always remembered one thing: "you cannot command respect; you must earn it." This is true in no matter what one does, or where one works – in order to get along with people one must respect each other! One of the best ways to learn and to earn respect is to regard information about students as confidential as possible. This is important always, but particularly if you are teaching in your old hometown. To be above board in all relationships with everyone in all that you do. If you are suffering from an unjust administrative decision, go to the principal and discuss the matter; spreading the news among teachers won't help. Never take requests to board members. Take them to your immediate supervisor. To be more than gracious to parents of the students always be willing to talk with them. They have a right to know about your work and the child's work. After all, they provide the children for teachers to teach and the salaries that support a living for teachers. You would never accept money from tutoring a student who is in your class. If you cannot give the necessary time and leadership, refer the student to someone else for tutoring. Never to speak slighting a member of your profession. (But sometimes they are very unjust)! That if you leave the school where you were employed, you should leave your materials in such shape that the new teacher will have little difficulty in taking up your work. That you shouldn't try to procure a teaching position which is already filled. Also, remember that your own contract is a big moral obligation. Your relatives' rating would be at the top of the social scheme. Think of all the men and women in the world. Are you fortunate or unfortunate? Now where is it truer that I get out of life just what I put into it than it is in the classroom – through teaching? If one treats every student with sincere respect, the chances are that one will, with reasonably good classroom management, be treated with equal respect. If one started teaching expecting the worst, there is good likelihood that one will get what one is expecting – EXPECTATIONS of you and others always come true! Every lesson is well planned so that each class period is adequately and constructively filled with learning activities, one has reutilized the mechanical procedures discussed previously and has made clear to the students a set of reasonable rules which have established conduct in each class. Like every other teacher, I, of all teachers, have my own individual case problems! Like all other inexperienced teachers, I do not regard disciplinary problems objectively, and this is not surprising when one realizes that few experienced teachers ever succeed in subordinating their personal reactions to such situations. However, it is important for one to realize at the outset that there is nothing new under the sun in behavior problems and that the particular troubles which one may have are not to be regarded as personal failures. It would be helpful in wishing for every young and inexperienced teacher to have a sympathetic principal or supervisor who would assist without discouraging. No one is fortunate enough to have someone of this sort to whom you can go to; do not hesitate to lay your problems before them, if you find someone of this nature. As a beginning teacher, one will learn that it is generally better to seek advice from those responsible for one's work than from a fellow teacher. Even though, sometimes one can seek advice from a fellow-teacher – just as wise! However, this depends upon the school personnel. At any rate, do not temporize if a discipline problem is becoming acute; the situation will be known eventually and you had better be the one to tell it and to seek out assistance, if needed. The first few weeks of teaching were very nervous in the passing. Just like another beginning teacher, I too, made many rash threats and nagged students into good behavior. Even though I tried my personal best not to yield to temptation! A threat once made must be carried out, and this often involves real difficulty for the teacher and sometimes much administrative disapproval. In anger, an ounce of caution is surely worth a pound of explanation.

Aside from the fact that the habit of nagging will ruin one's personality and make one unfit for human companionship, one will find that it also shatters your efficiency as a teacher and robs one of any pleasure in one's work. Commend students for good work; pass over failures in silence. This is a good rule to follow at any time, and it is particularly valuable in the classroom, because it directs the attention of your students to do good work and to make the atmosphere of the classroom more pleasant than it could otherwise be. Though one is a genius in classroom management and a paragon intact, one will still have some behavioral problems to worry about. Parenthetically, a good course in mental hygiene or personality problems will give you insight into some of these behavioral tangles and transform them for you from objects of worry into subjects of fascinating interests. This is a rule that tells us that the punishment should fit the misdemeanor. It is believed that the best punishment for a youngster who will talk in class is to have them report to you after school and talk to you on any and every subject as your time will permit. One rule should hold true: "the student must not stop talking to permit thinking, or the student has to start talking against time all over again." Using this punishment with some success with high school students, but it is risky. The first "time in" for talking carried a penalty of three minutes of constant talking with no time outs for thoughts. The second penalty was five minutes; the third was for 10 minutes, and so on. Students may recite poetry; The Gettysburg Address, or whatever; but they must not stop talking until time is called! After that, the student keeps quiet in class until he is called upon to respond in the lesson process.

A punishment of this sort has advantages because there's nothing meant about it to rankle the mind of the student. Most students will admit the logic of reasoning; if they can talk during class time, when it annoys the teacher, they should be willing to talk to the teacher for amusement after school, even though it causes them some discomfort.

If a student is too critical of other students or of the teacher, showing every desire to prove him/herself right and others wrong, give that student so many opportunities to perform and to carry conspicuous responsibilities that he/she will be glad when he/she can retire to comparative obscurity and silence.

If a student is idle when they should be working, place them in a prominent place in the classroom for a couple of class periods and allow them to do absolutely nothing. The student will be glad to return to his/her desk after he/she can do nothing except think of the work that they were going to have to make up.

There are but a few routine behavioral problems which each and every teacher encounters, and the punishment in each case is based upon the well-known principle that if a horse runs away with you, there is only one thing to do…hang on until the horse is tired, and then make the horse run a lot more. In other words, give the students what they enjoy doing, but enough to make them sick of doing it.

Always remember that the most strategic place in the classroom for the teacher in time of trouble is in the rear (as it was). The moment your class becomes restless, saunter to the rear of the classroom, if your lesson possibly permits it. The students cannot turn to face you, every troublemaker is sure that you are staring at them, just them, and you have an excellent view of all the students. The teacher who confines themselves to the front of the classroom is usually an amateur who moves about freely, up and down the aisles, and frequently. Take your stand in the back of the classroom. You'll have much less trouble with discipline if you do find your place in the back of the classroom for good management. It is understood that one knows that one should never give schoolwork as a penalty and that one should keep your hands to yourself. This little rule reminds me of a story which was   told to me just last year by an acquaintance who had, before her marriage, taught school in a small city community school. In your attitude toward this true story, you may find your own philosophy of school discipline. This was an actual occurrence, the sort of thing which might happen to you or to me, or to others – out wits forsaking us!

Mrs. R, a teacher in a small city community school, one day in a bit of a temper slapped one of her students while in English IV class, in the face. The student, a very nice young man, cried to himself quite a bit, which Mrs. R. no doubt considered it good for his soul. At any rate, the student was obviously not hurt, and she forgot the matter as class time went on. That afternoon, after school had been dismissed and the teachers were in the teacher's lounge getting ready to go home and/or leave for the day to do other things, a very well-dressed woman entered into the lounge. Mrs. R.? The well-dressed lady asked politely. Mrs. R. realizing that this woman must have been directed to the teacher's lounge from the main office, stepped up with her very best professional smile to greet the woman, who then upon reaching out and struck her full in the face.

A lady stated: "I wanted you to know how it feels to be slapped in the face in front of your friends," and the woman announced to the stunned group of the teachers and the hysterically weeping Mrs. R. with which words she marched out of the building and into her car and left. I shall not give you full details of Mrs. R.'s humiliating defeat in her attempt to take legal action against the boy's mother. Even the principal of the school said that she had insulted a child and had suffered the unusual experience of having the tables turned upon her in an exactly analogous situation. The superintendent of schools declared a bit more bluntly that every teacher worthy of a position should know the difference between a reproof and an insult, and if she did not know, she should not cry when she was shown. Now most teachers will rise to high fever over this story. Think it over. It will suggest several very obvious lessons for each of us. If you're teaching in a community and it's a common habit for parents to visit the school where you are teaching, you may know that you will have your quota of visitors. Now visitors are a disrupting force in any school and furthermore, a classroom, but if they are anticipated, they need not be a source of anxiety to you or anyone else.

The first day of school will not be too soon to tell your students that when visitors come into the classroom, they will be expected to behave well (better than usual); that there should be no whispering; that the person nearest the visitor should offer them a book, seat, etc., and that all students must remember that they are being disrespectful to the visitor, as well as to themselves, if they do anything less than their best – adjustments will take place following departure of the visitor. In this one case I think you are justified in making a threat; that if any students do not follow the above directions, the entire class will have to stay one hour after school or perhaps miss a complete play period. Yes, I know that this is against the rules of modern pedagogy, but retaining an entire class after school in extreme cases is an effective defense for the teacher against children who might, through perverted humor, cause the teacher some very embarrassing moments in the presence of outsiders. You can respect this little pep talk once a week or more often, until you are sure that the students understand beyond all possible doubts just when and what is expected of them if visitors do arrive in your classroom for any reason.

QUEEN OF THE STREET

It was my maiden voyage as a teacher – if a 19-year-old young man can be considered a maiden and a trip into the Mid-Western corn-fed part of Kentucky can be considered a voyage. I had signed a contract with a small community city independent school system which rose from a corn field and somewhat in the hills of poverty, or among three or four other small towns during a flood or winter storm. Jollytown, as we shall call it, was the type of town one would not expect to be among the first hit of World War II. It consisted of a grain mill, coal mines, a small but active drug store, and a feed store; that just recently was taken by fire. Also, a large but small group of little houses huddled around in a grove of planted trees along the riverside. The population of Jollytown was around 4,000 in all, including somewhat 60 percent retired farmers, miners and 30 percent on the Happy-Pappy Plan (welfare); well, as for the other percent – I guess you could say that they were the educators of the Jollytown community. You will most likely ask next: "What about the other one percent?" It's like this…the other one percent is and was the Gossip Queen membership! It was that classic little town where a school teacher is still looked upon as a sour little old maid punching bag. However, it would have to be home for me for the next several months!

Most of the merchandising stores reeked of nails, bib overalls, and bananas, but it was home to the several old fogies who spent their summers on the benches out in front of the courthouse and their winters in chairs or on kegs around the oil burner near the scoop shovels and fork handles—a place to spit and philosophy through mangled black teeth. Since it was also a newspaper stand, the town pump, a bakery, and the advertising agency, it was at the general merchandising store that everything took place. It was also at the general merchandising store that I found out about the only landlady available to young, single, male school teachers; Mrs. Handover, we will so call her.

Mrs. Handover had her fingers on the pulse of the community. She worked part-time in the general merchandising store; she was a part-time telephone operator at the local exchange; and was a part-time employee of the local post office, when she could push her way into the shop, in order to help and/or just to be the boss! She had her hair done every Saturday at 4:00 p.m. at Yvonne's Beauty Salon – "Saloon" to the local folks. After I was employed at the Jollytown School District of Jollytown 101 for only several weeks, things went very well.

As for Mrs. Handover, she was always talking about her son, (the most outstanding man in the town and of the world). Even when it was time for bed, she would come into the television (setting) room and start talking about her son. As we all know, when you hear something for the first time, we all enjoy it, but when you hear something over and over it gets old and quickly becomes out of place (character).

Mrs. Handover only had one son; and her husband was still living, and he would do anything for her that she demanded! He always said, "Well, it keeps me out of trouble and away from her."

But to fully understand the landlady, a bull session with the boys at the general merchandising store was not enough – one had to understand Mrs. Handover's house! The place had more windows than any house of its size that I had ever seen. All the curtains appeared to move as I parked out in front of the house or, as I eventually learned, whenever anyone walked by on the sidewalk. There were no trees in the yard, but flowered bushes came up just below the windows – like lowered eyelashes, if you know what I mean! Most of the flowers in the yard were displayed in such a matter that no matter how you looked at them all you could see were flowers—no grass.

My bedroom was up on the second floor in the big house, and the bathroom was next door to my bedroom. Every morning it was a "mad race to use the bathroom, get dressed, and be to school on time.

All the clocks in the big old house were electric and didn't tick; her husband never spoke above a whisper, even the termites worked with muted nippers. Both the landlady and the husband, known only as "Pa," tiptoed about the house in their stocking feet after sundown, and often they would sit noiselessly in the dark, peeping out – possibly waiting for something to happen or to take place, I can't say or figure out just what!

There were thirty-seven molded brasses scattered on the street where I lived. While I would dare say that they were on every available surface, and there were fifty-eight cactus plants of all sizes and with stick abilities. In a strange old way, several different things started to add up and I slowly started to open my eyes as my personal awareness came about.

Before the daily dusting, the couple would always talk about taking a Western trip that started all the dust and that it was still settling in the central park (jail yard) of Jollytown. Also, outside of the house one could see many old, polished rocks and cheap souvenirs, but for daily dusting of this layout—forget it!

The only well-worn chairs in the whole house were the one by the telephone in the living/bedroom, and another one out in the back hallway. This was the one in which Mrs. H would always eavesdrop on (not just myself; but all the other good citizens in town, too) just to save the embarrassment of asking what was that all about?

Mrs. Handover would be my publicity agent – my contact with the town; I knew that? But when, after about two or three months with the couple, I was told of a rumor growing throughout Jollytown, that I left my pants hanging on a chair at night, weekends, etc., and of another worse rumor about my underwear, I know that my landlady and I were destined to clash. Time was the only verbal that interrupted the clash for the moment.

As minutes and hours wore on over the next approaching months. The Handover's had what I would say 'a home away from home,' and most everyone was welcomed to come in it, your own reputation in the public-esteem was at-risk. They were well-known for keeping student teachers, traveling insurance people, and other individuals who came from other places to town to work or on business trips or for a short while.

After living with the Handover's for about five months, they had a female student teacher to come and live with them for a short time. Well, all I can say is …Auk! And Oh! As from the time she arrived and until the time she left the Hanover's, questions were asked of all of us about the young lady. Answer…I had none!

The SUPER rumor about this one house while I lived with the Handover's was, "this student teacher on weekends did not come in, and she stayed with some of her friends." But I did not know about this until it was too late and the young lady returned to campus. Because the same weekend I had plans to be out of town, too. Again, what I did not know was that the Handover's checked to see if the student teacher was in for the night and I was too.

Within two days of returning from the weekend trip, the SUPER rumor that I was up to hanky-panky with the student teacher was nipped in the bud, and a rumor that I was engaged to girls in five different states replaced it, satisfying the party line, the general merchandising store and putting a twinkle into the eyes of the patrons at Yvonne's Beauty Salon.

In order not to insult them with the fact that I know about all the rumors, in a round about way, I found an apartment and moved into it around the middle of December. The apartment was small, but just right for the living habits of one single male school teacher. The students at school were more than helpful, as always to help me move! Several of them helped paint and fix up the place and worked all hours of the night. But this too had its problems. For next door, the lady was very sick in bed and in the head, (I found out later) and a sister of my former landlady.

After about a week, this lady next door called my new landlord, Mr. A.J., and told him I had a drinking party and that it had lasted all hours of the night and weekend too, and that she could not sleep or rest the whole time. This was really hard to understand, as I am not a drinker of spirits. So, one thing led to another and Mr. A.J. called me to the side one day when I was in his general merchandising store and said: "I had a complaint that you have had a lot of parties and are keeping my other renters from resting." Well, I said nothing back, I just let it pass – this was my mistake; as you will see as time moves right along…school was out, and depressingly did trouble really start!

Why the first thing I knew I was about the worst person that ever hit the small community of Jollytown. For most of the town people were talking about me…in one form or another. For that summer I worked in the town, and you will learn about this later. Well, would you believe that by the end of the summer my mew landlord, Mr. A.J., was trying to make me pay for some old pipes that were damaging his roof over his general merchandizing store? As you can see, now this many had to put his shoes on the correct feet. In about seven more weeks he was gone from my mind, and I had moved for the third time in Jollytown. This time the people were the people like my own personal family…that is…it was like my home with them. No matter what happened, when things had to be done, I joined in and did my part of the work. As a matter of fact –I think I did a little more than the teenage sons. But this was just fine! Perhaps not everyone trips into a situation of this setting, but if I did not have parents of my own, I would like living with these people – because they are my family now (away from home) – I will always remember them as such. Thanks Davis family!

The family, we shall call them "The Davis" family. Mrs. Davis was always talking of the Bible and sizing up things to present, past, and things to come that were in the Bible. But I really loved her for this, because she always found the time to talk with you and to do something special for you.

She would always let me use her kitchen for something that I would want to do or needed for school – knowing that I loved to cook. As for Mr. Davis, he was the type of person that knew just what to say at the right time, and he never said anything unless he was spoken to first. As well as giving advice when he was asked for it. To me, his advice always had excellent judgment. However, young son "Lucky" never paid any attention to anyone – no matter what the subject was about. Lucky is now the only child at home – and I might add, that the young man has his own way – to come and go when he pleases. Sometimes, this is good and sometimes it is bad. But as a member of the family, I tried my best to speak only when spoken to; repeated no family discussions outside the home and I watched all the eyes behind draperies as I would walk the street to and from school.

RECALLING THE GOOD LIFE

Often, we do not see our misfortunes until we are told about them by others. Just as often these enlightened ones miss or overlook quality elements in our "disadvantaged" lives. So, I guess advantages and/or disadvantages are in the eye of the beholder.

Not until I was in college and had begun listening to evaluators in our nation's capital, did I become aware that I had lived a disadvantaged childhood. These people had spent their lives and many tax dollars developing theories about quality of life, so they were supposed to know what they were talking about, but I wonder?

The first twelve years of my life were spent in a small town, on the farm, eight-room house on the flat land of Shelby County, Kentucky. The first house in Lexington had no running water at all while the second had running water in the kitchen and excellent plumbing water throughout the house, too. In the first house our water was carried from a well in the backyard. The absence of the indoor water not only forced us to carry all our drinking, cooking, and washing water, but ensured the existence of that little house in the back. Most of you know the one I'm talking about, the tall, slim building with a half-moon cut on the door and set as far as possible away from the main house as possible.

Now, most of the trips to this half mooner were not all that bad, but the ones on a cold winter morning tended to pick up speed. The powers that be might consider trips to the outhouse as training techniques for sprint events in the Olympics. I am quite confident that this would work very well. However, with one second home we had full indoor plumbing with a bath and a half.

Too, during those early years, there were always gardens to the left of our house. To this day I can almost always tell the difference between fresh, homegrown food and that which has been hot housed or bought in a can. Gardening was more than just running out and harvesting those goodies when they were ready. There was a great deal of work that went into those gardens and still today I grow a healthy garden and enjoy all of the good vegetables grown.

I remember once when I was about ten or eleven, my father was ill, so the only ones to prepare the garden were my mother and her siblings. For days, it seemed, our mother would have us to use "spade forks" to turn about two acres of earth. Each day we experienced a "good tired," but knew that the "garden stuff: that year would be especially tasty, and it really was.

Those experts who frowned down upon the existence that many rural Americans have gone though have disappeared. Their theories prove to contain some degree of truth, but something was missing. The true experts on rural living are those who survive those lives on fact, not theory.

I don't agree with the statement that life in the country, in small towns, or on riverbanks proves to be difficult. I agree with the contention that this life was bad. If I had it to do over, I would want to grow up in the same way that I did and in the very same place. Carrying that water, spading that garden, and making those early morning runs to the little shack out back developed self-ability and self-reliance. I think it prepared me more for life than anything else I can remember. I am confident that anyone would benefit from a childhood in rural America. Of course, I am a bit prejudiced on this subject.

LET'S LIGHT ONE

Every normal boy or girl feels that he/she must smoke something, and nearly every child growing up has acquaintance of smoking something, harmful or otherwise. Just how we escaped poisoning I do not know, but nearly everything that even resembled smoking materials was tried. For some strange reason people of all ages think there is something big about puffing smoke out of one's mouth and especially out of one's nostrils, though I must confess that we did not try inhaling the smoke of the things we used in our younger years.

There are gradations of respectability in smokes, just as there are grades of tobacco. Corn silks are mild and make a good beginning for the fearful and sissy. But grape vine, with its savage bit, satisfies for years.

I recall that my sister and I smoked some rolled up paper towels one day and we got so sick and got scared that we hid beneath one of the upstairs beds in the house. When we were found sick under the bed our parents had to take the bed apart to get us both out from under it.

Our grandfather used a corncob pipe, we boys made our own, stem and all, rather clumsy affairs. But they gave us a thrill that comes to boys, old and young, when they think they are doing something naughty. We tried to make cigarettes from our mullein and tobacco, but with rather poor success, for the paper we used was likely to be coarse wrapping paper that tasted a bit strong.

But one just had to have a cigar-like smoke. That helped along with the case for grape vines. Another kind of cigar was made from a buddy whip, for it was porous and would draw well. I cannot recall what flavor that smoking yields.

Isn't the whole experience funny? Just why one would want to disturb the pleasant taste in one's mouth by smoking or chewing tobacco is a puzzle that I will never understand. Just maybe the pure bitterness of it makes life endurable to some!

HOPE

I've been thinking about hope lately, and the importance of it in a person's life when one has hope.

Sometimes – most of the time – life can seem a bit disappointing even for me. Even the greatest lives are full of profound loss and heartbreak. It seems that pain is inevitable, and while we may say that we know that good can come out of it, what hurts is still hurting.

In the process, one can quite easily lose hope: in life, in God, and even in oneself. Despair is often cyclical, spiraling one into depression and helplessness, leading to even greater despair. The result is that one sad thing leads to another and so on, until we feel that we can't possibly break free. It can all be a bit too much for our souls to handle.

As humans, we need hope. We can't live without it. It is the lifeblood to our spiritual survival, and the only thing that pulls us out of the deep trenches of pain and hurt is life with hope.

This theme of hope is so evident in great music, poetry, and art, that it's almost taunting us. We know that we need hope, and yet it can seem so far away.

Hope comes when one realizes they have inadequacies and learns to depend more fully on God.

There has been, throughout my life, a time that I had no more energy to fight. My ability to care about walking with God seemed to not only vanish but vaporize, leaving no trace of its existence. I wanted to give up, throw in the towel, and not ever look back. Though God, in His infinite kindness and love "laid beside" me and "gently whispered hope." His whispers of hope brought back to life areas that were dead. I was reminded that I am the one who is broken and in need and wanting hope.

Some say that hope is all a part of "grace" – that God would come to us when we're looking our worst and gently whisper hope to us. It's such a beautiful concept – the kind of beauty that makes you want to cry just for the sake of how overwhelming it is. In our most dire moments, when our failures have outweighed our triumphs, when sadness has seemed to overcome any joy left in us, we need hope. In those times, I believe that God sends the least expected people and circumstances into our lives to reinvigorate our spirits and remind us how good life still is.

We all share an "already" and a "not yet" dimension of our salvation. What happened through Jesus at his resurrection were the first fruits or the beginning of all that will happen when the Church is resurrected and given immortality. Jesus is the beginning of redemption; we will be the ending of it. He is the first fruits; we will be his final harvest. Although we presently, as Paul says, sit in heavenly places, we do not yet have all that is promised to us. We do not yet physically sit in heavenly places. Christ now has the immortality we will have in the end. We possess this immortality only by faith. By faith we trust in Christ. By faith we are "in Christ." Being "in Christ" we share in his victory. It is "in Christ" that we possess these blessings. Jesus Christ possesses all power in heaven and earth now. However, all the power and blessings will not be fully ours until He returns. The promise is now; the final reality is "not yet."

This is why hope is so important in the Christian life. It is the future aspect of our faith. Hope is not "I hope the Lord returns," or "I hope I'm ready when He comes." It is the settled confidence that what God has promised is true. When we say we hope, we mean that we are *sure* that Christ will return and that He *will* save us, who trust in Him.

Therefore, since we have been justified through faith, we have peace with God through our Lord Jesus Christ, through whom we have gained access by faith into this grace in which we now stand. And we rejoice in the hope of the glory of God. Not only so, but we also rejoice in our sufferings, because we know that suffering produces perseverance; perseverance, character; and character, hope. Hope does not disappoint us, because God has poured out his love into our hearts by the Holy Spirit, whom he has given us. (*Romans* 5:1-5 NIV)

For the grace of God that brings salvation has appeared to all men. It teaches us to say "No" to ungodliness and worldly passions, and to live self-controlled, upright and godly lives in this present age, even while we wait for the blessed hope – the glorious appearing of our great God and Savior, Jesus Christ, (*Titus* 2:1-13 NIV)

Any scheme or view of the end-times which is more filled with fear or terror than it is with hope is leaning away from the Gospel. The end-times are not about the Anti-Christ. They are about Jesus Christ. We are not to live in fear and awe of the Beast. We are to look with hope and reverence to the Lamb. The teaching of the Second Coming of Jesus should be a comfort to children, and not a frightening tool to bring them into the church out of fear. Hope is that which grasps the promises of God before they are realized. We hope because God has promised and given us His Word. We are taught in the Book of Revelation of Jesus Christ that there is war between the Beast and the Lamb. The Lamb wins! That is why we hope.

We yearn for all of our salvation now. That is to be expected. This present age is never satisfying. At times it is painful, trying and even grievous. This is how the Christian life is. There are two dimensions to the Christian life. We have this "treasure in jars of clay." On the one hand we are forgiven, given the Spirit, made alive in Christ, and set free from the power of sin. On the other, we struggle with the Evil One, we fight out flesh, and we wrestle with principalities and powers. We still feel pain and shed tears. Our loved ones still die. This is the reality of living in the "already" and the "not yet."

But we have this treasure in jars of clay to show that this all-surpassing power is from God and not from us. We are hard pressed on every side but not crushed; perplexed, but not in despair; persecuted but not abandoned; struck down but not destroyed. We always carry around in our body the death of Jesus, so that the life of Jesus may also be revealed in our body. For we who are alive are always being given over to death for Jesus' sake, so that his life may be revealed in our mortal body. (2 *Corinthians* 4:7-11 NIV)

But we are not stalemated. We are more than conquerors. We sit in heavenly places in Christ. We march in the victor's parade. We are joint heirs with Christ. We are able to do "immeasurably more than we ask or imagine, according to his power that is at work within us…" (*Ephesians* 3:20 NIV) The ultimate victory is ours, because Christ has already won it. But the final celebration and the full sharing of the spoils will *not* take place *until* Jesus comes again.

Today, we nobly march toward what is ours – into what awaits us. We expectantly desire to grasp what has been promised. Through faith in Christ, we boldly move toward what our Father has laid up for us. But, on that Day when our Lord begins his holy peregrination from Heaven, in that eternal moment, all will be changed. We will receive the glory which Jesus secured us through his Passion!

Dear reviewers, now we are children of God, and what we will be, has not yet been made known. But we know that when he appears, we shall be like him, for we shall see him as he is. Everyone who has this hope in him purifies himself, just as he is pure.

One might ask, "Well if most of what we are living for is in Heaven, why would anyone want to live this life out? Wouldn't it be better to forego this life and go straight to Heaven?" I must ask a question in response, "Doesn't the knowledge of our inheritance to come make living this life more special?" To me, this life only has meaning because we are heading into a certain future where Christ will rule and we will be clothed with immortality. Everything we do is filled with purpose because it matures us and prepares us for our future life. All that we do for others in service is not lost in the "ugly ditch of history." It does matter whether we are heroes or villains. It makes a difference that we help instead of hurt. The one without hope lives for the now only. He or she lives for what is personally expedient. They don't think life is any more than their own personal survival and well-being. But the person who has a future can live for others. Life is about more than me and mine. It is about a cosmic plan of the Creator in which I have a part. Therefore, why fight over the little stuff? The one with hope in the life to come can share what they have now, but they have so much for which to look forward.

There is a reason why, when God saves us, He does not resurrect us straight to Heaven. There is a reason why this life is necessary and must be lived out. God has a purpose for us here. Paul stated, "For I am in a strait betwixt two, having a desire to depart, and to be with Christ; which is far better: Nevertheless, to abide in the flesh is more needful for you. (*Philippians* 1:23, 24 KJV) We have a service in God's plan that we must perform in this mortal life. He gives us just enough of our salvation now to do what He has called us to do. Then, He gives the hope of the world to come to direct and strengthen us in what we are called to do. He fills our little lives with the profound meaning of the life to come, in order to energize us in our mortal work now.

Since death is hanging over the world, how do we, as believers, live our lives fully in a dying world? I believe a powerful answer to this can be found in a story from the life of Christ. In reading *John* 11:1-16 we see that Lazarus was an everyday ordinary person like all of us. But life "killed" him. Maybe it was an accident that got him, or an illness. Maybe he just worked himself to death. Whatever – something killed him. The Bible says that we are all under the power of death because we have sinned. You are dying…and so am I. We die a little every day. Just look in the mirror. Check out pictures from ten years ago. Things are happening every day, killing us by degrees: A career crash, a failed marriage, a fatal disease, a child gone astray. Death comes upon all men. The world is groaning under this death we have brought upon it. Jesus groaned over Lazarus.

When Mary and Martha intercepted Jesus, He comforted them with the Gospel: "I AM THE RESURRECTION AND THE LIFE!" But they did not understand this. Their grief blinded them to the good news. They thought he meant something which fit better into their preconceived religious notions. In essence, they responded, "I know you could have healed him," (past tense) or "I know he will rise on the last day." But Jesus was saying that he is the Resurrection for RIGHT NOW! The resurrection of Jesus has meaning for the "already."

Jesus, once more deeply moved, came to the tomb. It was a cave with a stone laid across the entrance. "Take away the stone," he said. "But Lord," said Martha, the sister of the dead man, "by this time there is a bad odor, for he has been there four days." Then Jesus said, "Did I not tell you that if you believed you would see the glory of God?" So, they look away the stone. Then Jesus looked up and said, "Father, I thank you that you have heard me. I know that you always hear me, but I said this for the benefit of the people standing here, that they may believe that you sent me." When he had said this, Jesus called in a loud voice, "Lazarus, come out!" The dead man came out, his hands and feet wrapped with strips of linen, and a cloth around his face. Jesus said to them, "Take off the grave clothes and let him go." (*John* 11:38-44 NIV)

Jesus raised him from death to live again. But Lazarus was not raised to immortality. After a time, he died again. Jesus raised him only to a mortal existence. WHY? Jesus didn't tell Lazarus, "This day wilt thou be with me in Paradise." He said, "Take off his grave clothes and let him go." In essence he said, "Let him go back to finish his life!" "Let him go back to his work, family, and friends!" HIS LIFE WAS NOT OVER. So often we give up when our life is not finished. Maybe it's your marriage. It could be your relationship with a loved one. It might be a career or a ministry. He redeemed you to resurrect your life and give it back to you, so you can finish living it.

Lazarus was not the only one raised to "mortality." That is what the resurrection of Christ is to our lives now. Although we do not have the fullness of the resurrection yet, that does not mean that Christ's resurrection is without power and meaning now. Christ's resurrection means that we can finish our lives. He raised us from the dead spiritually in order to send us out into the world to do the work of His Kingdom.

When Jesus entered the ruler's house and saw the flute players and the noisy crowd, he said, "Go away. The girl is not dead but asleep." But they laughed at him. After the crowd had been put outside, he went in and took the girl by the hand, and she got up. News of this spread through the entire region. (*Matthew* 9:23-26 NIV)

As he approached the town gate, a dead person was being carried out – the only son of his mother, and she was a widow. A large crowd from the town was with her. When the Lord saw her, his heart went out to her and he said, "Don't cry." Then he went up and touched the coffin, and those carrying it stood still. He said, "Young man, I say to you, get up!" The dead man sat up and began to talk, and Jesus gave him back to his mother. They were all filled with awe and praised God. "A great prophet has appeared among us," they said. "God has come to help his people." (*Luke* 7:12-16)

Once Jesus had raised these to live out the rest of their mortal lives, they were forever touched or impacted by the resurrection of Christ. They were not just "dead men walking." They were alive in Christ: as for you, you were dead in your transgressions and sins, in which you used to live when you followed the ways of this world and of the ruler of the kingdom of the air, the spirit who is now at work in those who are disobedient. All of us also lived among them at one time, gratifying the cravings of our sinful nature and following its desires and thoughts. Like the rest, we were by nature objects of wrath. But because of his great love for us, God, who is rich in mercy, made us alive with Christ even when we were dead in transgressions – it is by grace you have been saved. God raised us up with Christ and seated us with him in the heavenly realms in Christ Jesus, in order that the coming ages he might show the incomparable riches of his grace, expressed in his kindness to us in Christ Jesus. (*Ephesians* 2:1-7 NIV)

The power of Jesus's resurrection is certainly a power culminating in immortality – eternal life: for God so loved the world that he gave his one and only Son, that whoever believes in him shall not perish but have eternal life. (*John* 3:16 NIV)

But whoever drinks the water I give him will never thirst. Indeed, the water I give him will become in him a spring of water welling up to eternal life. (*John* 4:14 NIV)

I tell you the truth whoever hears my word and believes him who sent me has eternal life and will not be condemned; he has crossed over from death to life. (*John* 5:24) NIV)

For my Father's will is that everyone who looks to the Son and believes in him shall have eternal life, and I will raise him up at the last day. (*John* 6:40 NIV)

I give them eternal life, and they shall never perish; no one can snatch them out of my hand (*John* 10:28 NIV)

We usually think of this "eternal life" as life in the future. Nevertheless, there is a profound present dimension to the resurrection power of Jesus. By the working of His Spirit within us, we are made to live out our mortal existence. Lazarus had not finished his mortal life. Therefore, Jesus raised him so he could finish it. Jesus wants to empower you and me through the Gospel – not only to live in eternity – but to live out or finish our mortal lives. When Christ gives you back your life it's to say, "Your life is not over." YOU HAVE TO FINISH IT!

I have been crucified with Christ, and I no longer live, but Christ lives in me. The life I live in the body, I live by faith in the Son of God, who loved me and gave himself for me. (*Galatians* 2:20 NIV)

The life we have to finish is now touched by the power of Jesus. We live our mortal life "IN CHRIST," and our purpose is to "reveal him."

If the Spirit of him who raised Jesus from the dead is living in you, he who raised Christ from the dead will also give life to your mortal bodies through his Spirit, who lives in you. "Romans 8:11 NIV)

For we who are alive are always being given over to death for Jesus's sake, so that his life may be revealed in our mortal body. (2 *Corinthians* 4:11 NIV)

Now, we are experiencing the powers of the world to come: "who have tasted the goodness of the word of God and the powers of the coming age." (*Hebrews* 6:5 NIV) We are like the Israelites who saw the lush and beautiful cluster of grapes brought back from the Promised Land by the ten spies. Now we gather weekly as the faithful flock. We come together to be reminded how to live in the "already" and to be refreshed about the "not yet." We hear the Good News. We worship our Savior who sits on His throne in the Heavenliest. But when Christ returns, then time will be no more, and all that will remain will be the fruit of the everlasting Gospel.

THE HAIR GROWERS (A DREAM)

One day about seven years ago I woke up and I had no hair on my head. For two weeks I had to wear a hat. Once day I went to a book sale and I bought a witchcraft book. I was looking for a potion that would grow me some hair. I looked for seven or eight hours through the book and finally I found it. The name was Super Hair Grow Potion. I took the recipe and I showed it to my best friends, Monte and Guy. I had to get one pint of peanut butter, 5 ounces of jelly and some milk. I had to mix it for 5 hours. I got it done the next day. I applied some on my head. The book said to use just a little, but I didn't listen to what I had read. I put it all on my head and then I washed it off with a shower. When I finished, I still was without hair. I took a nap and when I woke up, I had at least an inch of hair. My friends said, "How did you do it?"

I said I'd tell them if they promised not to tell any other soul on earth. They promised, so I told them I had used the recipe from the book. They were really surprised. Suddenly, I got a crazy idea, "why don't you put some on your face and grow a beard they both replied. I didn't think they would want to but then they said, "Sure, we'll do it!" They said, "Are you really going to grow a beard?" I said, "Yes," with a quick answer. So, I told them, "Okay, it's your face." The next day my hair was 5 feet long, and my friends both had beards, and they were about 7 feet long. We were all really scared. But the next day our hair was even longer. We all walked to school and when we got there, we had to trim my hair every 8 minutes because it was growing so fast. Our teacher got really upset with each of us and sent all three of us to the office for detention for the rest of the month.

Soon everyone heard about us. One day on the way home from school we got kidnapped by a power madman. He wanted to cut our hair to make wigs, to sell. Another day I got loose for a couple of minutes, and I called Monte. I was trying to tell him the way here, but the madman caught me and made me hang up. My friend, Monte, looked for us but he couldn't find us, so he went home. The man was selling the wigs for $27.00 each. My friend Monte was still trying to find us, but he looked, and he couldn't find us again, so he went home again. Finally, one day Guy and I both got loose, and we ran home, and we told Guy and he called the police. They went to the warehouse to find the man, but he wasn't anywhere to be found.

The police had doctors run tests on me and Guy, but they found nothing wrong with us, so they let us go home. Our hair kept growing and growing so we went to the barber shop to get a haircut and to get his beard shaved, but their tools all broke trying to cut the hair because it was too thick. They finally cut 50 feet of mine. We made rope with it and sold it for $50.00 a foot because we wanted to make a bad thing into a good thing. We made over $5,000.00 from selling the hair.

In thirteen days, it was going to be Christmas, and we were so happy because we were out of school for twenty-nine days straight. Boy, did we all have fun! One time I went sledding, but my hair got caught in a tree and most of my hair got pulled out, but it did not hurt one bit. A couple of seconds later, my hair grew back. My friend Guy got a giant root beer float, but he got it all over his beard and none in his mouth.

Then one day I heard a myth about a great witch on the top of the tallest mountain in the world. So, we went there to ask her if she knew a spell to stop our hair from growing so fast. But when I got up there, there was a sign on the door, and it said: "Gone on vacation to Florida and be back in two weeks." So, we hopped on a plane and flew to Florida and found her. She said to go find a special flower called a gorilla flower and a tarantula. So, the next day we had to find the flower which was almost gone because it's so beautiful and everyone picks it. Next, we had to find a tarantula. We couldn't find any in the wild, so we went to a pet store and bought two of them. We took the flower and the tarantula to the witch, but she said she needed one more ingredient, a hair from George Bush's head. We had to sneak into the White House and take one when he was asleep. After we got it, we ran to catch a plane and finally got back to Florida. We gave it to the witch, and she mixed everything together. But it blew up, so it was only enough for one. I said that Guy could have it. As soon as he put it on, his beard disappeared. Somehow, it had worked. She said we would not have to pay her, but we did have to take her to lunch. While she was eating, she remembered another cure using jelly and ants, but it didn't always work.

We got the jelly and ants for her anyway, and she put it on my head. My hair stopped growing, too.

We went home and told my friend, Monte, about our exciting trip, but he said, "No way!" He didn't believe it. Then we went to the police station, and we told them what the kidnapper looked like, but they said they didn't believe us either. It didn't matter because we were happy just to be home and back to normal. We never forgot about this experience, so it was a special secret between Guy and me forever.

The best thing I remember about this complete experience was that it was all a dream!

Source: unknown

THE DOUBLE LIFE

Leading a double life – sounds great for a school teacher, doesn't it? I think it should be great! I really believe that your success as a teacher will depend in a large part on your happiness in out-of-school activities. One should have a large enough circle of friends of your own age and leaving enough pastimes that you won't have that on-the-shelf feeling and looks that makes teachers so bitter. It is so easy to follow the pattern of going in to school and coming home from school to the after-school naps, eating dinner, marking papers, or going to the movies, etc., and soon to bed. It is, however, fatal to one's ultimate success as an individual or as a teacher.

Our schools are filled with disappointed women and men who venture their unhappiness over their personal situations on defenseless children. Some manage to sublimate it. One doesn't want to have to do either. Don't count on forces outside yourself to prevent one from becoming morose; the answer to the problem of keeping out of a rut lies in developing one's own mental and physical resources.

An individual just can't be too stodgy if you exercise enough to keep yourself healthy and vital. One probably participates in three or four active sports. Make up your mind that you will hold to one of them for the future and practice it faithfully, even when you feel tired and good for nothing but that after school snooze. The fatigue which you feel from teaching is mental fatigue, and a game of golf, swimming, a good ride on horseback, or a set of tennis will make you feel refreshed and ready for life again. You see, teaching is filled with a number of minor annoyances which, added together, can bother you to a point beyond belief and return.

It is very trying to be with children all day, no matter how much you may like those children. The vitality of thirty to one hundred and fifty youngsters using one classroom on a sunny mid-May is something with which to cope. There is, to my mind, only one way in which to meet the situation; keep your own vitality at a high voltage level. You will need a spring in your own step, or you will be so upset by the child who starts to race through the corridors. If a game is scheduled for you right after school, you will understand the importance of some of the children getting out of the door quickly.

Knowing nothing is as poisonous and sterile as the mind that confines itself or formal academic pursuits to any young learner. Life is full of a number of good things, and the teacher who can find nothing outside of books to fill the many free hours is in a bad way indeed. Teachers need activities to offset the sedentary hours in the schoolroom. They need to get out on the fairways and into the woods. They need plenty of sunshine and the companionship of people within the same age or range of interests and hopefully all of this will take place in pleasant surroundings.

So far as social life is concerned, certainly teachers should be allowed the freedom accorded any other respectable citizens. This hypocritical "teachers-just," "teachers-just-don't," "teachers-just-don't smoke," and "teachers-just-don't-drink," and "teachers-just-don't whatever," attitude is nauseating to teachers who believe that teachers contribute something to civilization and also to parents who hope to give their children a true set of values for life.

Is it too much to assume that you, with your background in education and the social life you currently enjoy and that you enjoyed in the past, have learned that in social life moderation and good judgment are the key words of social conduct? Certainly, you will not go beyond the bounds of good ease in your social life, not because you are a teacher, but because you respect yourself. If you cannot control yourself in your social life, it follows quite logically that you would not control your temper of self within the classroom.

You should have a wholesome social life and much as you can achieve for yourself. The modern teacher knows that a sidecar is not always found on a motorcycle and that not all screwdrivers have handles, and one enjoys music, comedies, and dances as much as students or other adults.

Granting the fact that taking a cocktail does not make a drunkard of you and that you are not imperiling the youth of America when you smoke a cigarette, you surely will not expect to do these things if you are teaching in a small community in which the citizens themselves do not believe in smoking at all, or in drinking anything stronger than fruit lemonade. If you have accepted a position in such a community, you cannot expect the citizens to smile upon manners which to them are foreign and fraught with danger. The fair-minded teacher can hardly object to having to conform to community ideals.

If, on the other hand, you are teaching in a community where one set of standards prevails for the citizens and another set for the teachers, RUN FOR YOUR LIFE! Conform to their expectations while you are there but make every attempt to get into a more cosmopolitan teaching location, not because you are missing so much in the actual compromises forced upon you, but because such communities rob you of your social rights and of your self-respect.

Last, but not least of importance, a second vocation or active vocation can make life much more interesting to you. The average teacher who feels trapped in an uncongenial calling has only his/her own laziness to thank for the situation. What hobbies does one engage in? Is it photography? Contesting? Producing marionette shows? Cooking? Hi-fi? Bridge? Bingo? Boating? Golf? Swimming? etc. It should be something active. It may be one of a hundred things. Measured in money, it may seem to be of little value to you but measured in terms of its effect upon personality, it is of inestimable value.

What has all this to do with teaching? It is very closely related to your interest in your work and to your success. The active, vital person who has a number of interests is almost certain to be a better teacher, all other things being equal, than the teacher who never reaches out for new experiences or for new friendships. The teacher who knows different types of persons and who is the cosmopolitan in his/her point of view, brings more sympathy and understanding into the classroom than the teacher who has more respect for his/her profession because he/she knows that teaching is more highly regarded by those outside the school(s) than by those in the school(s), and furthermore, he/she knows something of the difficulties encountered in other lines of work.

Take stock today! What mark would you give yourself on personality, breath of interest, health, vitality? Have you planned a well-rounded and well-balanced program of activities for yourself outside-of-the-school? If you haven't, do you think that somebody else will do it for you? Maybe some will if you are lucky, but very doubtful.

Cultivate your own interests! Enjoy life! You will be better company for yourself and others, for your contemporaries, and certainly for the children who must spend a period of each school day with you! Just think about the amount of time you spend with yourself. Is it a happy time?

Source: unknown

DESIGN OF LIFE

When life seems to be settling down into something resembling a design of living, there comes a call from the superintendent's office, the principal's office, or from your activities director, depending upon the organization of your school system, a request of you for additional services. It seems that you have been chosen for a single honor. You are, in the opinion of the authorities, (because no one else would do the job), especially well prepared to sponsor the so call Umpty-Rumpty Club, the senior class party, the debating team outing, drama team, the yearbook, the school newspaper, selling at breaks and/or ballgames, or even selling the school's newspaper ads, among many other things!

You instantly realize that this is what happens to teachers who are not yet tenure. Don't blame your superintendent or the local school board members. There is nothing which you can do about this situation expect to be a good scout and to serve your time and say to yourself "…in three years…". You may or may not be compensated for the extra work in time or money. If you are wise, however, you will always remember that the extracurricular activity is secondary to your school work. The very fact that it is named extracurricular makes is so – less important than that of instruction and teaching.

Strangely enough, after you get into extracurricular work, you will find that it has compensations of its own, and you may actually enjoy the activities it entails to the extent that you would not willingly give them up. You become an integral part of students' life as you could not otherwise become, you learn to know the students, and you enjoy a certain prestige.

However, you find your Saturdays and evenings melting into extracurricular work, if you have a major activity/event, you begin to feel that in every evening you spend for your own pleasure, you are robbing the school (the instructional program).

Now all work and no play still makes a dull teacher and an uninspiring teacher, and you will need a sane sense of balance if you are to juggle a teaching schedule, extracurricular schedules, and a personal life, too. Insist upon that personal life! It is absolutely essential to your success as a teacher and as an individual. If you bury yourself beneath a mountain of routine work connected with extracurricular activities that no one else will do, thereby neglecting your own professional, personal advancement, and growth, you will deserve what you get, your opinion outstanding.

As justification for those rather strong words, which are, as you may have guessed, based upon a wealth of observations and experiences in this particular field of education. One should say in answer to the contentions of those armchair reformers who serve the secondary schools so admirably at comfortable distance. If the extracurricular activities have the outstanding values you claim for them, it is really believed that they do have, why aren't they not placed into the continuum and allotted regular time and credits earned towards graduation? There are certainly many dying subjects whom they could replace without any problems and approval of any school board.

MEMORIES OF CHRISTMASES PAST

In Kentucky during the mid-40's and 50's, Christmas was an enjoyable, drawn back celebration of the birth of Jesus Christ. It began in earnest about ten days before December 25 and lingered in the mind until well after New Year's Day. It was not a commercial rat race as it is today. There were no blaring radios and televisions. The "Little Drummer Boy" wasn't beaten half to death on the airwaves. Nobody wished that the "Partridge in the Pear Tree" had been shot 12 days before Christmas. The stores didn't offer valentines a week before Christmas. Santa Clause was a plump, jolly fellow engraved on the minds of the believing children, and not the pitchman with the sweat-soaked, artificial beard, found in numerous stores of today.

For the most part, a Kentuckian's degree of prosperity at Christmas time was pegged to agriculture: hemp, corn, rye, tobacco, hogs and milking cows. The money-on-the-pocket crop that paid for Christmas was tobacco, with auction sales coming the two or three weeks before the big holidays. Hemp was grown for the making of rope, not for its marijuana connection of today. Sometimes, the sale of Kentucky whiskey made its way to the public and had big sales. Of course, tobacco, horses and whiskey were the big three, plus coal mining, and they were Kentucky's principal cash crops of income until manufacturing plants began mushrooming in the state as World War II got under way in the late 1930s.

The Christmas celebration started with "pitting up" the tree. In some homes, the finding and cutting of the tree was an important ritual in which all the family took part. The trees, pine and cedar, were cut from farms of relatives and/or friends. The tree was placed near a large window and away from the heat of the open fireplace or stove, or the tree had to be placed in a room that was 'shut off' from other rooms in winter. At times the decorating of the tree was a shivering" undertaking. A couple of days before Christmas Day and a couple of days after, the tree room was kept warm.

A large box stored away since the previous Christmas was pulled from its hiding place. In the box there would be tinsel, paper chains with colored links, candles, candle holders and clips, stars, crescents, diamonds, and a large cross or star, all covered with tinfoil. The foil had been peeled off cigarette package wrappers and a few strings of colored lights added.

Next came the making of new ornaments for the tree. Home grown popcorn was shelled, popped, and strung on heavy sewing thread in strands about six feet long. The corn was usually popped in a wire basket with a long wooden handle on it. The box was held over an open fireplace or placed on top of a stove. The wire box was shaken as the corn heated so as to lessen the change of the corn burning before popping.

Pinecones and gourds were cleaned and dabbed with whitewash. White hen eggs were "blown out." A sewing needle was used to peck a small hole in each end of the egg. The lips were pressed to one end of the egg. Air, forced into the egg, caused the yolk and white to stream out at the other end. The eggshells were colored and strung on sewing thread. Sometimes the shells were decorated with snips of wallpaper. Colored gumdrops were strung on thread, about three to a strand. Peppermint sticks, two at a time, were crossed and tied together. The tinsel, paper chains, popcorn and eggshell strings were draped on the tree. The pinecones, gumdrops, peppermint sticks, stars, crescents, and diamonds were suspended from the branches. The large tinfoil star or cross was anchored at the top of the tree. The candle holders with candles were burned for brief periods, if at all. Illumination for the tree came from sunlight, through the large window, or by night from an open fireplace, oil lamps, or from electric bulbs that cast a pale-yellow light.

With the Christmas tree up and decorated, then came the waiting for Christmas Day, with the time passing slowly for children and passing fast for adults. Our mother and father had to make and/or buy gifts, sneak Santa Clause loot into the house, and prepare for the food festival of Christmas Day. Sending Christmas cards was not a headache or expensive. The relatively few cards that were mailed needed only a one-cent stamp per card for postage.

Food preparation was mostly "from scratch." Much dough was kneaded by hand until they 'felt right.' Seasoning was by pinches –

some foods needing small pinches, others large pinch. Walnuts and hickory nuts, gathered in the fall, were cracked and picked from the shells by family members who were gathered around a stove or sat in front of an open fireplace.

Pre-Christmas cooking became a frenzy of cookies, cake, and candy making. Our mother would make divinity, fondue, and fudge for the family and as gifts for friends. Real cream and butter were used. No bake fruitcakes were made and wrapped in flour sacks that had been soaked in whiskey. Popcorn balls, held together by a honey or molasses mixture, were made and stored in dishpans. Taffy candy had to be pulled.

Snowfall was more frequent, and the snow stayed on the ground longer during those days than today. Just about every home with a child had a hand sled. It was not uncommon to see a sleigh pulled by a horse that spewed 'steam' from its nostrils as it trotted in the cold, crisp air.

I remember very well how our older brother would tell us about "no Santa Clause" that it was all just made up. Of course, he took all of the fun out of Christmas at a very early age for me and my sister.

THE TEACHER'S ROOM

Of all the rooms in the building, the teachers' classroom is probably the one most attractive to the teacher (but not me); if you are teaching in a modern school building. Here you may relax in your free period, have a coke or coffee, and relapse into your original human state.

Every teacher's classroom should have on the door in bright, RED BOLD letters, "NEW TEACHER – BEWARE!" How is it that, in your first exuberance of teaching, you will most likely make yourself ridiculous by talking too much; here you may in one short sentence insult more teachers than you normally talk to outside the classroom in one word. As the old song goes, "Little one, little one, little one, watch what you say!"

It is a wise beginning teacher who is a good listener in the teachers' lounge. School politics are usually exceedingly devious, and remarks do gain momentum and importance as they travel downward to the central office of the school district. There may be one or two delicate personal situations represented in the group of which the new teacher is blissfully unaware.

As a new teacher, you have an excellent excuse for not talking by applying yourself to a set of papers to be marked, --you, at once – gain the reputation of being a conscientious teacher and, in addition, you can listen with one ear to the conversation which is sure to be underway. You should have very few opinions.

One of the worst mistakes you can make is to talk about your romances or the romance with another young teacher in the classroom and/or teacher's lounge. Aside from the fact that this is genuinely bad practice and shows a lack of judgment, it is a particularly bad mistake to make in a group of fellow teachers.

Be certain that you are not sitting in the best chair, and monopolizing the chaise lounge or the newspaper, or in any way presuming upon the rights and privileges of older members of the staff. Teaching has a queen and king effect upon us; trifles are indeed no trifles to most of us and when we encounter a situation which we cannot adjust by a snap of the fingers and a few terse words, we suffer from a sense of frustration which is almost unbearable.

In short, be reserved and properly humble. See all, head all, know nothing, and criticize no one. Attend to your own work and business! LISTEN! Therefore, you will find yourself so busy that you won't have the time to pick up on these other things.

TURNING MISTAKES INTO PRODUCTIVITY

What? Can one make a mistake in productivity? How could that be? A mistake is objective evidence that a student "doesn't know" or can't do." As such, it alerts us to the fact that something needs to be learned. Without that mistake, the learner's problem might go undetected and therefore remediate with the resultant possibility of more serious problems later on. A mistake uncorrected is the same as a mistake undetected; both could eventually swamp a learner. A product mistake is one which is correct, and the right response learned thereby leaving the student stronger, with more confidence in his/her own ability and more ego strength to support him/her in the future mistakes which are inevitable.

When a learner makes a mistake there are two things he/she doesn't know. He/she doesn't know the answer to the question that was asked and/or he/she doesn't know the question to which his/her incorrectly answered really belongs.

WORKING WITH JERKS IN THE OFFICE

Well, what do you know; I'm working with a bunch of jerks. They may be the boss, peers, or even subordinates. However, the common denominator: THEY GO OUT OF THEIR WAY TO MAKE YOUR LIFE MISERABLE.

Quite a group, aren't they? Chuck asked the question in that quasi-rhetorical tone some spouses use to give their mates an opening to either say what they really think or tactfully duck the issue. It was obvious from the set of her shoulders and the grim, straight ahead stare that Barbara would be ducking no issues this time. She was just taking her time, framing a response.

What followed was the longest, most audibly silent seven blocks. Church could ever remember having driven. Preceded as it was by the longest, most annoying office Christmas party he had ever endured, he had a strong hunch about the nature of what he was going to hear and steeled himself for it. Still, he honestly wanted his wife's take on his new boss and colleagues.

As the car slowed for a stoplight, Barbara gave up the struggle to find a delicate way to put it. "Okay, here it is" she sighed. "All along I kept thinking: My God, is it me? Or, has Chuck really fallen into a snake pit?"

It was pretty much what he had feared. But he wanted all of it, so he pretended not to understand. "What do you mean?" Barbara shoots a disbelieving glance at him but decides to soften it a little. "Well," she began, "they'd been drinking, so maybe I'm not being fair. But if they're at all like that when they're sober, I don't know how you stand being around them all day. I'm sorry, honey, but if the people I work with at the hospital were as catty and nasty as the people you work with seem to be, I'd turn in my stethoscope and take up another profession. Is he a hermit, maybe?"

Until that moment Chuck has been clinging to a desperate hope that everything would work out – eventually. "There is always a period of adjustment on a new job," he'd been telling himself. "It takes time to fit in, to feel at home in a new outfit. Okay, so it's been four months. That's a lot longer than it's ever taken when I switched jobs before. But eventually it has to work out. Doesn't it?

But now Barbara has seen the ghastly mismatch between Chuck and his new crew. She had confirmed it, given it substance, and made it a fact instead of a feeling. He was working for a jerk – a jerk who showed a definite talent for hiring in his own image, and who had done so in the case of six of Chuck's nine office mates. There were the people he had to work with closely every day for…Well, for the foreseeable future. How does it happen?

We could candy-coat the concept (and pretend we're being "scientific" by coining some pasteurized, psycho babbling phrase like "interpersonally dysfunctional persons. "But what the hell, let's call a jerk a jerk. Or rather, let's use "jerk" instead of several less printable epithets as a broad term to cover people who are out to get you. We're discounting paranoia on your part (check with at least one person you trust) and any enemy who has a specific, legitimate grudge against you. Jerks, for our purposes, are those individuals who seem to go out of their way to make your life – any usually other people's lives – miserable.

They come in a hundred varieties. They come as bosses, peers, and subordinates. But you know who we're talking about. So how do regular people – good people, like you and me – end up working with jerks?

First of all, there is the luck of the draw. There's simply no 'guarantee' that a new job won't put you in regular contact with one or more jerks. Now it's true that no one ever promised we'd spend our entire working lives in the company of people we absolutely adore. The object of work, after all, is primarily commercial, not social. On the other hand, the workplace is a social environment. It can be grim if you wind up working with a major league jerk or, worse yet, a whole gaggle of jerks.

Chuck is a big boy, ambitious, savvy, no baby in the woods. He went through the attention process sober, aware of his surroundings and certainly not under duress. He met several of his prospective. You could say he had ample opportunity to size up the people and the situation. He may indeed have discounted the telltale signs of 'jerkdom' he saw at the new company, but he did so at his own peril; going for the goal has its inherent risks – which could not be a given disadvantage or advantage.

But there are other ways to end up working with jerks – ways that are less volitional. Most are, in fact, accidental (Who, but over-eager Chuck would have ignored the signals and gone to work for a jerk on purpose?) Many are downright unavoidable: Your boss leaves and is replaced by you-know-what. The "downsizing" ax falls on the co-workers you thought the world of, and you, you lucky survivor, get transferred to "corporate," land of the weird and home of the Gila monsters. Then there's the naked fact that you do need a job – some kind of job – and you'll take the most promising one you can get; if a jerk comes with the package, so be it.

Centralization, decentralization, leveraged buyouts, acquisitions, delaying, hostile takeovers, changes in political administrations – there's no end to the list of changes that can leave you working under, over or beside some genuinely appalling people. When it happens, you'll be reluctant to believe it. For a while you'll amble along, unsure of the problem's source ("Is it me?"), maybe even mystified about why you feel so whipped all the time. But finally, as in Chuck's case, someone you trust implicitly will turn to you and ask: "How do you stand it? How do you spend eight hours a day dealing with that jerk?

An important principle: Not all jerks are created equal. It's corollary: The majority of jerks you are likely to have to cope with in the workplace are temporary or situational jerks. These are people who, for one reason or another, act jerky once in a while, especially when you first meet them, but who turn out to be relatively inoffensive – or even diamonds in the rough.

A typical situational jerk move is to walk into your cubicle on your first day and ask, "So where did you go to school Chickadee? Just what were you doing at Cyber corpse that made you such a great candidate for this job?" It doesn't take whopping portions of insight to see where this situational jerk is coming from. He/she, sex being no barrier to jerk hood, is worried about some real or imagined threat you pose to his/her little corner of the ecosphere. Depending on the situation and how you both handle it, this relationship may very well smooth out.

More forbidding is the genetic jerk. This is the individual who wears jerk hood with the pride of any Eagle Scout flaunting a merit badge in advanced taxidermy. By and large, your genetic jerk is colder, more ruthless, more calculating than the situational jerk an example. Let's say that you, the genetic jerk and your boss are in a meeting with your boss' boss to discuss new ways of attacking the sales training problem. The genetic jerk (GJ for short) lies in wait until you have presented your carefully planned proposal for criterion-based training – the one he/she has known for weeks you were working on – then chimes in with: "Oh, Chester! Hasn't anyone told you that sort of thing is taboo at this company? Didn't you now your predecessor tried to do self-directed sales training and was run out of the "town on a rail???"

A more detailed typology of jerks is described in the companion story on the following pages, but let's spend a little time on those two basic varieties, 'Situational Jerk –remember that a situational jerk may be making your life miserable right now, but eventually he/she will stop. Trouble is, when you're up to your knees in quicksand, you don't know whether there's a solid bottom a few inches away or if you're sinking into a bottomless morass. So, it's important to look for clues that will tell you whether you are dealing with a temporary or a permanent jerk.

It is also worth pointing out that some rather bad bosses don't really indeed to be jerks – they just don't know how not to be. "Most bosses never get any training at all. Others are promoted to being boss because of their technical talent or expertise." Both situations sometimes lead to the same result: Bosses who act like jerks because they don't know any better.

Most of the time bosses like these are trainable, but it isn't a good idea to start "teaching" your boss to be a better manager. The things he/she doesn't know about being a good manager are the same things that ensure he/she will take offense at your attempts to be helpful. Indirect approaches whereby you fight the boss' jerkiness by being a sneaky little jerk yourself – unsigned notes hinting at his/her failings or newsletter items naming him/her.

THE OLD MERCHANDISING STORE

Over sixty years ago I would visit once in a while the old merchandising store in a small community town just a few miles down the road from where we lived. This store was in business long before wage and hour laws, before overtime, before plastic packaging, before television and before the customer did the work of collecting and bringing the groceries to the checkout counter.

The old store was a two-level store. Upstairs, at one time, was a department store with all of the merchandise that anyone would wish to have—clothing, furniture, finer things of life and sometimes one could find something very special. The floor level entrance had many barrels – crackers, pickles, candy and along the way, was some hardware, tools, farm items of interest just to name a few.

The store name was just "Yancey's Store," the building was old sixty years ago and the family kept selling from it until it finally fell down and no longer can be seen.

I noticed that the family clerks were the scanners and price recorders. They wrote the prices of items on brown paper bags, added the figures, and then write the totals on the paper bags, then gave the customers a turn at checking the accuracy of the clerk's mathematic skills. Most customers were good enough at math to check the accuracy of the figures. Some were not, gave fleeting glances to the figures and then nodded approval of what had been added.

The store had a very old cash register (before its time) and when the clerks cashed out a customer, if the total was $19.19, they would press a key for $10, another one for $9 and one on the ten cents key and one on the nine-cent key for the sale. All these keys were depressed simultaneously. The four metal tabs appeared behind glass at the top of the cash register showing the amount of the sale. It was up to the clerk to figure how much change, if any, was due to the customer, whose sales slip was the column of figures written on the brown paper bag.

It was a well-known fact to becoming a grocery clerk in those days you have to be good at math, strong back, strong arms, strong feet, and clean-shaven along with neatness.

Strong feet were needed because of the 'miles' a clerk walked while at work. The customer usually stood at the checkout counter while the clerk gathered items needed on the order of the customer. Sometimes the clerk would pick up two or three items on the way to get another item for the customer.

All the stores in those days managed to keep most requested items near the cash register. Sometimes the clerks would need to use a step ladder to secure merchandise from upper shelves. Other times they would use a stick with a hood on it that was used to tumble a roll of toilet tissue down to the clerk. Toilet tissue was a slow mover in the old store because everyone had a Sears catalogue at home to take care of "the need." Of course, some individuals use large oak leaves, corn shucks or a corn cob. This tells me why senior citizens today must use Preparation H!

The old merchandising store was on Main Street of this little county town and just next door was the Baptist Church, a post office to the left of the church, a business that cured and processed country hams next to the post office, and the school was just down the street a few 100 feet.

Regardless of the season, the store always had ice cold drinks, cakes, cookies, ice cream and all kinds of candy to make your taste buds happy.

Sixty years ago, the old store received most items in bulk: potatoes, coffee, dried beans, dried fruit, hominy grits, rice, sugar, crackers, cookies, lard, fresh fish, vinegar and kerosene.

These items, for the most part, were shipped in 100- or 50-pound bags and the clerk would weigh out what the customer needed. Kerosene came in a 50-gallon drum, commonly called coal oil. The clerk would pump out the amount requested by the customer and usually in a container supplied by the customer.

Lard (called cooking oil today) was received in metal cans that held 50 pounds. It was sold by the pound to customers who brought their own small, large buckets to the store. Vegetable oil sales were then second to lard sales. In those days very few customers worried, or even knew, about cholesterol and triglycerides.

The busiest days for the old store were Saturday each week and the third Monday of each month, which were days on which the little town had court day. One of the best sellers to men in those days around noon was a dime's worth of cheese and crackers or bologna.

For the customer's dime, he/she got about five ounces of rat cheese (or bologna) and a handful of soda crackers in a brown paper bag. For a nickel more they could get a 12-ounce bottle of pop (called soft drink today). Sixty years ago, Bologna was not filled with additives and other by-products as it is today.

Wieners (hot dogs) came in processed animal guts. The cheese, bologna, wieners, boiled ham and souse meat loaf were kept in a large ice refrigerator. Wieners (hot dogs) sixty years ago would come into the store about a dozen to a string.

In those days, clerks were not encouraged to wash their hands because I saw one clerk go outside to pump gasoline and return to the counter to prepare a sandwich for the same customer. Today the inspector would fail the store for something that major.

So, I observed the clerk's time filling the list of items needed. For instance, his hands sacked the cookies, then the dried fruit, then the wieners, and then the fish. The coal oil can was filled last, followed by hand washing.

When the clerk waited on kids just spending ten cents on candy, there was no pleasure. However, some clerks enjoyed watching the ordeal demonstrated by the kids. The kids usually wanted a penny worth of ten different candies. In those days, the nickel Three Musketeers consisted of three bars: chocolate, vanilla and strawberry. A half pound Baby Ruth cost five cents.

On rainy or very cold days customers would come into the old store and stand around the stove in the middle of the floor. As the customers and clerks would huddle around the stove they would have stories about family, members of the community, church activities and sometimes the clerks would have difficulty moving about the store to get customer needs.

In a store of this nature the clerks had many opportunities to hear choice bits of gossip if he/she kept his/her ears alert.

BLADDER CANCER

Back in October of 2010 my regular doctor, through several tests, found blood in my urine. As he was concerned his office made an appointment with a urologist.

In meeting with the urologist, after doing several tests and exams and not finding anything, he made me an appointment with Bluegrass Regional Imaging for a full boy scan in late December.

This old body was found in very good shape as everything looked normal.

In January, I went back to the urologist, and he performed a cystoscopy procedure and found a 2.5 cm papillary tumor on the lower right lateral wall of the bladder. As the doctor then said that I completed my hematuria work-up. No other significant findings were made.

In February, I went back to see my regular doctor for decision-making and his review/interpretation of all the reports, along with his blessings for the surgery.

Following this meeting I contacted the urologist and scheduled an appointment for the surgery.

The surgery will take place on Monday, March 14 at 10:00 a.m., but I must report at 8:00 a.m. for prep work prior to the surgery. This will all happen at St. Joseph Hospital on Harrodsburg Road.

No one knows anything about the blood in the urine to-date.

Overall, the urologist was most complementary as he stated: "the patient appears a bit younger than his stated age." Therefore, something must be good about farm life!

Monday, March 14, 2011, 4:00 p.m.

Well, we got home at 4:00 p.m. and I put him right to bed. The doctor said that all went well and that he removed all the tumor and that everything looked good, but we will wait for the pathology report. We will find out the results on Wednesday or Thursday. He came home with a catheter, so I get to play nurse and remove it tomorrow! (He will definitely not be going to the Refuge Clinic to work tomorrow.) He has to eat light for a day or two and has pain medication and medication to prevent infection to take place. He will be out like a light the rest of the day.

Thanks for all your thoughts and prayers. I have to go gather eggs and then I will be off to Kroger's to get his medication. Thanks again!

Friday, March 18, 2011

Pathology Report

Well, we had an associate of Jim's surgeon call today to give us the results of the test on the tumor. It was malignant! He said that since the surgeon got everything there would be no type of follow-up treatment. Jim will have to be checked every three months for a year to make sure that it does not come back. This sure was the opposite of what we were told before the surgery, but we will deal with it. Please keep the prayers going for a complete recovery with no return tumors. He has a follow-up appointment for April 14 with a new surgeon. Also, he will need to continue to have monitoring visits to the doctor every three months for a period of two years to check the bladder to learn if anything returns.

Jim is starting to do more, but he is tired today after supervising a couple of fellows working at finishing cleaning off the garden and flower beds. His constipation is over, and he feels better because of that. He says he will sleep well tonight.

Thanks again for all good thoughts and prayers. They are very much appreciated

The following is with a different doctor.

As results of my annual physical (blood test), I learned that I had bladder cancer. I had to follow up on these findings which the next step was to see a doctor. He performed surgery to remove the cancer cells. This doctor had poor bedside manners nor did he say anything about a follow-up plan. Afterwards, I did not have a good feeling about everything that had taken place. I had a feeling in my stomach; therefore, I got a second opinion.

In meeting with the new doctor and talking with him about what took place previously, the decision was made to test one more time. After the test the doctor reported that all of the cancer cells were not removed from having the first surgery. Surgery was scheduled as soon as possible. After surgery the doctor provided a follow-up plan involving radiation and chemo treatments. The doctor told me that I would lose my hair, appetite and feel nauseated. All of the treatments went well and were completed several months later. Thanks Dr. S. for giving me back my life.

More: I never experienced any of the problems of hair loss, feeling sick or otherwise.

YES, I am cancer free today!

Love to all,

Kathy and Jim Cole

DIVING FOR THE CROSS

I haven't been sick my whole life, and this within itself is a **Reason for HOPE**. Oh, some would say that you had bladder and appendix surgery years ago, but I have not really been sick.

This story of courage will step up the importance of cancer being in the body and you can only hope and pray for a better day to come but through tragedy comes hope. No excuses or simplistic solutions here. You'll come to understand why the 'good" and "evil" stereotypes the media uses when describing any type of cancer don't really apply to most cancer situations.

You will learn why, in some instances, those stereotypes actually delay individuals from recognizing cancer behaviors and taking the necessary steps to get help for you or your loved ones involved. You'll find difficult truths, complex personalities and tough challenges in these stories – courageous people describing how they turned anger and despair into a journey of hope to whip cancer.

The Reason for HOPE is a Christian evolved prayer that strives to integrate your very soul diagnosed with developmental delays and neurologically typical of thinking to go on and on while you are undergoing treatment!

The Reason for HOPE uses principles of Applied Behavior Analysis (ABA) and/or Speech and Language Therapy to facilitate learning among ourselves. Much research has demonstrated that Applied Behavior Analysis is the most effective intervention in the treatment plan.

The Reason for HOPE first, would be to strive to provide exemplary intervention treatment plan to cure the cancer and keep their families in a positive Christian environment while they experience and live through this ordeal. Second, **The Reason for Hope** strives to cultivate learning about the cancer by providing a learning Centre that focuses on academic, social, language and coping skills within a Christian environment.

I personally felt that I was diving for the cross when the doctor informed me that I had bladder cancer, for that day my life was changed whether I wanted it to be or not!

At 67 years of age, I sat around thinking to myself trying to describe this experience of grasping for the cross in the murky waters somewhere beyond my reach and control.

The cross has been a huge aspect of my faith, and it's a blessing of God, how the cross just landed in my hand through prayer and the cross feels like it was chosen to direct me. Every night I sit and think and pray all through this cancer experience.

This is the story of Marshall Duke, Charles Thomas Southworth, II and his son Luther Soutworth. Charles Thomas Southworth was our great, great, great, great, great grandfather.

This article is taken from *"The Georgetown Times,"* Monday, September 18, 1899.

TERRIBLE TRAGEDY

TWO MEN KILLED AT STAMPING GROUND

MARSHALL DUKE KILLS THOMAS SOUTHWORTH AND IS HIMSELF KILLED

WHO FIRED THE SHOTS?

A terrible double tragedy occurred at Stamping Ground Monday evening between half past six and seven o'clock in which Town Marshall C.R. Duke and Tom Southworth of Harmony, Owen County, were both almost instantly killed. Southworth and his son, Luther, had been to Georgetown and were on their way home in a buggy. Southworth had been drinking freely and as they passed through Stamping Ground, he began to curse and yell, calling on Duke. The Marshall was at home at supper and hearing Southworth, came out and caught hold of the horse telling Southworth to stop his noise. The latter continued to curse, and Duke attempted to place him under arrest. Southworth resisted and the shooting began. The Southworth's were out of the buggy at the time. There was no eyewitness except the son and very little could be gotten out of him about the affair. There were five or six shots fired, and some say they heard seven. Southworth was shot four times, once through the breast, once through the side of the head just behind the ear, once through the cheek and once through the ear. The first three shots went entirely through him and anyone of them would have been fatal. Duke was shot through the lower part of the heart. Both men died almost instantly where they lay, Duke living a little longer than Southworth. A singular thing is that while Duke's pistol was found to be empty, every chamber of Southworth's weapon was filled with a cartridge, and it showed that it has never been fired. Who killed Duke? Was it young Southworth or was a third part engaged in the affair? Such questions of blood poured from Southworth's wounds that his body was covered from head to foot and he presented terrible sight.

Coroner Ashurst was notified and went to Stamping Ground and held an inquest the same night. Young Southworth testified that he was holding the horse and did not know anything about the affair except there was shotting and he didn't have any weapon or do any shooting himself. He seemed to take his father's death very hard and moaned piteously, calling on his father to speak to him. There were several other witnesses, colored men, who were some distance away. They could see two men, see the flashes of the pistols, but could not tell who was shooting. They heard the Marshall call his brother and the brother say he was coming. When he reached him he was on his hands and knees. The brother caught him around the body and the Marshall dropped down without uttering a word. It was evidently the last shot fired that killed Duke. The colored man say after the four shots were fired there was a pause and then another shot of a different sound. Duke was about 45 years of age and unmarried; he has a brother living at Stamping Ground and other relatives living at Richmond, Virginia. He has been Marshall at Stamping Ground for about two years and was a brave and fearless officer. Southworth was 41 years of age. He leaves an invalid wife and seven children: five boys and two girls. He killed Green Barr at Harmony a few years ago and was regarded as a dangerous man. He was acquitted for the killing of Barr. Young Southworth is about 20 years of age.

The verdict of the coroner was that Southworth came to his death by bullets fired by Duke and that the bullet that caused Duke's death was fired by an unknown party. There is great excitement at Stamping Ground over the affair, the community being shocked at the tragedy. The dead Marshall will be buried at Lexington Cemetery today. Southworth's body was taken to Harmony to Beechwood Cemetery.

"The Lexington Leader"

September 21, 1899

Georgetown, Kentucky

There were new developments in the double tragedy at Stamping Ground Monday evening in which Town Marshall Charles Duke and Tom Southworth were almost instantly killed in a battle on the street. Southworth's son Luther is under arrest, charged with murder. Two eyewitnesses to the affair have been found. They state that a terrible struggle took place between the three men, and the Marshall was getting badly used up when he shot and killed the elder Southworth. It is alleged that young Southworth then tore the pistol from the Marshall's hand and shot him through the heart with his own pistol. It was not at first known who killed Duke, as Tom Southworth's pistol was found loaded in every chamber.

At the Coroner's inquest young Southworth swore that he was unarmed and fired no shot, and an unknown party was believed to have done the deed. Young Southworth was arrested at the conclusion of his father's funeral in Owen County, and will be brought to Georgetown, where he will have an examining trial.

"Georgetown Times"

Under $15,000 Bond Luther Southworth Held to Circuit Court

Charged with the Murder of Marshall C.R. Duke who killed his father, Tom Southworth

At the time the account of the terrible double tragedy at Stamping Ground was presented in the "Times" last week, it was not known who fired the shot that killed Marshall Duke. Later two eyewitnesses were found, Messrs R.J. Thomasson and K.T. Oliver, who live near Switzer, Franklin County. They were driving home in a buggy and were passing through Stamping Ground and saw the killing of Duke, but not Southworth. They say young Southworth fired the fatal shot, which was done with Duke's own pistol after he had killed Tom Southworth and while the Marshall was down on his knees and holding his hands above his head.

Young Southworth was taken into custody at his father's funeral Wednesday and brought to Georgetown Friday morning and the examining trail was held before Judge Yates. There was a large crowd present. The County Attorney was assisted by Mr. V.F. Bradley, who conducted the examination of the witnesses. The prisoner was defended by Mr. James Steel of Owen County.

The evidence for the prosecution was substantially as follows:

Olie Jameson – I heard shots and went to where the shooting took place. Saw both Duke and Tom Southworth lying on the ground. Southworth was dead. Duke was still breathing. I heard hallooing just before in center of town. There were two folks, one of them in the buggy said, "Where is Duke?" There was some time between yelling and shooting. There were two voices. They were coming from Georgetown and passed my store. Shooting occurred below my store about the little branch. There were about five shots. It was about 6:30 o'clock. I didn't know who the parties were. There were no others hallooing but these parties.

John Cook – the day after the shooting I saw a bruise on the side of Duke's face. I hear hallooing just before the shooting. I was at Jerry Haner's corner. I heard two voices. They were going through town from Georgetown. I went on to depot and didn't hear the shots. They kept hallooing after they passed me.

W.H. Green – I was in the drug store; heard someone calling for Duke. There were two in buggy. Said, "Oh Duke," I didn't know who they were. There was an interval between the first shots and the last one or two. I didn't hear any other hallooing but this. It was about 7 o'clock. There were three or four rapid shots and then an intermission.

Sam Beagle – Heard shooting and hallooing. There were four or five minutes between the shooting and hallooing. I was in Calvert's store. I heard men hallooing, "Where is Duke," and a little afterwards shooting and then an interval before the last shot. Two or three times they hallooed for Duke, I saw the buggy go by at that time but did not hear anyone else hallooing.

Mr. Wilkerson – I was in the store and heard shooting. I heard hallooing for Duke before. I heard several shots and then an interval and then one other. There was no other hallooing. I thought there was only one person hallooing. It was between 7 and 8 o'clock I guess. "Where is Duke?" I was hallooing. They seemed like drunken yells.

Mr. Darnell – it was deputy Marshall under Duke for a while. The shooting was in the limits of town. The men came by hallooing very loud. They began to call for Duke. He said, "Where are you, Duke? Come out here duke, G-D you." I was in front of the Coleman Hotel. In a little while the shooting began. Shooting was near a branch in hollow. I could not tell who they were. Hallooing continued until just before shooting. Then I heard someone crying. I didn't know whether both men were hallooing or not.   At the place of the shooting, I recognized the horse and buggy. Two men came along just behind and stopped. They asked who the parties in front were and said they came near running into them. The hallooing commenced about the town hall. They yelled, "Who we." If the buggy has a top, it was down. The horse was grey. I think there were some other buggies there when I got there. Young Southworth was at his father's head. He was crying.

R.J. **Thomasson** – I live near Switzer, Franklin County, was returning home with K.T. Oliver in a buggy. I was passing through Stamping Ground. Saw one shot fired. I heard the hallooing. We stopped when shooting commenced and then went on. We were about 30 yards off. They were in a pile. The young man pulled away from Duke. Duke raised his knees, and the young man shot him. I told him twice not to shoot but he did. Duke was on his hands and knees. Duke held up his hands in front of him about his head as if pleading and said something, I don't know what. When shot he fell on his face. Young Southworth attempted to shoot again, and I grabbed him. I took the pistol and gave it to Sam Beagle. Young Southworth said it was his father who was killed. Then I saw Tom Southworth lying there. He was dead. I didn't examine the pistol to see if all the loads were out. Southworth's body was very bloody. It was not searched in my presence. The boy stepped around from the side of Duke to the front of him and pointed the pistol at him. I hallooed to him, "Don't shoot the man, don't shoot him," and jumped out of my buggy, but he fired before

I got to him. Mr. Thomasson then identified the black handled revolver as the one with which Duke was killed. It showed dried blood stains on it.

Beagle recalled – Mr. Thomasson left the pistol with me. It was Duke's pistol. I did not examine it at first but did afterwards and found all the chambers empty. It was not out of my possession.

K.T. Oliver – I was in a buggy with Thomasson and saw the shooting. We were going through Stamping Ground and heard four or five shots. When we got there, we saw young Southworth and Duke scuffling. The boy jumped back with the pistol and fired. Duke was trying to get up. He was on one knee and had his hands up, holding them above his head.

Thomasson hallooed to the boy several times not to shoot and jumped out of the buggy. He ran and caught the pistol. Young Southworth tried to shoot Duke again, and had the pistol pointed at his head. Duke fell on his hands and knees and then on his face. The parties passed up on the road. It was a grey horse. They almost ran into us as they passed. We almost caught up with them again. I didn't hear the young man say anything. I didn't know the other man had been killed till the crowd came up. Afterwards I found Southworth had been killed. Duke had nothing in his hands. His hands were up like he was reaching up. Duke had hands up when the shot was fired. He had his blue uniform on. After the shooting young Southworth said, he killed my father.

Alfred Poindexter – I was in front of Calvert's store. Heard yelling and hallooing. I thought it was Tom Southworth. I saw them ass. It was a grey horse. I heard the hallooing. "Duke, Duke where are you?" and after a little while I heard the shooting. I saw the buggy at the scene of the shooting. I recognized Tom Southworth as the man wo did the hallooing. I recognized his voice. I hadn't heard it for almost four years. But I told Calvert it was Tom Southworth when they went by. He hallooed "who wee."

The prosecution rested his case here and the defense offered no evidence.

Arguments were made by Messrs. Settle, Bradley and Sebree. The Court held the prisoner over to Circuit Court and stated that in view of the testimony before him he could not allow bail. After the witnesses were recognized and Court was almost about to adjourn, Southworth's attorney stated that he had just received important evidence in the boy's favor and asked that the case be reopened. He said a colored man had just come to him and that he saw the affair was willing to testify. The attorney also stated that he did not believe the boy's mother would last through the night unless he came home. The Court refused to reopen the case, but in view of the statements of the prisoner's attorney, the County Attorney was willing to allow bail provided it was made large enough and said nothing less than $15,000 would be satisfactory. The defense signified his willingness to give $25,000. On the suggestion the County Attorney, the Court then approved the bond of $15,000 which was given by the boy's relatives and friends, and he was released.

Mr. Bradley was employed by the citizens of Stamping Ground to assist in the prosecution.

Young Southworth is twenty years of age and is not bad looking. He did not seem to realize the gravity of his condition.

Mr. and Mrs. Charles Thomas Southworth had a baby boy, Power, born to them just three days before the father was killed.

Duke was buried at Stamping Ground, in the presence of a large number of friends. It is said that the citizens of that village were to erect a monument to his memory.

Charles Thomas Southworth, II, was buried in the Beechwood Cemetery in Harmony, Kentucky, on top of a hill. Southworth was a landowner (former), retail store and hotel owner and operator.

A SILENT TEAR FELL

This is a story about a man named Clifford. I'm telling his story as follows:

It was not more than forty-eight years ago when his wife gave birth to the first child. I still remember that night.

I stayed out all night long with my friends as we were all home from college. It was a night filled with useless talk, and worse, with backbiting, gossiping, and having fun with people. I was mostly the one who made people laugh; I would tell stories about others, and my friends would laugh and laugh. I remember on that night that I'd made them laugh a lot. I had an amazing ability to imitate others – I could change the sound of my voice until I sounded exactly like the blind man I was mocking. No one was safe from my biting mockery, even my friends; some people started avoiding me just to be safe from my tongue. I remember on that night; I had made fun of a blind man who I'd seen begging in the market. What was worse, I had put my foot out in front of him – he tripped and fell, and started turning his head around, not knowing what to say. I am still sorry today for doing that action! I went back to my house, late as usual, and I found my family waiting for me. They were in a terrible state, and said in a quivering voice, "Clifford…where have you been?"

"Where would I be, on Mars?" I said sarcastically, "With my friends of course."

She was visibly exhausted, and holding back tears, she said, "Clifford, I'm so tire. It seems the baby is going to come soon." A silent tear fell on her cheek.

I felt that I had neglected my wife. I should have taken care of her and not stayed out so much all those nights…especially since she was in her ninth month. I quickly took her to the hospital; she went into the delivery room and suffered through long hours of pain.

I waited patiently for her to give birth…but her delivery was difficult, and I waited a long time until I got tired. So, I went home and left my phone number with the hospital so they could call with the good news. An hour later, they called me to congratulate me on the birth of LaCinda. I went to the hospital immediately. As soon as they saw me, they asked me to go see the doctor who had overlooked my wife's delivery.

What doctor? I cried out, "I just want to see my daughter, LaCinda!" "First go see the doctor," they said.

I went to the doctor, and she started talking to me about trials, and about being satisfied with Allah's decree. Then she said, "Your daughter has a serious deformity in her eyes, and it seems that she has no vision." I lowered my head while I fought back tears…I remembered that blind man begging in the market that I'd tripped and made others laugh.

You get what you give! I stayed brooding quietly for a while…I didn't know what to say. Then I remembered my wife and daughter. I thanked the doctor for her kindness and went to see my wife. My wife wasn't sad. She has a strong belief she was content…How often had she advised me to stop mocking people! "Don't back bit people," she always used to repeat…We left the hospital, and LaCinda came home with us.

In reality, I didn't pay much attention to her. I pretended that she wasn't in the house with us. When she started crying loudly, I'd escape to the living room to sleep there. My wife took good care of her, and loved her a lot. As for myself, I didn't hate her, but I couldn't love her either.

LaCinda grew. She started to crawl and had a strange way of crawling. When she was almost one year old, she started trying to walk, and we discovered that she was crippled. I felt like she was an even greater burden on me. The years passed, and LaCinda grew, and her brothers grew. I never like to sit at home, I was always out with my friends…in reality, and I was like a plaything at their disposal (entertaining them whenever they wanted).

My wife never gave up on my reform. She always made small talk for my guidance. She never got angry with my reckless behavior, but she would get really sad if she saw me neglecting LaCinda and paying attention to the rest of her brothers. LaCinda grew, and my worries grew with her. I didn't mind when my wife asked to enroll her in a special school for the handicapped.

I didn't really feel the passing of the years. My days were all the same. I would work, sleep, and consume food and stay out late with my friends. One Friday, I woke up at 11 a.m. This was early for me. I was invited to a gathering, so I got dressed and perfumed, and was about to go out. I passed by our living room and was startled by the sight of LaCinda – she was sobbing! This was the first time I had noticed LaCinda crying since she was a baby. Ten years had passed, and I hadn't paid attention to her. I tried to ignore her now, but I couldn't take it…I heard her calling out to her mother while I was in the room. I turned towards her and went closer. "LaCinda! Why are you crying?" I asked.

When she heard my voice, she stopped crying. Then when she realized how close I was, she started feeling around with her small hands. What was wrong with her? I discovered that she was trying to move away from me! It was as if she was saying, "Now, you've decided to notice me? Where have you been for the last ten years?" I followed her…she had gone into her room. At first, she refused to tell me why she'd been crying. I tried to be gentle with her…LaCinda started to tell me why she'd been crying, while I listened and trembled.

Do you know what your daughter wants?! Her brother Charles, the one who used to take her to the playground, was late. Because it was Jimmy's prayer time, LaCinda was afraid she wouldn't find a place in the first row. She called out to Charles…and then she called out to his mother…but nobody answered, so she cried. I sat there looking at the tears flowing from her blind eyes. I couldn't bear the rest of her words. I put my hand over her mouth and said, "Is this why you were crying, LaCinda?!"

"Yes," she said.

I forgot about my friends, I forgot about the gathering, and I said, "Don't be sad, LaCinda. Do you know who's going to take you to the playground today?"

"Charles, of course," she said, "…but he's always late."

"No," I said, "I'm going to take you."

LaCinda was shocked…she couldn't believe it. She thought I was mocking her. Her tears came and she started crying. I wiped her tears with my hand and then took hold of her hand. I wanted to take her to the playground by car. She refused and said, "The playground is near…I want to walk there." Yes, by Charles, she said this to me.

I couldn't remember the last time I had entered the playground with her, but it was the first time I felt fear and regret for what I'd neglected in the long years that had passed. The playground was filled with children, but I still found a place for LaCinda in the first row. We listened to the other children playing together, and she prayed next to me. But really, I was the one praying next to her.

After the prayer, LaCinda asked me for a brail Bible page. I was surprised! How was she going to read when she was blind? I almost ignored her request, but I decided to humor her out of fear of hurting her feelings. I passed her a brail page. She asked me to open the page. I started flipping through the pages and looking through the index until I found it. She took the page from me, put it in front of her, and started reading the page with her eyes closed! She had memorized the entire page.

I was ashamed of myself. I picked up a brail page…I felt my limbs tremble…I read, and I read. I asked God to forgive me and to guide me. I couldn't take it…I started crying like a child. There were still some people in the church play area praying…I was embarrassed by their presence, so I tried to hold my tears. My crying turned into whimpering and long, sobbing breaths. The only thing I felt was a small hand reaching out to my face and then wiping the tears away. It was LaCinda! I pulled her to my chest…I looked at her. I said to myself…you're not the blind one, but I am, for having drifted after immoral people who were pulling me to hellfire. We went back home. My wife was extremely worried about LaCinda, but her worry turned into tears of joy when she found out I had prayed with LaCinda.

From that day on, I never missed the congregational prayer in our church. I left my bad friends…and I made righteous friends among people I met at the church. I tasted the wetness of man with them. I learned things from them that distracted me from this world. I never missed out on gatherings of remembrance, or on the written prayer. I recited the entire group of old friends, several times, in one month. I moistened my tongue with the remembrance of God, that He might forgive my backbiting and mocking of the people. Here is another example of how **Love was Understood**! I felt closer to my family. The looks of fear and pity that had occupied my wife's eyes disappeared. A smile now never parted from the face of my daughter, LaCinda. Anyone who saw her would have felt that she owned the world and everything in it. I praised and thanked God a lot for His blessings.

One day, my righteous friends decided to go to a faraway location. I hesitated about going. I prayed for a long time and consulted with my wife. I thought she would refuse…but the opposite happened! She was extremely happy, and even encouraged me…because in the past, she had seen me traveling without consulting her, for the purpose of sin and evil. I went to LaCinda and told her I would be traveling. With tears, she wrapped me up in her small arms.

I was away from home for three and a half months. In that period, whenever I got a chance, I called my wife and talked to my children. I missed them so much…and oh, how I missed LaCinda! I wanted to hear her voice…she was the only one who hadn't talked to me since I'd traveled. She was either at school or at the church whenever I called them.

Whenever I would tell my wife how much I missed her, she would laugh happily, joyfully, except for the last time I called her. I didn't hear her expected laugh. Her voice changed. I said to her, "Give me to LaCinda," and she said, "God is working in a good way" and was quiet.

At last, I went back home. I knocked on the door. I hoped that it was LaCinda who would open the door for me, but was surprised to find my daughter, Karen, who was not more than four years old. I picked her up in my arms while she squealed, "Baba! Baba!" I don't know why my heart tensed when I entered the house.

I sought refuge in God from the accursed evil as I approached my wife…her face was different. As if she was pretending to be happy. I inspected her closely then said, "What's wrong with you?" "Nothing," she said. Suddenly, I remembered LaCinda. "Where's LaCinda?" I asked. She lowered her head. She didn't answer. Hot tears fell on her cheeks.

"LaCinda! Where's LaCinda?" I cried out.

At that moment, I only heard the sound of my daughter, Karen, talking in her own way, saying, "Baba…LaCinda went to paradise, with Father…"

My wife couldn't take it. She broke down crying. She almost fell to the floor and left the room. Later, I found out that LaCinda had contracted a fever two weeks before I'd returned, so my wife took her to the hospital…the fever got more and more severe and didn't leave her…until her soul left her body.

If this earth closes in on you despite its vastness, and your soul closes in on you because of what it's carrying…call out, "Oh Father!" If solutions run out, and paths are constricted, and ropes are cut off, and your hopes are no more…call out, "Oh Father." God wished to guide LaCinda's earthly father on the hands of LaCinda, before LaCinda's death. How merciful is God!

SOME FUNNY THINGS

THIS IS FOR ALL THOSE BORN BEFORE 1945

We are survivors!!!

We were born before television, before penicillin, before polio shots, frozen foods, Xerox, plastic, contact lenses, Frisbees, going to the moon, I Pad, and the PILL.

We were before radar, credit cards, split atoms, laser beams and ballpoint pens, before pantyhose, dishwashers, clothes dryers, electric blankets, air conditioners, drip-dry clothes and before man walked on the moon.

We got married first and then lived together. How quaint can you be?

In our time, closets were for clothes, not for "coming out of." Bunnies were small rabbits and rabbits were not Volkswagens. Designer Jeans were scheming girl's names Jean and Jeanne, and having a meaningful relationship meant getting along well with our cousins.

We thought fast food was what you ate during Lent, and Outer Space was the back of the Riviera Theatre.

We were before house-husbands, gay rights, computer dating, dual careers and commuter marriages. We were before day-care centers, group therapy and nursing homes. We never heard of MF radios, tape decks, electric typewriters, artificial hearts, word processors, yogurt, and guys wearing earrings. For us, time-sharing meant togetherness – not condominiums; a 'chip' meant a piece of wood; hardware meant hardware and software wasn't even a word!

In 1940, "made in Japan" meant junk and the term "making out" referred to how you did on your exam. Pizzas, McDonald's and instant coffee were unknown.

We hit the scene when there were 5 and 10 cents stores, where you bought things for five and ten cents. Sanders or Wilsons sold ice cream cones for a nickel or a dime. For one nickel you would ride a street care, make a phone call, but a Pepsi or enough stamps to mail one letter and two postcards. You could buy a new Chevy Coupe for $600.00 but who could afford one: a pity too, because gas was only 11 cents a gallon.

In our day, cigarette smoking was fashionable. GRASS was mowed. COKE was a cold drink, and POT was something you cooked in. ROCK MUSIC was a grandma's lullaby and AIDS were helpers in the principal's office.

We were certainly not before the difference between the sexes was discovered but we were surely before the sex change; we made do with what we had. We were the last generation that was so dumb as to think you needed a husband to have a baby!

No wonder we are so confused and there is such a generation gap today! BUT WE SURVIVED!! What better reason to celebrate?

SAD, BUT TRUE...

Everything is farther away now than it used to be. It is twice as far to the corner, and I notice they have added a hill.

I've given up running for the bus; it leaves faster than it used to. It seems that we are making stairs steeper than in the old days, too.

Have you noticed the smaller print they use in the newspaper now? There's no sense in asking anyone to read aloud; everyone speaks in such a low voice I can hardly hear them. The material in clothes is so skimpy now, especially around the waist. It is almost impossible to reach my shoelaces; I can't figure out why.

Even people are changing. They are so much younger than they used to be when I was their age. On the other hand, people my age are much older than I am. I ran across an old classmate the other day and she'd aged so badly she didn't even know me. I got to thinking about the poor thing this morning and in doing so I glanced at my own reflection. Really now, they just don't make good mirrors anymore.

Do you get lonesome? Living alone? I live with four men and I'm thankful they do not eat too much. I get up with Charley Horse; have lunch with Arthur it is, spend the day with Will Power and go to bed with Ben Gay.

Source: Unknown, but it sure fits very well with us today!

DON'T DO THAT!

Before you roll your eyes, look at your own exacting behavior standards or take charge of your own style to accomplish things. You might not realize how your behavior can control, manipulate, intimidate or humiliate someone.

In the 1950s and 1960s no one knew what a bully was or eve the term, "bully."

What does this have to do with education? Most unfortunately regardless of how you view the situation, plenty as bullying increases in today's school. There is a culture of bullying within education and its profession that many of us have experienced first-hand. Mostly it is called "relational aggression" – the use of a relationship to hurt others.

Relational aggression is not physical, like the kicks and punches of childhood aggression, so it can be overlooked, disclaimed or ignored by administrators who are in a position of control.

If you ask an aggressor why he/she treats him/her co-workers so shabbily, chances are they'll be shocked to hear you suggest that he/she ever does such a thing. They might describe him/her as a student who has high standards and expects no less of others, but a "bully"?

It's been said that bullies live the good life – they take dream vacations on your mind, spend quality time with your friends and family and explore the world as they make fun or pick on you from one to the next. My goal is to ensure you get the most out of your helpline against bullies. That's why I'm excited to unveil a program for bullies to be branded from school once found and allowed to take part in the good life.

Every school has a "King" or "Queen" bully I have taught, described them as "driven." Similarly, a friend of mine works with a classic manipulator, but that person says she's a "people person" who knows how to "get results." Little do these individuals know that everyone else considers them to be bullies.

While any one of us on any given day can act aggressively, a bully will constantly use aggressive behavior. They convey an outlook through body language as well as verbal. Every individual in the school knows the meaning of raised eyebrows and heavy sighs. Sometimes there's a group of aggressors and the venom increases exponentially until the entire classroom turns toxic.

Bullying another student adversely affects learning and measurable outcomes, job performance and absenteeism. It's the last thing you want to do, so it pays to step back and take a hard look at your own behavior. You may be quite surprised by what you observe.

Do any of these examples sound familiar?

- Giving another student and/or coworker the silent treatment
- Spreading rumors

- Putting down another student/coworker, usually regarding his/her knowledge and skill.

- Failing to support another person because you don't like them

- Refusing to share information with one another and setting someone up for failure

- Excluding another person from on or off the job socializing

- Repeating information shared by one staff out of context so it turns against another staff

- Sharing a confidence, you were asked to keep private, and you twisted the information a bit

- Making fun of another student or co-worker appearance, demeanor or other traits

- Manipulating or intimidating another student or co-worker into doing something for you

- Using body language (such as eye rolling or head tossing) to convey an unfavorable opinion

- Saying something unfavorable, then pretending you were joking

- Calling names

- Making a student/co-worker look bad in front of patients, other staff/supervisors, etc.

- Teasing another person for his/her lack of skill, knowledge, leadership, etc.

Individuals rarely think of themselves as too aggressive, but in reality, every person has the potential to use these behaviors and probably has on occasion, at one time or another.

What really makes a bully a bully? All too often, you go through your daily routines without much awareness of your behavior. In many ways, it's an adaptive mechanism; without it, you would have to figure out how to do your job anew each day. The problem with this, though, is that you can slide into behaviors that aren't healthy for you or those around you. Eventually, those behaviors become who you are, and unless you receive a pretty intense wake-up call, you won't do much to change.

Reflecting on your behavior and thinking about what's driving it are keys to your success. Are you planning a big event? Worried about cutbacks at your job? Suffering from too little sleep? Chances are you may be grouchier than usual, less ready to volunteer for overtime or work a game after school is out for the day or not your usual self when a student can't seem to figure out how to solve a problem.

In addition, there are many overt stressors that come with working in the field of education: for starters, the sicker and quicker syndrome, chronic staff shortages and information overload. Then, what other profession expects employees to go for hours without food, drink, or bathroom breaks? Where else are you "trapped" in a small space (called a classroom) where it's impossible to avoid your aggressor? What other environment is constantly noisy and always changing as administrator's drop-in for evaluations, etc. Having time to compose yourself from one situation to another has you ready to pop be a rare privilege for most teachers, as is going out for lunch to de-stress. Instead, you're expected to tolerate all the above with a pleasant smile/attitude and a willingness to take on more students if asked.

What do you do to undo bully behavior in your classroom? Okay, so this given student is a bully sometimes. Not sure how to stop or what to change about his/her behavior. Once you understand where they are coming from and are able to acknowledge your students' behavior you will need to take the first step in effecting changes. The next step would be to alter the behavior of the student in some way. You will require fortitude, as it's not easy to dig out of a rut as the student has practiced the behavior for years. One relatively easy-to-make change is to focus on positive talk, and this will be difficult to do with all the other students around. Teach the students to walk away when someone comes up with a saucy tidbit of information or tell them directly that you don't want to hear.

Gossip is a particularly negative communication style, and negativity breeds negativity. All it takes is one busybody person to sour an entire staff. Most individuals are prone to seeking out a spicy story, embellishing it and passing it along, especially because people respond to negative information. That's probably because the gossiper is doing the impression that he/she trusts you enough to share vital information.

When positive, respectful relationships are promoted among staff members so every individual feels needed and important, the team will coalesce. Each person must matter in order to have the team matter, and everyone's goals must be focused on the instructional program overall.

You have the power to change the emotional environment of your workplace every day. You are challenged to start bringing out the best in your students and staff around you and stop obsessing over flaws.

You can be the one who helps students have a vision, and every day someone can find your presence is a blessing. It is promised this will change more than just your career – it will change your life!

SENTENCES WHICH ACTUALLY APPEARED IN CHURCH BULLETINS

1. This afternoon there will be a meeting in the south and north ends of the church. Children will be baptized at both ends.
2. Tuesday at 4:00 p.m. there will be an ice cream social. All ladies giving milk please come early.
3. Wednesday the Ladies Literary Society will meet. Mrs. Johnson will sing "Put Me in My Little Bed" accompanied by the Pastor.
4. Thursday at 5:00 p.m. there will be a meeting of the Little Mother's Club. All wishing to become little mothers meet the Minister in his study.
5. This being Easter Sunday, we will ask Mrs. Johnson to come forward and lay an egg on the altar.
6. The Services will close with "Little Drops of Water." One of the ladies will quietly start and the rest of the congregation will please join in.
7. On Sunday a special collection will be taken to defray the expense of the new carpet. All wishing to do something on the carpet will please come forward and get a piece of paper.

YOU ARX A KXY PXRSON

If you'll read what follows all the way to the end you may feel rewarded and think more highly of yourself. The author is unknown on this write-up.

"Xvxn though my typxwritxr is an old modxl it works quitx wxll of thx kxys. I wishxd many timxs that it workxd pxrxctly wxll xnough, but just onx kxy not working makxs thx diffxrxncx.

Somxtimxs it sxxms to mx that our organization is somxwhat like my typewritxr –not thx pxoplx arx working propxrly.

You may say to yoursxlf, "Wxll, I am only onx pxrson, I wan't makx or brakx a program." But it doxs makx a diffxrxncs bxcausx any program, to bx xffxctivx, nxxds thx activx participation of xvxry mxmbxr. So thx nxxt timx you think you arx only onx psrson and that you xfforts arx not nxxded, rxmxmbxr my typxwritxe and say to yoursxlf, "I am a kxy" pxrson and I am nxxdxd vxry muxh."

CHILDREN LEARN WHAT THEY LIVE

If a child lives with criticism, he* learns to condemn.

If a child lives with hostility, he learns to fight.

If a child lives with ridicule, he learns to be shy.

If a child lives with shame, he learns to feel guilty.

If a child lives with tolerance, he learns to be patient.

If a child lives with encouragement, he learns confidence.

If a child lives with praise, he learns to appreciate.

If a child lives with fairness, he learns justice.

If a child lives with security, he learns to have faith.

If a child lives with approval, he learns to like himself.

If a child lives with acceptance and friendship, he learns to find love in the world.

- The masculine pronoun is used for economy purposes only; no sexual discrimination is intended.

BE A PROFESSIONAL

The rudiments of good salesmanship are universal, and date back to Ben Franklin's era, but there are many salespersons who still try to underestimate the consumer's level of intelligence. Either they condescend to him/her as if they were selling to a small child, or they try to "flim-flam" his/her with fast-talking, high-pressure tactics.

This salesperson may make sales, but the repercussions of such myopic techniques are far-reaching and some fatal. The most expensive, well planned marketing strategy isn't worth two cents if your salesperson isn't doing a "professional" job. Here are a few basic sales techniques – says snap, crackle and pop – that successful care histories have proven sound:

A good salesperson knows his/her product – its uses, specifications, price and marketing success. By arming him/herself with a surplus of knowledge, he/she can answer any question from a prospective customer with poise, thus affirming the customer's confidence in him/her and his/her company.

Know the competition, too. Find out everything you can about the latest innovations and events within the industry. Update your knowledge at every opportunity by reading trade journals, news releases and talking to experienced industry personnel.

Part and parcel of this knowledge is being familiar with your company's advertising and marketing programs. Kay your special promotions and displays to your advertising for wider coverage and instant identification.

Know your firm's special services and after-sales procedures. Be up on what credit programs are available and delivery service, rates, warranty, and service practices.

Good grooming is essential. It builds confidence – both your and the customers. The old adage holds true: When you look your best, you do your best. Besides, if you were unsure of buying a new gas range, who would you turn to, the salesperson in a clean shirt and tie or the fellow with his sleeves rolled up and his shirt hanging out of his/her pants? Avoid nervous habits like smoking, biting your nails or whistling while trying to make a sale. Make a note of your idiosyncrasies and then eliminate them. When speaking, be bright and alert, with a crisp delivery and genuine concern for the customer.

Groom your store, as you do yourself. Product displays should be easily accessible, cheerful and informative. Point of purchase materials are helpful but remember: Too many promotional pieces on a product may hide it. Displays should be kept in order; price tags should be neat and current. When you have a minute, straighten up the floor and put yourself on firmer selling ground.

THE BEAN STORY

Our father would tell this story to everyone visiting the farm.

The following story has been placed in this volume for the pleasure of reading and as we all have the problem. Our father would tell this story to every person visiting the farm.

Once upon a time, there lived a man who had a maddening passion for baked beans. He loved them, but they always had a very embarrassing and somewhat lively reaction on him. Then one day, he met a girl and fell in love. When it became apparent that they would marry, he told himself, "She is such a sweet and gentle girl; she will never go for this kind of carrying on." So, he made the supreme sacrifice – he gave up beans. Shortly after they were married.

Some months later, his car broke down on the way home from work and since he lived in the country, he called his wife and told her he would be late tonight because he had to walk home. On his way home, he passed a small café. From the café door came an overwhelming odor of freshly baked beans.

Since he still had seven miles to walk, he figured he would work off any ill effects before he got home. So, he stopped at the café. Before he left, he had eaten three large orders of baked beans.

All the way home, he putt-putted, so when he got there, he was reasonably sure he had putt-putted his last. His wife seemed excited to see him and exclaimed delightfully, "Darling, I have a most wonderful surprise for dinner tonight." She then blindfolded him and led him to his chair at the head of the dinner table. He seated himself, and just as she was ready to remove the blindfold, the telephone rang. His wife made him vow not to touch the blindfold until she returned, to which he agreed, and then she went to answer the phone.

Seizing the opportunity, he shifted his weight to one leg and let one loose. It was not only loud, but ripe as rotten eggs. He took his napkin from his lap and vigorously fanned the air about him. Things just returned to normal when he felt another urge coming on, so he shifted his weight to the other leg and let another one go. This one was a prize winner.

While keeping his ear on the conversation the hall, he went on like this for ten minutes or so, until he heard the farewells on the phone meaning the end of his freedom. He placed his napkin back on his lap and folded his hands on top of it.

While his wife returned apologizing for taking so long, he was the picture of innocence, smiling contentedly to himself. She asked him if he had peaked, and of course, he assured her he had not. At this point she removed the blindfold and there was his surprise – twelve dinner guests seated around the table for a birthday party for him.

TEST YOURSELF – ARE YOU A LEADER?

Do you have what it takes to be a leader? Do people turn to you for guidance? Men and women who can inspire others are urgently needed for management jobs in industry, commerce and the professions. Leadership ability is also important at home and even in social functions.

The following activity will assist you to determine your leadership qualities:

1. Glance at these lines of numbers and GUESS whether lines a, b, or c – will add up to the greatest sum. TIME: 10 seconds.
   a. 08360157
   b. 5190035140
   c. 4190514
2. Glance at these lines of letters and GUESS what line contains the most letters.
   a. Lghwxkledc
   b. Ellfdhgfhfei
   c. Uwvmnowqmn

The following questions will be answered TRUE or FALSE)

3. Directives from superiors should never be openly questioned.
4. Some people are not worth bothering with.

5. A man or woman in a top position should not delegate responsibilities

6. Most people work better and produce more under criticism.

7. True leaders do not need suggestions from those who work for them.

8. "The end justified the means."

9. To operate effectively each day guarantees future more than long-range planning does.

10. It is a sign of weakness to confess your mistakes.

11. Good leaders will try to know the personal problems of those around them.

12. A sense of humor is a healthy, helpful attribute for leadership.

13. In a pinch, a good leader should be able and willing to do the tasks assigned to others.

14. Everyone should strive to be a leader.

15. It is desirable for the leader of a group to be older than the other members.

16. All decisions should be discussed democratically.

Note: Provided by Unknown

(Answer Key)

To

TEST YOURSELF

Following are the answers to the "Test Yourself... Are You a Leader?"

Answers

a. A (30)

b. B (12 letters)

3. False

4. False

5. False

6. False

7. False

8. False

9. False

10. False

11. True

12. True

13. True

14. False

15. False

16. False (No time for discussion if the building is burning).

THAT SHAGGY OLD DAY – SNOW BALL
III

I must have passed by that old farm house hundreds of times while I was growing up, maybe three or four times some weeks. There was nothing special about it that might catch the eye of a passerby person.

It was just a common old house by the side of the road, except that, thanks to progress, it now sets closer to the narrow rural road; progress in the form of a heavier traffic flow which called for the widening of the road due to development of subdivisions close by. The road encroached on the small year, but the house remained defensively staunch and firmly in place, despite the road's threatening encroachment.

There is one single tree in the front yard today, a tree seemingly as old as the homestead itself. In the summer it presents a meagre but leafy shade to its root system. Today, however, the tree is rapidly balding in appearance. In the winter months, the tree is as bare as Adam was in the beginning.

Perhaps the most appealing feature of the house is the inviting front porch. It seems as if it is just waiting for someone to come in and sit down in the creaky old rocking chair or sing, which has held no guests for a number of summers. There have been no guests perhaps since an aging, matronly lady, Mrs. McKinley, once set there shelling butter beans, or the overall clad old farmer shared one entrancing tale after another of his younger and more carefree years.

The only constants about this old house anymore are that inviting front porch, and the old shaggy dog lying in the front yard guarding the place as usual with the name of "Snow Ball." Snow Ball was white and with a tail that had a double curl in it which made up his wonderful happy dog personality.

In earlier days as I would go by the house, the shaggy old white dog was merely a playful pup, temping in the front yard, or musing to himself about chasing the next cat down the road or the family of squirrels living in the top of the old tree.

Today, Snow Ball is an old dog and is almost immobile. He lies in the shade of that one old tree in the summer and heddles in a shaggy clump around the roots of the tree during the winter months. Occasionally, he may be seen behind a nearby shed to fend off the old north winds that rush our way.

Sometimes, when he is seen slowly walking along, his hind legs barely support the weight of his frail body as they did in olden days.

The most of his days now find him lying in the shade of that lone tree, dreaming perhaps of days gone by when he would go hunting for rabbit or other game. Though he seldom moves any more, his dreamy eyes still follow the movement of each and every car which passes, possibly pondering the bygone days in which he had thoughts of giving chase. Even his eyes do not reveal as much of his sparking personality as in earlier days. Unkept shaggy hair now all but hides those once youthful and alert eyes.

To me, as I pass by once again, it is not the front porch which is enchanting to me. It is that shaggy white dog, who must be 15 to 18 years old, which in dog years would be around 130. I ponder and I wonder how much longer those soft eyes and panting red tongue will be around to greet me as I pass by.

Then again, as he watches me hurriedly drive by each day, he may be wondering the same about me.

It now becomes a very good question. Which of us will go first, me, now in my late 60s or that dreamy-eyed old shaggy white dog named: "Snow Ball?" This is a very good questions, yes indeed; and only time will tell, and it definitely will.

RIDE THE PONY

Some sixty years ago when we lived on the farm, we each had a pony of some type that we would ride, and my sister had a pony that did not want to leave the barn once we were saddled up and ready to go riding.

On the other hand, after we finished riding the ponies, her pony knew we were finished riding for the day, and it would take off running back to the barn just as fast as she could run.

As best as I can remember, Vicki never took a riding lesson on learning how to ride horses. One of the great things to do on a farm is different than anywhere and that would be to have optimum horsy lifestyle. Sometimes we would see Vicki going barefoot and she made sure that the horses were well fed.

On things that Vicki learned on summer was that she had to listen even though she was capable of riding. Listening is one part to know before riding horses and the other part would be to respond to instructions for her well-being and enjoyment. It is never safe to bring an undisciplined or irresponsible child to a farm.

Every summer we would have relatives to come down and visit us on the farm and many would stay for several weeks and the children would ride the ponies and horses too, This one summer my cousin, Vicki, was visiting us and we had been taking her riding every day, but this one day we all had so much farm work to do that we failed to take her riding. Later that day we were milking the cows later in the afternoon just before sun set and we had built a new milk room out back for general storage – such as saddles, bridles, work harness for the mules and horses and all kinds of work tools.

Our father went over to the old milk room to pick up several small tools for work on a wagon and when he entered the building my cousin Vicki was busy riding a saddle. It's more to it than just riding the saddle. Vicki had collected some buckets and stacked them on top of one another to get some height from the floor and then she placed a saddle on top of the buckets and there she was a big as life riding a certain horse. As my father entered the building, he heard Vicki say, "Getty up horse, Getty up, let's go!"

Our father was so surprised that he yelled at her to stop and get off before she hurt herself! In the process of all taking place so quickly, Vicki wet her pants, and it ran all down her legs. Many hours afterwards we learned the reason she wet her pants was because our father scared her when he yelled at her.

Vicki would always groom the ponies and/or horses as she loved all ponies and horses. She would brush, brush, and brush each one time after time until she would almost brush the hair off the body. Vicki would even take the time to plat the mane and tails of the horses if she had time. Most times she did an excellent job!

Many years have gone by and when we all get together to visit and still get a good laugh from telling and laughing about the story of Vicki riding the tin horse in the old milk room.

Even as Vicki got older our family always looked forward with excitement when we learned that Vicki was coming down to the farm for a visit with us.

Vicki is now grown and married but she still has several horses of her own today that she rides for pleasure and contentment. She takes real good care of her horses as I have made several visits to her home for other important things over the years and her houses always are in tip-top shape!

Vicki learned early on that trail riding was something that she enjoyed doing and even more so with other riders tagging along. She never wanted to miss out on an extraordinary all-inclusive vacation down on the farm as she always went home recharged, refreshed and invigorated. Our parents and her parents would work together to help plan the trip and to store up memories to last a lifetime with our endless array of activities, including horseback riding, fly fishing, trap shooting, archery, paddle boats, camping, hiking, biking, swimming, dancing, campfire and much more. Vicki never had to worry about her lodging and meals, clean clothes or anything else – she worried about nothing, not even the atmosphere!

SIBLING FIGHTS AND ARGUMENTS

During those growing up years my brother and I were into fighting all the time. We actually would fight sometimes over nothing.

The most aggravating fights were the ones when he would catch me off my guard and he would reach over and grab a handful of my tit and skin, squeezing it very hard. It was not only a squeeze and grab, but he had a way of twisting the skin while delivering more and more pain. Naturally, following all this a fight would start and go on for a while.

With all these fights going on I never understood why our parents did not step in to stop the fights. We never got a whipping, but we were only told to stop fighting or else. Many of our fights would end up having pitch forks, sticks, brooms, twine, rocks or anything that one could get a hand on to help bring about self-defense and to equal the strength to offset the difference in age.

At that time, I could never figure out how and when my brother knew just the perfect timing to set me off with a word or two or hit me on my arm very hard or even turn his eyes just so to start me and much later in years. I figured out that he did all this to me because he enjoyed doing things to me. I never started a fight because I did not care to fight but I was not about to allow someone to run over me at the same time.

Again, when our parents would leave the farm and go to town to do business and our brother would get his BB gun and start shotting me and my sister. Many times, with the season, we would both run into the tobacco field and hide from him because we knew that he would not shut into the tobacco as it would tear the leaves up and our father would notice as soon as he returned from town. Our brother would always make up some big story to save himself from getting into big trouble with our parents.

"I don't understand it. The techniques my parents used so effectively just don't seem to work with us in those days." Does this statement sound familiar to you? A lot of parents today are wondering what to do with their children and are frustrated because the old techniques just don't seem to get the job done any more.

Parents want to enjoy their children, have fun with them, and enjoy a less stressful family life. But even if their children are trouble-free right now, they fear what may come in those teenage years.

At no time in history have parents been unsure of their parental role. Even the best are not all that sure about whether they are using the best techniques. They say that their children don't appear to be much like the ones they knew in years past.

A lot of conflicting philosophies have been presented over the last 30 years. Many of these sound good, but don't seem to do the job of helping children become respectful, responsible, and a joy to be around.

Many ideas, offered with the best of intentions, center around making sure that children are comfortable and feeling good about themselves in order to have a good self-concept. However, parents have discovered that self-confidence is achieved through struggle and achievement, not through someone telling you that you are number one as this is something that one must earn. Self-confidence is not developed when children are robbed of the opportunity to discover that they can indeed solve their own problems with caring adult guidance.

There is, however, an approach to raising children that provides loving support from parents while at the same time expecting children to be respectful and responsible. This idea is based on the experience of a combined total of over 75 years working with and raising children.

Many parents want their children to be well prepared for life, and they know this means children will make mistakes and must be held accountable for those mistakes. But these parents often fail to hold the children accountable for poor decisions because they are afraid the children will see their parents as being mean. The result is they often excuse bad behavior, finding it easier to hold others, including themselves, accountable for their children's irresponsibility.

We should "lock in our empathy, love, and understanding" prior to telling children what the consequences of their actions will be. The actual teaching of the parents is how to hold their children accountable in this special way. This Love and Logic method causes the child to see their parent as the "good guy" and the child's poor decision as the "bad guy." When done on a regular basis, children develop an internal voice that says, "I wonder how much pain I'm going to cause for myself with my next decision?" Children who develop this internal voice become more capable of standing up to peer pressure.

What more could a parent want? Isn't that a great gift to give your child? Parent child relationships are enhanced, family life becomes less strained, and we have time to enjoy our children instead of either feeling used by them or being transformed from parent to policeman.

The Love and Logic technique in action sounds like this:

Dad: "Oh, no, you left your bike unlocked and it was stolen. What a bummer. I bet you feel awful. Well, I understand how easy it is to make a mistake like that." (Notice that the parent is not leading with anger, intimidation, or threats.)

Dad then adds, "And you'll have another bike as soon as you can earn enough money to pay for it. I paid for the first one, you can pay for the additional ones."

Love and Logic, parents know that no child is going to accept this without an argument, but Love and Logic, parents can handle arguments. Jim Fay advises "just go brain dead." This means that parents don't try to argue or match wits with the child. They simply repeat, as many times as necessary, "I love you too much to argue." No matter what argument the child uses, the parent responds, "I love you too much to argue." Parents who learn how to use these techniques completely change, for the better, their relationships with children and take control of the home in loving ways.

What is Love and Logic?

Love and Logic, is a philosophy of raising and teaching children which allows adults to be happier, empowered, and more skilled in interactions with children. Love allows children to grow through their mistakes. Logic allows children to live with the consequences of their choices. Love and Logic, is a way of working with children that puts parents and teachers back in control, teaches children to be responsible, and prepares young people to live in the real world, with its many choices and consequences.

Almost everyone will benefit from the Love and Logic approach. Our products especially help parents and teachers enjoy working with children through easy-to-use techniques. The Love and Logic approach helps children develop and grow in a healthy way, provides them with confidence and dignity, and teaches them how to become more responsible. The possibilities are limitless.

Love and Logic offer adults an alternative way to communicate with children. The Love and Logic techniques produce immediate results because the techniques are simple, practical, and easy to learn.

The concepts behind Love and Logic place a heavy emphasis on respect and dignity for children and at the same time allow parents to grasp simple approaches instead of learning difficult counseling procedures.

What is sibling rivalry?

Sibling rivalry is jealousy, competition and fighting between brothers and sisters. It is a concern for almost all parents of two or more children. Problems often start right after **the birth of the second child.** Sibling rivalry usually continues throughout childhood and can be very frustrating and stressful to parents. There are lots of things parents can do to help their children get along better and work through conflicts in positive ways. Read on for tips and resources to help you keep the peace at your house.

What's the upside of having more than one child?

Most likely your children's relationship will eventually develop into a close one. Working things out with siblings gives your children a chance to develop important skills like cooperating and being able to see another person's point of view.

What causes sibling rivalry?

There are many factors that contribute to sibling rivalry:

- Each child is competing to define who they are as an individual. As they discover who they are, they try to find their own talents, activities, and interests. They want to show that they are separate from their siblings.

- Children feel they are getting unequal amounts of your attention, discipline, and responsiveness.

- Children may feel their relationship with their parents is threatened by the **arrival of a new baby.**

- Your children's developmental stages will affect how mature they are and how well they can share your attention and get along with one another.

- Children who are hungry, bored or tired are more likely to become frustrated and start fights.

- Children may not know positive ways to get attention from or start playful activities with a brother or sister, so they pick fights instead.

- Family dynamics play a role. For example, one child may remind a parent of a relative who was particularly difficult, and this may subconsciously influence how the parent treats that child.

- Children often fight more in families where parents think aggression and fighting between siblings is normal and an acceptable way to resolve conflicts.

- Not having time to share regular, enjoyable family time together (like family meals) can increase the chances of children engaging in conflict.

- Stress in the parents' lives can decrease the amount of time and attention parents can give the children and increase sibling rivalry.

- Stress in your children's lives can shorten their fuses, and decrease their ability to tolerate frustration, leading to more conflict.

- How parents treat their children and react to conflict can make a big difference in how well siblings get along.

How can I help my children get along better? The basics:

- Don't play favorites. This one is a "biggie."

- Try not to compare your children to one another. For example, don't say things like, "Your brother gets good grades in math – why can't you?"

- Let each child be who they are. Don't try to pigeonhole or label them.

- Enjoy each of your children's individual talents and successes.

- Set your children up to cooperate rather than compete. For example, have them race the clock to pick up toys, instead of racing each other.

- Pay attention to the time of day or other patterns in when conflicts usually occur. Are conflicts more likely right before naps or bedtime or maybe when children are hungry before meals? Perhaps a change in the routine, an earlier meal or snack, or a well-planned quiet activity when the children are at loose ends could help avert your children' s conflicts.

- Teach your children positive ways to get attention from each other. Show them how to approach another child and ask them to play, and to share their belongings and toys.

- Being fair is very important, but it is not the same as being equal. Older and younger children may have different privileges due to their age, but if children understand that this inequality is because one child is older or has more responsibilities, they will see this as fair. Even if you did try to treat your children equally, there will still be times when they feel as if they're not getting a fair share of attention, discipline, or responsiveness from you. Expect this and be prepared to explain the decisions you have made. Reassure your children that you do your best to meet each of their unique needs.

- Plan family activities that are fun for everyone. If your children have good experiences together, it acts as a buffer when they come into conflict. It's easier to work it out with someone you share warm memories with.

- Make sure each child has enough time and space of their own. Children need chances to do their own thing, play with their own friends without their siblings, and to have their space and property protected.

Be there for each child:

- Set aside "alone time" for each child, if possible. Each parent should try to spend some one-on-one with each kid on a regular basis. Try to get in at least a few minutes each day. It's amazing how much even 10 minutes of uninterrupted one-on-one time can mean to your child.

- When you are alone with each child, you may want to ask them once in a while that are some of the positive things their brother or sister does that they really like and what are some of the things they do that might bother them or make them mad. This will help you keep tabs on their relationships and also remind you that they probably do have some positive feelings for each other!

- Listen – really listen – t how your children feel about what's going on in the family. They may not be so demanding if they know you at least care how they feel.
- Celebrate your children's differences.
- Let each child know they are special in their own way.

Resolving conflicts:

- Research shows that you should pay attention to your children's conflicts (so that no one gets hurt, and you can notice **abuse** if it occurs.) Try to see if your children can work out their own conflicts but remember that younger children will probably need you to intervene and help structure the problem-solving. Try not to take sides and favor one child over the other. Get them settled and calm first, then ask questions about what happened before dispensing discipline.
- Help your children develop the skills to work out their conflicts on their own. Teach them how to compromise, respect one another, divide things fairly, etc. if you give them the tools, eventually they will have confidence that they can work it out themselves.
- Don't yell or lecture. It won't help.
- It doesn't matter "who started it" because it takes two to make a quarrel. Hold children equally responsible when ground rules get broken.
- In a conflict, give your children a chance to express their feelings about each other. Don't try to talk them out of their feelings. Help

your children find words for their feelings. Show them how to talk about their feelings, without yelling, name-calling, or violence.

- Encourage win-win-negotiations, where each side gains something.
- Give your children reminders and advance warnings (for example, counting to three). When they start picking on each other, help them remember to state their feelings to each other. Help them solve the problem themselves. You can offer suggestions but let them decide what the best options are.
- If you are constantly angry at your children, no wonder they are angry at each other! Anger feeds on itself. **Learn to manage *your* anger**, so you can teach your children how to manage *theirs*.
- Teach conflict resolution skills during calm times.
- Model good conflict resolution skills for your children when interacting with them and with other family members.

When to intervene:

- Dangerous fights need to be stopped immediately. Separate the children. When they have calmed down, talk about what happened and make it very clear that no violence is ever allowed.
- If your children are physically violent with each other on a regular basis, and/or one child is always the victim, is frightened of the brother/sister, and doesn't fight back, you are dealing with **sibling abuse**. You should seek immediate professional help and guidance.

- Involve your children in setting ground rules. Ground rules, with clear and consistent consequences for breaking them, can help prevent many squabbles.

Here are a few ideas:

- In a conflict, no hurting (hitting, kicking, pinching, etc.) is ever allowed.
- No name-calling, yelling, or tattling is allowed.
- If the children fight over a toy, the toy goes into time-out.
- Any child who demands to be first will go last.
- No making fun of a child who is being punished, or you will also be punished.
- No fights in the car or you will pull over and stop until all is calm again.
- If arguing over who gets first choice of bedtime stories or favorite seats in the car is a problem, assign your children certain days of the week to be the ones to make these choices.
- If borrowing is a problem, have the child who borrows something from a brother or sister put up collateral – a possession that will be returned only when the borrowed item is returned.

What are family meetings, and how can they help with sibling rivalry?

If you have older children, call a family meeting every once in a while. A family meeting is a meeting for all family members to work together to make family decisions. Parents, children, and others who live in the home and have a stake in decisions affecting the daily life of the family should take part. Choose a time that works for everyone. Establish a set of rules (for example, no yelling or name calling, everyone gets a turn) and allow everyone to have a say, even if members don't agree.

The purpose of the family meeting is to recognize that everyone's opinion makes a difference. The meeting allows the family to share their opinions, seek understanding, and find resolutions to problems. Family meetings help to build cooperation and responsibility and make anger and rebellion less likely. Also, it is a time to share love, develop unity, and build trust and self-esteem. The social skills and attitudes that children develop within the family circle are the skills and attitudes they will carry with them for the rest of their lives.

Sick of those constant fights over toys, the remote control or who farted? Buy as many $2 rolls of nickels as you have children and write one name on each roll. When someone squabbles, no matter who's at fault, the bickerer loses a coin. At the end of the week, each kid gets to keep the money that's left in his/her roll. The only downside is that you may never know the true identity of the family's secret porter.

Somewhere we got this romantic notion that our children would practice patience, empathy and compassion toward each other. Squabbling and wrestling would be rare. Politicians would never lie.

The history of mankind is littered with examples of sibling fights (and worse). We all want children who can get along, problem solve and handle conflicts.

Three critical questions:

We want children who can control themselves. Can you control yourself? Do you find yourself yelling at your children? Can Dad stay calm when things go wrong? If not, how can you expect your children to control themselves?

Do you and your spouse know how to handle conflict? Do you actually solve problems? Or do you run away, act like they don't exist and hope they go away, or become controlling and try to "fix" everything away?

Have you taught your children how to control themselves and problem solve? Or do you just yell at them to stop fighting, separate them, or make them apologize? Our children will never learn to get along if we don't teach them.

Sibling Arguments: How to Stop Children from Fighting with Each Other Knowing how to stop children from fighting with each other is valuable information in the parenting world. "How do I stop my children from fighting with each other?" Is a question that many of us with more than one child close in age will eventually ask? My experience so far is with siblings around two years apart and under six years of age. I have learned a great deal about how to stop children from fighting with each other in the past three and a half years through research.

The first step in stopping children from fighting with each other is to keep in mind the age of your children. If your children are between the ages of two years old and six years old, they are going to fight. Most of the fights will be over toys. Go ahead, accept it. There, now you are ready to begin learning how to stop your children from fighting with each other.

First, do not heed the advice to "let them work it out alone." With small children it is not safe to do that. Use the times that your children are arguing to teach lessons about sharing, kindness and the golden rule. As your children get older, they will become better equipped to "work it out" between (or among!) themselves. For them to get to that point you must be ever present and step in to squabbles often. If you go ahead and prepare yourself to help them work things out, you will be pleasantly surprised when they work some things out all by themselves.

Next, be proactive. To stop children from fighting with each other you must know their triggers. Set them up for success. Don't pull them in a situation together (playing too closely to each other, etc.) that will cause them to argue with each other. Give them time away from each other every day with a daily quiet time. This space from each other allows them to play comfortably without being on edge about having to protect their space and their toys. Know that from time to time their fighting may not be about each other or a toy, but instead they are hungry or tired or even bored.

An important factor that will stop children from fighting with each other is whether or not they know what to do instead of fighting. Give them acceptable words to say to each other. This is easier with three-six years old than with two years olds. However, if you start giving your child the words to say when he or she is under the age of two (you do this by saying the words for them before they are able to talk), by the time they are three, with reminders, they can produce polite conversation and problem solving with their siblings.

For example, if Child A wants a toy that Child B is playing with, Child A should say, "Child B, may I have that toy when you are finished?" As opposed to grabbing the toy, demanding the toy or whining about the toy. Child B should say, "Yes, when I am finished you may have it." As opposed to whining about Child A wanting the toy or simply telling Child A "no" and not sharing at all. A five- or six-year-old who has been taught good sharing habits will hand over the toy when he is finished in a reasonable amount of time. A younger child may need for you to tell him, "In three minutes you will need to be finished with the toy so that Child B may play with it." Be prepared to help a younger child transition to playing with another toy and reassure him or her that in a certain number of minutes he or she will be able to play with the toy again.

Taking away toys when young children fight over them is not the right way to stop children from fighting with each other. It is a lazy way to parent. It is so crucial that your children learn from you how to solve problems. Take every single opportunity that they give you to teach them how to share. Do it over, and over, and over again. Taking a toy away from fighting siblings teaches only that next time they must be more aggressive so that the other party either hands over the toy or leave them alone before mom or dad can come in and take the toy away. You can either take toys away one hundred times per day or you can show your children how to share properly one hundred times per day. The first will lead to having children who never learn to share or solve problems. The last will lead to less fighting and more politeness between children as they get older.

When it comes to knowing how to stop children from fighting with each other and saying means things, the process is the same. When they first say something mean or hurtful to each other, ask the offended party to say how the mean words made him or her feel. Both children need to realize that words hurt and should be chosen wisely. The offender should offer an apology but realize that words cannot be taken back. If a child has empathy for his or her sibling, he or she will not want to say things that hurt. Again, be sure that tiredness, hunger or boredom are not factors in the behavior. Sometimes after a verbal assault your children might feel more comfortable playing apart.

More than anything your children need you to show them how to stop fighting with each other. Set a good example with your partner and other people in your life. Remember that children are very likely to do what we show them and less likely to do what we tell them.

Our parents kept telling my brother not to pick on me or fight me that someday I would end up whipping him. I was in my sophomore year of school when he left for the Army and I had matured over the last two years as I was doing all the farm and barn work and my father would help milk the cows.

Not knowing or realizing, with my brother, that I had developed and was very strong and he should have never picked a fight with me. But I would never have continued to fight unless my father said to do so. The last fight that I recall was the one when my brother was home from the service on a furlough for several days and we were milking the cows in the afternoon.

We were just starting to milk, and in order to get the first cows milked we had to wash the udders off prior to putting the milker on the cows. In that process I was washing the cows, and I suppose that I was not moving fast enough, and my brother grabbed the washcloth and started to wash the rest of the cows to start milking. When my brother grabbed the washcloth, he pushed me down into the manure ditch (cow waste as it was winter and would keep the cows up in the barn 24/7) and of course, I had stuff all over me and that made me mad!

For once in my life I came up fighting and did not let up. Our father came through the rows of cattle in the barn, and he said, "Okay, you two, you've wanted to fight it out for a long time, so go to it." When I heard my father say those magic words, I truly took advantage of the situation and gave it all that I had as this was my one chance!

That was all it took, and the major fight of all years was on! It went on inside the barn and somehow, we ended up on the outside of the barn and finally I gave the final blow when I hit him with my FFA ring just above his right eye (where he has a scar today) and the fight was over because he saw blood. My brother went to the house and asks my mother where the gun was because he was going to shoot me. My mother told him, "Your father and I have been telling you for years not to fight your brother that someday he would end up whipping you."

She did not let him have the gun and he packed his clothes and headed back to the Army that night.

The fight was never talked about after that night until this day as I am writing about the fight of all time!

At our state conference in Marketing, I was awarded **Outstanding Teacher of the Year**. I was the first teacher to receive this honor. The award was sponsored by the Kentucky Consumer Finance Association of Lexington, Kentucky. At the same time, I was teaching adult education and serving as an off-campus teacher for Western Kentucky University, Bowling Green, Kentucky.

SANTA CLAUSE FOR SENIORS

Back in the late 60s (This is a true story) when I was teaching at Pendleton County High school and I had a homeroom of senior students. One girl (Anita) in my homeroom had a sister (Sandy) that I taught with and her husband (Marvin) who taught English to junior students. Also, I ran around on weekends, when he was home, with the brother (Gerald) of Anita and Sandy as he was a junior or senior at Eastern Kentucky University at that time.

As the school year went on and getting close to Christmas the parents (Banjo (a farmer) and Dorothy (a bus driver for the local school board) asked me to play Santa Clause at their home for all the friends of Anita as they were giving them a Christmas party. How could one say no?

I already had a suit for Santa to wear and that made the event all so easy to undertake. As time rolled around, I wanted to make sure that none of the students would recognize me. There I cut all my fingernails off, brushed my knuckles with black pencil lead as I did not have white gloves to wear. As for the weather, it really was cold with a low of 20 degrees and no moonlight to see with and the atmosphere was very still overall almost as if we were about to get a big snow.

When the time arrived for me to play Santa Clause I drove out to the farm and parked my car in the tobacco barn and closed the doors. Then

I got dressed and just waited until all the students arrived for the party. To let me know when everyone had arrived Dorothy and I agreed that she would go outside and call the cows, and it worked as that was my clue to come on in.

Following the call, I went up to the house, knocked on the door, Anita opened the door and when she saw me, she said, "Oh my God, Santa Clause is here," and all the other student surrounded me at the door. Several students went outside to check and see what Santa Clause drove or flew in on and where he landed.

After telling me to come in and I did, I made sure that I disguised my voice and did not let anything slip. This was a real experience getting seniors in high school telling Santa what they wanted for Christmas and me knowing every one of them! As each student had a visit with Santa and told him what they wanted the other students would have a good time laughing, but everyone had a turn with Santa. Once Santa left, he had to change clothes and get cleaned up to make his appearance at the party.

All the time while Santa was talking to each senior, on his lap, all the other seniors were talking together and trying to figure out just who Santa was. I heard some say, "No, that's not Mr. Cole, because he has longer fingernails than that person." And just look at his knuckles, they are so dark he must do construction work. Of course, the discussion went on and on for a great while.

After Santa Clause left the group, I showed up about 45 minutes and made the statement, "had I missed all of the fun?" The food was excellent – punch with homemade cookies of all kinds, brownies, and homemade candies.

All the students were excited to tell me that I missed seeing Santa Clause and the opportunity to tell him what I wanted for Christmas. Little did they know that I had already received my Christmas gift when I played Santa Clause for them!

Of course, the longer I stayed the more they talked about Santa's visit and one thing led to another and finally, the secret was out, and they all had a good time, laughed and were blessed!

Needless to say, once returning to school after Christmas break was over, the students and I talked and laughed about the event for several months to come.

THE COTILLION AND HOP CLUBS

Years ago, growing up on the farm, we never had much time for a social life but as we each became of age (dating and 16 years of age) we were allowed to go to dances in town once in a while.

This organization, formed 100 years ago, was called the Girls Cotillion Club. The club hosted events for new members and had casual parties/dances at area clubs. The Girls Cotillion Club also hosted debutante balls. The ladies wore formal white gowns, and the gentlemen wore white dinner jackets. The club provides high school students with the opportunity to learn dancing, manners and etiquette and is open to students who achieve high standards in academics, athletics and the arts.

The organization for men was a membership of fun and community minded activities as they worked and made contributions to many of the planned community events.

Cotillion sessions are geared to entrance into the world of college, college admission and college scholarships. The club helps students develop self-esteem and self-confidence by teaching what is expected of them in the world, and how to conduct themselves and the finer points of interacting with others.

Young people felt really important at that time if you were a member of one of the top clubs in Shelbyville – young men would join the Hop

Club, and young ladies would join the Cotillion Blub and these two organizations were hard to become members.

When my brother came of age, he wanted to become a member because the group had outstanding dances at Christmas, Valentine, 4th of July and fall dance. He applied to become a member and was accepted at once. Then he started attending all the wonderful dances and my sister, Mary, finally turned 16.

When Mary applied to become a member of the Cotillion Club, she was black balled (that meant you will not become a member of the club). To be blackballed resulted from a secret vote. The voting took place as follows: a basket with white and black balls would be passed around and each voting member would take out (under cover) a white or a black ball. Another basket would be passed for the actual voting, and this is when members would cast individual votes by dropping in the white or back ball in the basket.

The next year she applied again, and would you believe that she was black balled for the second time, after the second turn down she did not bother applying another time as she left for college. After all, she had participated in beauty talent contests as a county participant for the county fair against the city girls that participated and were strong members of the Cotillion Club! I never could figure out what the problem was or was there a problem?

All this time my brother would fix her up with guys that were members of the Hop Club, and she still got to attend all the dances right along with him. He would also fix me up with some girl so I could go dancing, too.

When I turned 16, I received notice that I had been accepted as a member (before I applied) and I was welcomed at all the dances and activities. Naturally, I attended as many Hop/Cotillion Clubs dances as possible until I left for college.

I must admit that when you went to one of the Hop/Cotillion Clubs you danced your ass off, and today this one television network feel that they have a great show, but the television show will never be compared to the dances I took park in back in the late 50s and early 60s!

When I finished high school, I attended a Baptist college and dancing was not allowed. However, I would sneak out of town with some other males and some girls would do the same and we would dance until we were worn out and everyone had a great time!

THE MAKING OF HOMEMADE WINE

Little did I realize that by making homemade wine that I would actually make someone get drunk! Let's see what all took place during one of my summers.

The story starts when the blackberries ripened. I went into the back side of the farm to pick many blackberries just for the purpose of making some homemade wine. However, not to get caught I provided enough for my mother to make a homemade blackberry pie for the family to enjoy.

Long before the blackberries were ripe, I started collecting old used ketchup bottles with the twist off/on cap. When no one was around in the kitchen I would take off the labels, clean and wash the bottles and dry them ready to use. Then I would store them in the basement (one had to enter from the outside) and line them up in the back of other canned goods that our mother had canned and stored in the basement for winter.

In making the blackberry wine, I put about a cup full of berries in each bottle, put some sugar, some yeast, and screwed the lid on as tight as I could and place the filled bottle back behind the other canned goods on the shelf. Once I got the cap on, I dipped each bottle in red wax to make sure that each bottle sealed its best.

As time passed, about three weeks, one night when we were in bed sound asleep, everyone in the house thought that we were fighting the Civil War again. If you could imagine bottle tops blowing off and hitting the bottom of the floor on the first level just under the kitchen in the middle of the night.

We all got up and checked the house out and then our mother said let's go down to the basement and check things out. As we entered the basement from outside, we noticed and heard tops continuing to blow off and the air smelled just like good wine. Not too much was said at that time, but the next day my job was to clear out all my private bottles and clean everything.

Our farm hand, Mr. Berry, wanted to help me with the cleanup and I welcomed the help. Little did I know that he was collecting all the unopened bottles and any other bottles that still had some wine left in for him to drink. After that day our hired hand did not show up for work the next day, but his wife told us that he had gone to Louisville. We knew from past experiences that when he would go to Louisville and he would be gone for about a good week as he would be on a drunk. His wife also told us that he had drunk all the homemade wine, and it was not enough to satisfy him, so he took off to Louisville as he wanted a lot more to drink. Our father would give Mr. Berry two or three days and then he would drive to Louisville and pick him up as Mr. Berry's wife knew where to get him.

PLANTING CORN AS A COVER UP

During the early summertime there was always corn planting time on the farm and our father sent my brother over to the corn field to finish up planting the rest of the corn as corn planting was not completed the day before.

My brother was in the corn field for hours getting the planting finished and finally he came to the house and told our father that he was through.

As time passed, several weeks passed and the corn was coming up and our father went over to the corn field to take a look, as to how well the corn was coming up out of the ground to learn if we had a good stand. As he checked the corn, row after row, in one spot he noticed that corn was coming up around this large rock. Therefore, seeing the corn coming up around this big rock, our father decided to pick up the rock and see what was going on. As he pulled the rock up from the ground, he noticed that under the rock were many kernels of corn not yet sprouted. After gathering all the facts, he came to the house and started questioning everyone about the corn and the rock. Of course, no one knew a thing about the situation until our brother arrived at the house. When our father questioned my brother, he started to tell our father that when he was planting the corn that he spilled some and rather than picking it up and planting it, he figured that he would just leave it and cover it up with that big rock.

Well, when the truth was all out, this started an all-new issue and from the other stories you have read, you know what happened at this point, place and time.

THE OLD WASHER RINGER

Our mother used an old Maytag electric ringer washer to do our laundry from week to week, and the ringer washer stored in the basement.

As I remember Mama would wash the clothes and run them through the ringer on top of the washing machine into the rinse water and then do the same process from the rinse water to get them dry enough to take out and hang the clothes on the clothesline.

Antique Maytag Electric Ringer Washer Washing Machine Pictured and Description and what is an old washer ringer machine?

Here we have today this Antique Maytag Electric Ringer Washer Washing Machne. I don't see a mode number on the machine itself, but there is some info on the motor (pictured). Another thing I don't see is damage or missing parts. Just some pain wear and VERY minor surface rust near the bottom of the legs mainly. The cord is not in great condition, so we are not going to plug it in to test it. If you want to come by, we will let you have the honors! Will be a local pickup (about 40 miles south of Kansas City), or email or the nearest pickup Hub if you are seriously interested. Residential delivery is an additional $75.00. I guarantee these item/items to be authentic and as described. Local Pickup is always FREE; our zip code is 64723. Please check our other listings, feedback, and NEAR PERFECT detailed seller ratings (DSR's.

First of all, we would like everyone to know that we are human beings, and we will occasionally make a mistake. It is inevitable! We deal in large volumes of merchandise of all types and try our very best to describe our products exactly as they are. We will NEVER intentionally attempt to mis-identify or hide a problem with an item!!! We are honest sellers. It is not only how we conduct our business, but how we live our lives as well. It you feel that an item you purchased from us is not as described and misidentified, or if there is a shipping issue.

We WILL literally bend over backwards to see that your problem is resolved in a VERY TIMELY MATTER!!! If for some reason we cannot take care of the problem, then feel free to leave whatever feedback you wish! Payment and Checkout Invoices will be sent out no later than the day after action close. It is usually best to wait for the invoice before paying, especially if you have won more than one item. If you plan on bidding on two or more items that end on different days, please let us know. If you receive an invoice for an item won and you plan on bidding on more items, just let us know, and if you win more, we will be happy to combine invoices and shipping costs. We will combine invoices and shipping for items won within 5 consecutive days.

In order to keep shipping costs down, we normally ship USPS Parcel Post. It is the most economical for you, our customer. But parcel post can take up to 14 days for delivery, so please do not email us after 6 or 8 days wondering where your item is. I have been using this service for over three years and have only had 1 package that did not make it to its destination.

We estimate shipping as close as possible to the national "zone" average and add only an additional $4.00 to $2.00 for packaging materials, supplies, operation costs, and labor. Most of the items we sell are on consignment, so we must cover those costs. Any personal items we sell have NO handling costs added. We do our very best to package your items in a way that will ensure their safe voyage! We take extra care in wrapping and packaging fragile items using bubble wrap, packing peanuts, and heavy-duty packaging paper. If you do receive your item damaged, please photograph it and contact us immediately. DO NOT throw away the original packaging! Our Customer Policy Without questions, the customer is our most valuable asset. Without you we cannot support our families! We care about your satisfaction and strive to deliver you a quality product in a timely manner! If for any reason you are not completely satisfied with our service, simply email us and give us the opportunity to make you happy. We will literally bend over backwards to see that you are completely satisfied with your buying experience with us!

The wringer, or ringer washer, is a precursor to the modern washing machine. Introduced in the early years of the 20th century, the typical ringer washer included a vat for washing clothing, a simple agitating system recessed in the vat, and a washboard and ringer combination. Considered to be an innovative appliance at the time, this type of clothes washer made the process of cleaning clothing a much easier task for many households.

In appearance, the ringer washer featured a body that was composed of a vat mounted on four legs. Many models included rollers or caster wheels on each leg, making it possible to move the washer from storage when needed. Built into the vat was a simple agitating device, located in the middle area. The agitator normally had two extended flaps that would move the clothing around during the operation of the washer. At the base of the machine was a drainage valve that made it possible to remove water from the vat once the washing process was completed.

The early ringer washer also included handy tools that were attached to the top of the vat, normally on one side. A sturdy washboard provided the idea place to scrub stubborn stains on shirts and other garments before immersing them in the wash water. In order to wring as much water from the clothing as possible before hanging them on an outdoor clothesline, a wringer composed of two sturdy rollers and a crank handle was provided. After the clothing was washed, it ran through the rollers, effectively squeezing out the excess water, which dropped back into the vat.

Original designs for the ringer washer used the newly harnessed electricity in order to operate. A single power cord equipped with a wall plug ran from the washer to the power source. Once the vat was filled and the clothing immersed in the water, washing soap was added and the device was turned on.

The agitator moved the clothing back and forth in the filled vat, helping to remove dirt and rime from the clothing.

Later designs mechanized the wringers, eliminating the hand crank. By flipping a switch, it was possible to start the motion of the ringers and run the wet clothing through with relative ease. Due to some accidents involving the electrical rollers, a hand guard was added to the last generation of these types of washers.

Draining water from a ringer washer involved opening the drain located near the base of the unit. Many models include a fixture where a hose could be attached, making it possible to control the flow of the water as it left the vat. Other models were set up to allow the water to drain into a bucket, which could then be dumped into the sink or out of doors.

Over time, the ringer washer was replaced by the modern washing machines of today with their multiple washing cycles and spin technology. However, it is still possible to purchase replica editions of the ringer washer from a few select vendors. The replicas are fully operational devices to clean clothes and may be ideal for use at a lake cabin or other location where plumbing or space restraints make the installation of a modern clothes washer impractical. This is good knowledge to know in case one may need it.

Now that you have some background on the old washer ringer, I will tell you what took place one early morning in June. Our cousin, Sonny, was visiting us for a month during the summer and our mother was in the basement doing laundry. She came upstairs for something and while she was away from the washer Sonny decided to try the machine out to see what it could do.

All at once we heard this loud scream coming from outside, we thought, but when we got to trying to find what was going and where we discovered that it was Sony in the basement with his right arm stuck in the ringer of the washing machine.

Our mother did everything that she could and finally reached around and unplugged the machine so it would stop slipping on Sonny's right arm as it was stripping the skin from his arm. After attempting time after time to get his arm out of the ringer nothing would give. So, Mama told us to run and get our father and tell him to bring some tools and what had taken place. Our father arrived and I first thought that he would physically kill Sonny for what he had done, but he cooled down and worked on getting Sonny out of the ringer.

Finally, with everyone working together we got Sonny out of the washing machine ringer (taking it apart and afterwards putting it back together) and Mama started to work on Sonny's arm by applying medication and wrapping it with sterilized cloths.

Over the next two to three weeks Sonny's arm healed, with Mama's nursing daily, and Sonny went home back to Lexington with his grandmother in mid-August as his school was starting the next week.

In closing, I tell you, if it's in good condition, it's probably worth something. You can go to eBay and just look under antiques ringer washer or type in ringer washer and get results quickly. There is also an antique book that lists all this stuff, last resort. Call an antique dealer or two and see what they say. Not that they will be totally honest!

ABOUT CLASS REUNIONS

Some people faithfully attend high school or college reunions. Others scoff and wonder if it isn't a bit crazy to fly halfway across the country to see folks who, except for maybe three or four, are not acquainted with who you are now and certainly don't really care. So why go?

My high school experience is best summed up as awkward and interminable. Though adulthood has shown me to be a clear-cut extrovert, I was unable to access that quality amid the agony of self-consciousness that drowned me in high school.

So – once a decade – reunions have become that rate opportunity for a do-over. I can mingle with people I was once too shy to speak to, be friendly, and be the person I wanted to be in high school. It's a chance to spruce up outdated recollections steeped in angst-filled teenage introspection and self-absorption. Rewriting history this way has become a big lure of reunions. But it didn't start out that way.

Because I have not lived in my hometown since I left for college, I went to my 10th high school reunion out of curiosity and even picked up an old date to go with me. I was depressed and a bit horrified to find many classmates still clinging to their outdated cliques: cheerleaders were still with cheerleaders. Same was found to be true with the bank kids and the outstanding athletes. I went to my 20th out of perversity, I suppose, with low expectations – and was delighted to discover my fellow grads had come to see that what bound us together was much more important than those small differences that separated us in high school. It was a fun night.

My recent 40th reunion included a tour of the old neighborhood by my best friend from grade school. I was shocked to see that the lawn space between his house and the next-door neighbors was tiny, 4 to 5 feet. I remember flying kites from that spot and learning to throw a rope there, in what I'd recalled as a vast expanse. How could all those bright memories fit into such a small space?

At our high school, where my friend and I were part of the first graduating class from a new school, I teared up as we pulled into the parking lot. Just think, 50 years ago this was a brand-new building. So were we!

We were embarking on complicated lives we could in no way predict. In that moment, the passage of 50 years was an exceedingly difficult concept to absorb.

But those experiences are why I'm willing to make the long journey home each time I attend my class reunion. What a gift it is for me to have another opportunity to come face-to-face with the tangible reminders of youth, which rekindle those priceless memories again. Even some of your classmates are just memories today and many are gone forever!

THE ALLOWANCE

What is an allowance? The dictionary states allowance as al-low-ance. An allowance is an amount of money set aside for a designated purpose. Allowing another… the material or equipment of the allowance in questions? Allowances for children al-low-ance will teach your child responsibility and money management by assigning age-appropriate chores and providing a regular allowance. Learn the best way to set your child's allowance and get help deciding whether to reward your child for helping out around the house.

Some other definitions of allowance are: the act of allowing, an amount or share allotted or granted, a sum of money allotted or granted for a particular purpose, as for expenses: *Her allowance for the business trip was $200*, a sum of money allotted or granted to a person on a regular basis, as for personal or general living expenses: *The art student lived on an allowance of $300 a month. When I was in first grade, my parents gave me a allowance of 50 cents a week and an addition or deduction based on an extenuating or qualifying circumstance: an allowance for profit; an allowance for depreciation.*

An allowance--a certain amount of money given on a regular basis – is a great way to get kids to learn about the value of money while also learning basic money management skills.

What is children's allowance? It is giving your child an amount of cash so they can use it every week for something they wish to do or purchase or save. The whole purpose for a kid's allowance is to educate them how money works in society. It also builds financial skills such as counting, saving, budgeting and making money. To give children allowance is to instill a sense of responsibility to them. This is how they are going to grow. By giving money for kids, you are giving your child practical uses of what money can do for them.

A children's allowance amount depends on how old they are. The general rule for allowances for kids is $1 per age. So, if they are 10, you would give your kid allowance of $10. If they are 12, you would give them an allowance of $12. An allowance for kids will teach them how much items cost as they grow up. Naturally as they get older, their costs increase, therefore, the children's allowance should also increase.

Now below are the main factors on how much an allowance for children given by the experts to give?

Age – As described above, a children's allowance depends largely on their age. Obviously, a child who is 16 will receive more money than a child who is 8. It's most likely because of their needs and wants cost more as they grow older.

Family Income – Allowance for children will also largely depend on how much you earn. A family which lives in more affluent areas or a higher-socioeconomic society will most likely have a higher kids allowance than a family which is in a lower one.

How many children do you have in your family? The more children you have, the more money you will have to divide up. So, a family with 4 children may each receive less than a family with only 1 child comparatively.

What other children are receiving as an allowance – you may ask around other parents on how much they give their child to give a fair idea on allowance for kids.

AGE OF CHILD

Below is a general outline of how much pocket money for kids you should give according to their age group.

TODDLER AGE 0 – 6

Usually, you don't have to start giving your child pocket money until they are about 6 years old. A children's allowance for this age is just so that they have an initial responsibility of money that is given to them. Don't give them too much, maybe $5 or $6 when they are 6 years old. Of course, you can start younger if you wish. They may understand the concept of money that it is used for goods in return. You can start them at 4 years old and give them $2 to hold in their backpack or pocket.

A great way to teach your children about money at this age would be to take them shopping with you. Show them what you are doing with each item such as looking at the price, and then what you do at the checkout counter. The allowance for kids can be used here as you allow them to buy one item at the shops. Teach them how much items cost and if the kids allowance either is below that cost or matches it, your child can buy that item.

AGES 7-12

Increase the allowance for children every year within reason. They may want to save money for something more expensive such as a bike. Or they will want to buy the latest Playstation game. Teach them how to budget properly in the age bracket. To give children allowance at this age means to trust them a bit more on what they do with their money. Allow them to make mistakes, as people usually learn better through these experiences.

As the parent, you are still solely responsible for all their needs and wants. Therefore, you are the provider for allowance for children and will need to teach them good spending and saving habits here.

AGES 13 – 18

At this age, you may want to increase the allowance for kids significantly. Why? You could give them the added responsibility to have a clothing allowance each month, so they are in charge of buying the clothes. Therefore, you will start shifting the responsibility from you to the child/teenager. Teach them that they must use it wisely or they will blow it all off in the first few days. A teenager's allowance needs to be thought out carefully as this is the stage where they will cement their money habits for life. Allowances for teenagers reaching adulthood will most likely be their first step into how the economy works as a whole and that money doesn't grow on trees but is hard to earn.

In conclusion, how much you give for allowance for children depends on you and your family's situation. A teenager's allowance is going to be much different than a younger children's allowance. At the end of the day a kid's allowance gives them an opportunity to be financially responsible and gives you the parent the opportunity to teach kids about money.

It is easy to lose sleep over the amount of allowance that you pay your child each week. By using these allowance guidelines defining the recommended daily allowance, you can feel confident that you are giving the right amount based on your situation and teach your kids about money.

What the Experts Say?

Most experts agree that a child should be given $1 per week for each year he or she is old. For example, an eight-year-old would receive $8 per week while a ten-year-old would receive $10 per week. However, the experts also agree that a child's allowance should be based on more than just one factor and that the advice above is simply a starting point or rule of thumb and does not need to be followed literally. The experts also agree that one of the most important factors in how much a child receives for allowance is what you want them to spend it on. The child should receive enough money to cover the normal expenses that they pay for (like lunch money) as well as have some discretionary money left over. This discretionary money will teach them the concepts of managing money, <u>saving and financial planning.</u>

Regardless of what the experts say, the fact is that you know your child best and you are the best judge of what they need for an allowance in order to learn the financial concepts that you think are important as a parent. When deciding whether you're eight-year-old should receive $3 per week or $20 per week, consider these factors in your decision.

Look at what you expect them to purchase during the week. For example, if you expect their allowance money to cover school lunches as well as toys and other discretionary items, be sure that you provide enough for those needs. Also, be sure to adjust as the needs change. For example, if the price of school lunches changes, adjust the allowance amount to cover that.

Consider your household finances; it makes no sense to offer your child an allowance that you simply cannot afford. If you want to pay your child $10 per week, but you cannot afford that in your budget, explain that to the child. This will help them appreciate that you also have to worry about money and that they will not always get everything they want. However, even if your budget is right, try to provide something as an allowance (even if it is only a couple dollars), so that they can have money of their own to learn with.

YOUR CHILD AND THEIR ALLOWANCES?   HOW OLD SHOULD KIDS BE TO GET AN ALLOWANCE?

Start as early as you and your child are comfortable. Kids often develop a very early fascination with money, so they will be very excited to have some money of their own. Kindergarten age is a good time to start – though some parents begin earlier if the child is ready.

HOW MUCH ALLOWANCE TO GIVE?

How much money should kids get? This depends on your own family budget restrictions and personal situation. One suggestion might be $2 for every year of age. So, a five-year-old would get five dollars, and a ten-year-old would get ten dollars a week. Or start with a certain dollar amount and increase it by $1 each year. Though, we would suggest giving an amount that is comfortable with you, based on your own child's spending habits, and your budget. The main point is to give a certain amount on a regular basis.

If your child is older, you might also start by asking your child how much money they wish to receive each week. If they don't know how much, you could ask them to see how much they might spend each week (which is also a good way to get them to think about budgeting). Then adjust that amount to something more appropriate if necessary.

HOW OFTEN SHOULD AN ALLOWANCE BE PAID?

Allowances do not have to always be paid weekly. Some parents pay their kids at the same time they get their own paycheck, which may be every other week. Others give a monthly allowance to encourage better budgeting skills. Though, we suggest a minimum of once per week.

HOW TO DEAL WITH BASIC MONEY MANAGEMENT SKILLS?

Allowances help teach basic money management and economic principles. For example, some parents find that their children often ask too often to buy something when they are out shopping. By giving an allowance, instead of putting pressure on you to buy something, you can let the kids decide to buy, if they have an allowance. "You get an allowance, so it's up to you to use your own money." This way they can begin to learn the concept that money is a limited resource.

CHORES AND ALLOWANCE< ARE THEY EQUAL? Should your child only make an allowance if they do chores? This is one approach that might seem appealing, but it is often considered a mistake.

Having a chore-allowance relationship is not recommended, since it takes away from the money skills that children might otherwise learn. Chores should be considered a family responsibility that should not be associated with money. Also, kids may not do their chores if they only have to give up a small allowance. The purpose of an allowance is to teach money skills, and this may be lost if it is strictly tied to chores, and if the allowance is not regular and consistent.

As a compromise, you may pay a base allowance and let your child make additional money if they complete additional chores for the week.

ARE YOU SAVING MONEY?

Of course, don't let your children buy everything they want immediately if they have the money. An important concept to teach is the concept of saving. By saving money, we can buy something more expensive tomorrow, if we save our money today. However, at the same time the money given as an allowance is now your child's, so you must let them decide how they spend it – its part of the learning process.

Though, you can still give guidance. For example, when you are shopping, and your child asks to buy something, always ask them if they are sure if that is what they want, and that they could save their money to buy something better.

Along with the allowance, you can establish some restrictions. For example, you should require the child to set aside a certain amount to save. So, if the allowance is $3, for example, then perhaps $1 should be placed in a piggy bank for saving, while $2 can be used for spending. You can even set aside a percent for donating as well.

To encourage even longer-term savings, you may want to give your child additional money to allocate to long-term savings. Long-term savings money should then be deposited to a bank account or other financial institution. Long-term savings could be for college or other long-term goals.

WHAT ABOUT CLOTHING ALLOWANCE?

For help with budgeting for different items or spending categories, it may be easier to help your child budget his or her money by setting up a special allowance. For example, for clothing you could give clothing allowance in addition to the normal allowance. Money for the clothing allowance is only to be spent on clothing.

ARE THE KIDS BANKING?

Some parents find it difficult to always carry around their child's money when shopping. In that case, it may be easier to start a kid's bank. With a kid's bank, the weekly allowance is 'deposited' into a simulated bank account. Then, your child can write a check when making a 'withdrawal' and you can directly give them the money.

 An extra benefit of this approach is that your child can learn basic checking skills, and practice math. See our <u>checking</u> category for blank checks and a check register to use for setting up a kid's bank.

ARE YOU GOING TRIAL AN ERROR?

Remember, kids will learn by trial and error. Don't be too afraid that your children will not spend their money wisely. It's much better that they make mistakes now, when they are young, rather than later in life – that's what an allowance is for.

Money skills are unfortunately not taught extensively in school, so it's up to you to help your kids learn about money and the value of savings!

An Allowance can help children understand the concept of budgeting and saving, but you have to teach them.

Now that we have a good understanding about allowance and dealing with the establishment of an allowance let's venture into the life of the story.

As each sibling reached the ripe age of 16 in growing up back on the farm we were given an allowance. Our parents started our brother out with $20.00 a week and that was when gasoline was only 25 cents a gallon. His $20.00 was spending money, dating, motor operations and whatever he wanted to do with his money.

It was not long before he was in trouble as we ran up a gasoline bill at one of the local service stations that our father charged gasoline, to the amount of $500.00 in one month. When the bill arrived in the mail, we thought our father would die! When our brother arrived home, he and our father got together for an understanding, if you know what I mean!

The one sad outcome to this event was when my sister and I each turned 16 we were given $2.00 a week for all the same reasons of management.

GROCERY SHOPPING

Every week growing up, after you turned 16 years old and got your driver's licenses, your first job after breakfast was to go to town and shop for the family's weekly groceries.

This chore started out being very big as we got to drive our father's car, but not our brother as he had a record of too many accidents. Just my sister, Mary, and I were allowed to drive Daddy's car.

Our father would make out the list of groceries that we needed, once review the local newspaper ads to see what was on sale. Once in the store shopping for the groceries on the list you made sure that you only got the things listed. If for some reason you arrived home with something that was not on the list our father would make us take the item(s) back to the store and get our money back. Once you did this it was a BIG embarrassment! Also, you would make sure that it never happened again!

Our father would go through the local newspaper to see what was on sale in the grocery store, then he would go to the section of the newspaper to cut our coupons and would collect and put with the grocery list any other special discounts that he possibly had at that time.

My sister started out when she was 16 and shopped for the family for 2 years and left for college, and by then, I had turned 16 and it was my turn to shop for the groceries.

My schedule included: getting up at 4:00 a.m. to milk the cows, eat breakfast, wash up the milk room, clean out the barn, change clothing, go to town to get groceries, return home with the groceries and then go about the rest of the day – crushing corn for cattle feed, feeding dry stock, and whatever else was on the agenda for the day. However, I remember one day I made a mistake at the grocery store, and I caught the mistake on the way home, but I figured that I would get away with the mistake. I do not remember what the item was, but I do remember that I had to go back to the store and make the exchange and having to explain what happened when I got home.

Sometimes, just like today, the store would be sold out of something that he had on the list to buy, but when we arrived home if we did not have the item(s) we had to explain WHY we did not have the item(s). Here was the opportunity to demonstrate that failure to get an item(s) on the list was not an option!

Our father would even time us to make sure that we were getting just weekly groceries and not running around doing other things. If we took too long in town to get what was on his list, he would ask us when we got home what took us so long? Telling him that the store was busy and the checkout lines were backed up was not a very good answer but it was the truth coming from the shopper.

SCHOOL DANCES

What is dance? Dance is an art form that generally refers to movement of the body, usually rhythmic and to music, used as a form of expression, social interaction or presented in a form of expression that uses bodily movements that are rhythmic, patterned (or sometimes improvised), and usually accompanied by music. One of the oldest art forms, dance is found in every culture and is performed for purposes ranging from the ceremonial, liturgical, and magical to the theatrical, social, and simply aesthetic. In Europe, tribal dances often evolved into folk dances, which became stylized in the social dances of the 16th-century European courts.

Dance is an art form that generally refers to movement of the body, usually rhythmic and to music, used as a form of expression, social interaction or presented in a spiritual or performance setting.

Dance may also be regarded as a form of nonverbal communication between humans and is also performed by other animals (bee dance, patterns of behavior such as a mating dance). Gymnastics, figure skating and synchronized swimming are sports that incorporate dance, while martial arts, kata are often compared to dances. Motion in ordinarily inanimate objects may also be described as dances (*the leaves danced in the wind*).

Definitions of what constitutes dance are dependent on <u>social, cultural, aesthetic</u>, <u>artistic</u> and <u>moral</u> constraints and range from functional movement (such as <u>folk dance</u>) to <u>virtuoso</u> techniques such as <u>ballet</u>. Dance can be <u>participatory, social</u> or performed for an <u>audience</u>. It can also be <u>ceremonial, competitive</u> or <u>erotic</u>. Dance movements may be without significance in themselves, such as in <u>ballet</u> or European <u>folk dance</u>, or have a <u>gestural vocabulary/symbolic</u> system as in many Asian dances. Dance can embody or express ideas, <u>emotions</u> or tell a <u>story</u>.

Dancing has evolved many styles. <u>Breakdancing</u> and <u>Krumping</u> are related to the <u>Hip Hop</u> <u>culture</u>. African dance is interpretative. Ballet, Ballroom, Waltz and Tango, Jitter Bug are classical styles of dance while <u>Square Dance</u> and the <u>Electric Slide</u> are forms of <u>step dances.</u>

Every dance, no matter what style, has something in common. It not only involves flexibility and body movement, but also physics. If the proper physics are not taken into consideration, injuries may occur.

Choreography is the art of creating dances and now that you have a good working knowledge of dancing let's get into the story.

We all loved to dance! My brother and sister both took Author Murray dance lessons one fall/winter and learned to dance really well. I never took lessons, but I would go with my parents when they took my brother and sister for lessons and watched.

When they took lessons, I was just entering high school, and the first dance was coming up and my parents made my brother take me and my date to that dance. To everyone's surprise I could dance! The school had a dance contest later that night and the only three couples left standing on the floor were: my brother and date, my sister and date and me and my date. Just imagine, even with a little hard work with no money you can do it!

These results went on dance after dance, year after year, until they graduated. Of course, our brother would always win the dance contest every time! Mary and I figured who cares as long as the title ended up in the family.

SNOW

Play in the Snow! Just because it's snowy doesn't mean it is dreary outside. Snow can be a lot of fun to play in! Don't use the excuse "It's too cold!" Get out there and have fun! There is no time to waste; snow only stays for a while! Then, it's summer and you can't play in the snow.

Bundle up! Jeans may be more stylish than puffy snow pants, but those snow pants will keep your legs nice and warm. Jeans are really bad with the snow when they get wet, they will get hard and maybe even freeze and you'll be left uncomfortable. Thick socks or stockings and snow boots are a must for your feet. Put on a coat with a sweater underneath. Wear a good hat that covers your ears. Wear a very warm pair of gloves, those yarn gloves or polar-fleece ones probably won't cut it. Waterproof gloves work best. Don't forget a scarf!

 Throw snowballs! Go outside, make snowballs and throw them at the mean neighbor's house (be careful not to damage property)! Start a snowball fight! Team up with your friends against your other friends and hit them with snowballs without being hit yourself! If you are an adult, then kids will probably team up on you, but you have brains on your side! If you're an adult, be friendly! You might miss hitting kids a couple of times or let yourself get hit by them.

Go sledding! Take a quick trip to a local store and get a cheap $5 sled (although the cheap round ones go the fastest, they tend to break easily, so buy spares) and join the kids in the popular sled hill. Or, better yet, buy a tube for a swimming pool. Make sure that it's big enough to fit multiple people at a time. Everyone will be begging for you to share! If you have money to burn, get a really nice sled with a steering wheel and brakes (about a hundred dollars). These will last you a long while and handle jumps pretty decently.

SELLING THE FARM

After I left for college, I decided to go straight through and finish in three years. Completing two full years (credit wise it equaled 2, ¾ years) and coming home for a short break in August following summer school my father asked me to go to the farm in Shelbyville as we were living in Lexington at the time.

Daddy and Mama had leased the farm out to a tenant. Daddy wanted me just to ride down and check things out with him one Saturday and to our surprise we learned that the tenant had left, and the cows needed to be milked, and all animals needed to be fed. Also, cows were having calves, and we had heifers having calves and coming into the herd as milking cows, too.

Daddy asked me if I would stay and take care of the work and he would go back to Lexington to get me some clothing, sleeping bed, cooking pots and pans, whatever items he and Mama could put together quickly. Of course, I took the challenge as I was in college and with no personal money at the time as I had been in school. This is where I made a mistake because I never discussed a salary with my Daddy for doing the farm work for five months to this point.

This challenge turned out to be a long fall and beginning winter as you will learn. Starting out, we have around 100 head of cattle that I had to milk and deal with daily along with feeding about another 50 or so animals. Along with putting up feed, crushing corn for feed, cutting yard grass and cooking for myself. At times, Mama really helped me out as she would cook ahead and make a supply of food items that could last for several days and save me much time in cooking and Daddy would bring the food with him as he traveled back and forth. I really had no time to visit, listen to the radio, talk on the phone, watch television, read the paper or run around for anything or with anyone that fall. Of course, by this time all the friends that I ran around with in high school were in college, service, married or no longer with us. I was so isolated that when President Kennedy was assassinated, someone locally drove into tell me what had happened in Texas that day.

During the next week Daddy and Mama talked about just selling the farm and we planned that the sale would take place in December just prior to Christmas. At this time, with the sale in December, it would allow my Daddy and I to get everything ready for the sale – farm equipment, cattle and any other miscellaneous items that needed to be sold.

As the days were numbered to the sale, the season changed daily, and a chill moved about with the weather and turned out to be a record low for that time of the year. The next thing we knew was Halloween then Thanksgiving and December were approaching quickly. We had pretty much made ready all the equipment for the sale and the cattle looked great and the other animals, too.

The day of the sale rolled around, December 20, and it was unusually cold that day with a little snow blowing around! Not much of a crowd showed up to buy equipment or cattle and Daddy took a financial beating but he did not allow the registration papers to go with the registered Brown Swiss cattle sold as they sold too far under the market price. Once the sale ended shoppers took the equipment and cattle home with them and we stayed the night, our last night in the big house and on the farm.

The next day, Daddy and I moved the furniture we had in the house and went back to Lexington just in time for Christmas. Daddy went to Shelbyville several days later to settle up with the signing of the land deed, finances and other related business items that needed to be done.

The whole family was home in Lexington for Christmas. It was a much-needed rest for me as I was in the process of getting ready to go back to college and earn my degree. I must admit that I was lucky in college to have my own car to travel to and from, but I always managed to have riders that I would drop off on the way home and pick up on the way back to school and they each would pay me enough money to buy my gasoline for the trip.

The day arrived for me to go back to college; of course, Daddy paid my tuition/board and expenses for my books but spending money was on me. Little did I know, as the fall passed, I never asked for any money from my father as I wanted him to save it for me to use as spending money for college. When I got ready to leave for college, I asked Daddy where my spending money was. Daddy handed me $250 and said, "Here you go, this should take care of it!" I was really shocked as I expected much more especially since I did not take any money all fall for a sum of five months.

Knowing that I wanted to finish college I said nothing and left as I did not wish to make him mad, because if I made any kind of statement at all I would have ended up in a situation that my brother experienced and that was not for me. Whenever I came home from then on for a weekend visit my sister and Mama would sneak money to me and reminded me to say nothing to my Daddy about the money. Did I say anything? No!

Even today, I have never understood why Daddy treated me the way he did about money. I worked very hard doing all the farm work for five months even without him being in attendance. Really, I isolated myself from the world until the farm was sold.

My father ended up buying in (not letting the animals go as sold in the sale) a limited number of calves and young heifers and then moved to Lexington on Versailles Road just near the Red mile. Later, he sold these animals privately as he found interested individuals desiring registered Brown Swiss.

CORDUROY PANTS

I was just old enough to recall this story about my brother. He came running into the house one night as white as a sheet from scared of something outside. As I recall, the night was very dark, and my brother told my parents that something outside was chasing him. My parents asked how you know something has been chasing you. He told them that he would run some, stop and listen, then he would walk some, stop and listen and then would run some more and stop to listen. He said every time he stopped to listen that they would stop running, walking or whatever, and that this went on until he got to the house.

At this point our father got his flashlight to look outside to see what was really going on. Daddy was gone for some time but upon his return he stated that he found nothing.

After Daddy had returned and our parents started questioning our brother again from the beginning, he quickly learned that our brother was wearing corduroy slacks. Every time that my brother took a step, his corduroy slacks would rub and create a sound as if someone was walking beside him.

What are corduroy pants? A corduroy is an alive teddy bear and a little kid, too. Corduroy The Bear is a bear that wears green corduroy overalls that wears two yellow or white buttons. Corduroy is a textile formed of twisted fibers woven and made to lie parallel to one another which gives the cloth its distinct pattern, which is called a "cord." Modern corduroy is most commonly composed of tufted cords, showing a channel in which the base of the fabric is visible between the crests of the cord called the tufts. Corduroy is in fact something like a ridged form of velvet. Until the 19h century it was mainly used for the clothing of livery and agricultural workers but later it became a common fabric for jackets worn in outdoor sports. During the 20th century it picked up its popularity as a casual fashion garment. Today it is seen in trousers and jackets. It is never in fashion so never out of fashion. Youth, middle aged and older age people all like to wear the fabric in the mid cold weather where it gives you enough warmth. It is not the fabric of choice for extreme cold conditions.

Corduroy pants are trousers or jeans made with corduroy fabric, a cut-pile fabric like velvet with ribs (narrow, medium or wide). From a distance, narrow Wale's corduroy pants look like velvet pants. Such pants or jeans are usually called corduroys. The word, "corduroy" was inspired by the French words, "corps du roi," which means it was a garment of the king.

Nowadays, French call that fabric, "velour's cotele." Translated in English word for word, it would mean "corded or walled velvet." Corduroy is usually 100 percent cotton.

Corduroy pants were worn for a few centuries by workmen in many countries because it was a durable fabric for active men. In Western

Europe and North America, some working men wore corduroy breeches. In the second part of the 20th century, corduroy pants and corduroy jeans were the most popular for college and university students. Scouts wore corduroy shorts, and it was part of the uniform in a lot of private school especially catholic schools. Workman still wears corduroys in some countries such as Germany (Zunft cord hose) and France. Since those pants were made in Manchester during the first part of the 20th century, the word Manchester was used in reference to corduroys. As an example, that word is used by Czechs for corduroys. Some British lads would call corduroys by the word, "Manchu."

For the same reason some men have developed a leather fetish, a few men have a corduroy fetish because of an accidental connection made between sexual pleasure and wearing corduroys. The famous British actor John Gielgud had such a fetish for corduroys. It was publicly known when his diary was published after his death. Erik Satie, the French composer, wore only corduroys suits. When he died, he had a closet full of corduroy suits. Such a fetish was common amongst gay men but there are also heterosexual men turned on by corduroys.

Corduroy is a <u>textile</u> composed of twisted fibers that, when woven, lie parallel (similar to <u>will</u>) to one another to form the cloth's distinct pattern, a "cord." Modern corduroy is most commonly composed of <u>tufted</u> cords, sometimes exhibiting a channel (bare to the base fabric) between the tufts. Corduroy is, in essence, a ridge form of <u>velvet</u>. The word, corduroy, originates in fact from medieval times, where kings would prefer to wear corduroy, so it was understandably named: *le cord du roi.* After years of bearing this name, it eventually became Corduroy due to mispronunciation or simplifying the word.

As a <u>fabric</u>, corduroy is considered a durable cloth. Corduroy is found in the construction of <u>trousers</u>, <u>jackets</u> and <u>shirts</u>. The width of the cord is commonly referred to as the size of the "wale" (i.e. the number of ridges per inch). The lower the "wale" number, the thicker the width of the wale (i.e., 4-wale is much thicker than 11-wale). Corduroy's wale count per inch can vary from 1.5 to 21, although the traditional standard falls somewhere between 10 and 12. Wide wale is more commonly used in trousers; medium, narrow, and fine wale fabrics are usually found in garments worn above the waist.

Corduroy is made by weaving extra sets of fiber into the base fabric to form vertical ridges called Wales. The Wales are built so that clear lines can be seen when they are cut into pile. The primary types of corduroy are:

- Standard wale: 11 Wales/inch, and available in many colors. This cloth is sturdy and practical.
- Pincord/pinwale/needlecord: Pincord is the finest cord around with a count at the upper ed of the spectrum (above 16) and has a feel as soft as velveteen.
- Pigment dyed/printed corduroy: The process of coloring or printing corduroy with pigment dyes. The dye is applied to the surface of the fabric, and then the garment is cut and sewn. When washed during

the final phase of the manufacturing process, the pigment dye washes out in an irregular way, creating a vintage look. The color of each garment becomes softer with each washing, and there is a subtle color variation from one to the next. No two are alike.

Did you know that we have a Corduroy Appreciation Day? The dates of 1/22 and 11/11 have been dubbed as Corduroy Appreciation Day, because of their visual similarity to corduroy Wales. The date of 11/11/11 is considered to be the "holiest" of Corduroy Appreciation days.

When is it a good rule not to wear corduroys? The answer: whenever it is dark outside and you are scared!

It is very important that the reader has a good understanding of corduroy fabric and how the fabric is put together in clothing to grasp the full sensation of this fabric rubbing to make a noise of someone walking.

If you know anything about corduroy slacks you know that they have cords (vertical) that will rub as you walk, run, or whatever.

With all the knowledge about corduroys one can quickly understand how a little one could be scared in the dark while running, walking or even standing in one spot.

DEDICATED TO DOT

I just arrived back from Hodgenville, Kentucky from viewing a layout of Mrs. Dorothy Newton Comer Boone Filiatreau who died several days ago at the young age of 97 and has always been a very dear friend of mine since 1971. To know Dot was to love her as she was one of the sweetest, most helpful and loving people that I have ever known!

Let's talk about funerals as Dot had outlived three husbands. Death has always been, but it is handled differently now than it was in the 1940's, 50's and 60's. Today a funeral home is plush, with thick carpet and all the modern conveniences. There are flower arrangements that go to all corners of the layout room. Organ music floats in, and the presence of visitors is noted in a guest register book. Currently, many people start cooking when they learn of a friend passing on so that members of the family will have lots of food to eat. Many years ago, one would have the layout and service in the home of the deceased, but it is not the same today with the large funeral home production.

At the end of the service day the sun set pink, the wind was chilled, as the chorus of "In the Sweet by and by" varied across the hills. The preacher led in prayer. There were more hugs, kisses and the neighbors and family drifted away, and all was quiet again in the cemetery.

In loving memory of Dorothy Newton Comer Booke Filiatreau, born January 29, 1915, and died March 21, 2012. God looked around his garden, and he found an empty place. He then looked down upon the earth and saw your tired face. He put his arms around you and lifted you to rest. God's garden must be beautiful; he always takes the very best. He knew that you were suffering; he knew you were in pain. He knew that you would never get well on earth again. He saw the road was getting rough and the hills hard to climb so he closed your eyelids and whispered: "Peace be Thine and come with me," it broke our hearts to lose you, but you didn't go alone. For part of us went with you the day God called you home.   --Rust Funeral Home, New Haven, Kentucky.

Thomas Filiatreau, I always called him Mr. Tom out of respect; was the father and local sheriff, his first marriage ended when his wife and oldest son who were going to church, his son was an ordained priest just several days, they stopped the car at a rail road crossing, with he and his mother inside, the car stalled and a train was coming, the train hit the car and both were killed. Other brothers and sisters are: Theresa, Johnny, Joe, Edna, Pat, Paul, Bill, Frankie, and Ann. Mr. Tom went on and had a second marriage, and she died within six months of marriage. I met the family while the last five children were still living at home. The name Filiatreau is an old French name. Mr. Tom passed on some fifteen years ago. It seems that the only time that all of us can get together is when a wedding or a funeral is taking place.

On the other side was Dot. She lost her first and second husbands and met and married Mr. Tom in time. Dot had three children with her first husband: Don, Rita and Ginger Comer.

Today is March 23, 2012, this story actually took place some 40 years ago in the fall of 1971 in Bardstown, Kentucky, when I started teaching in a new community and started a new educational program within that community at the Nelson County Senior High School – Distributive Education with a student organization named DECA (Distributive Education clubs of America).

To fully implement the program, it would take me three years to phase in and to have senior students in a coop program. Meanwhile, I was assigned to teach other subjects within the business education curriculum to have six offerings. One of those subjects happened to be typing (keyboarding) and in one of my classes I had the son of the local sheriff (not knowing when school started) but into school about five to six weeks this one student was talking with me (Bill) and he invited me out to have supper with the family. I never realized at the time that by accepting an invitation for dinner that night I would find a family that I needed for support, and they needed me.

During supper that night, Mr. Tom was telling me about how he asked the children several nights ago how they were doing in school. Of course, when he got to Bill, Bill only told him about five of the courses that he was taking. Mr. Tom pressed the issue and said, "Bill don't you have another class?" Then Bill said, "yes I do but the man is a mean SOB!!" Right at that time if Bill could have found a crack in the table he would have crawled into it quickly.

I soon learned that Pat (the planner) was attending the University of Kentucky; Paul (superman) was attending Elizabethtown Community College. Bill (the thinker) was a junior in high school, Frankie (easy going) was in the eighth grade and Ann (loved adventure) was in the seventh grade.

Mr. Tom and Dot had been married only several months when I first met up with them. Dot could not fill up the children when she first started cooking for them. She was an excellent cook. As for desserts, she would bake many cakes while the children were in school and freeze them later as they would all be gone in just several days. Another issue was salad dressing and mayonnaise. I forgot which one that the children would not eat (salad dressing I think) but when Dot went shopping, she would buy what was on sale and that was always the one that the children did not care to eat. She would save the old jars from mayonnaise and put the salad dressing in those jars and the children never knew the difference as they would eat the salad dressing on sandwiches, etc.

The family was very much self-contained with farm products to eat. Bill and Paul were responsible for milking the cows, as they had two to milk during part of the year as the other cow would be dry (not milking).

Dot had a big green rocking chair that she would use to take a break with the two windows up in the kitchen for a good breeze blowing to stay cool. In that process Bill would be at the barn milking the old Jersy cow and many times dot would hear some language used that no one wished to repeat as he would call the old cow "you old rip," and a few other words that I do not plan to write. I would be out for a visit and Dot, and I would listen at the window and have a healthy laugh or two on Bill and he never knew we were listening to what he was saying.

Frankie and Ann were always into it with words only about whose turn it was to wash dishes. They both would carry on so that Mr. Tom had to get involved to break it for the girls to wash dishes.

On many Sundays, I would go out to the farm and take a walk over the farm and one Sunday I found a baby pig in its nest. The sow had her litter of pigs and left this one small pig in the nest to die. Beint a farm person, I picked the pig up and took it to the house. We fed it and it felt very well and then we named it Betty. Betty was a lot of joy as she grew and grew and grew. During that summer, Dot would go out into the backyard to snap green beans for supper and Betty would lay down in front of her and Dot would prop her feet up on Betty's back.

One time Mr. Tom, Dot and I went to visit the monks and when we returned Betty met us at the end of the road, about a mile from the house. Dot rolled the car window down and said, "Betty you get on home where you belong." Betty takes off running all the way home on the side of the road! Paul and Bill loaded Betty in the cattle truck one day and took her to the stock yard in Louisville (see Betty had a bad back right leg that she favored some) but the girls ended up getting the money that Betty sold for at the stock yard that day.

Mr. Tom would often take Dot to Louisville for surgery from time to time and would ask me to stay at the house (to have a referrer of some sort) until he got back with Dot. I would go and stay for a week to two weeks at a time and help the girls cook, clean and the boys do the farm work that had to be done.

The second year I knew that family, during Thanksgiving I was helping them to kill hogs. I also had Tinker, a dog belonging to my mother and father who had gone on vacation, and I had to keep the dog. I went out to the farm and let the dog out, and as soon as I had let the dog out, he found a pile of cow dodo and rolled in it and then quickly jumped back into my car. Cow dodo was all over the car inside and had to be cleaned. I ended up taking the dog home later that day and giving him a good bath as I had to keep him for another week. That was one time I was glad to see the dog go home when my parents returned from vacation.

We went on with the hog killing and I ended up cutting my left thumb open with the back of a knife while cutting up meat to render lard from. I recovered quickly with the help of Dot and her first aid as she worked at the hospital in surgery.

Ann was a pest growing up and just not to me, but generally everyone. One hot summer day I was out visiting after supper was over and Ann would not let up pestering. I verbally warned her several times that if she did not stop that I would throw her in the cattle watering tank. It was not five minutes until I had her up in my arms taking and dropping her in the cattle watering tank. She came up with some sort of green slim all over her body and was she ever mad. Mr. Tom steps in and tells her that I warned her many times to stop, but she would not listen, and that is what you get.

One of the funniest occurrences on Ann was one Saturday morning when her father was in Louisville with Dot for surgery. She got out of bed and was in one of those moods that no one wanted to deal with. She continued into the kitchen to fix her breakfast, and she made the decision that she was going to have French toast. She did very well but the only thing that went wrong that morning was that she used a rotten egg to dip her bread in to cook to make her French toast. After she had finished cooking the French toast she smelled something that was not just right. She asked all of us to smell. Without question, we all smelled what she smelled and about that time she took a bite of the French toast, and she exploded!

Pat, Bill, Frankie and I all started laughing and laughing until we each cried and then she really got mad at all of us. Later during the day Ann cooled down and returned to her old self, and all was at peace again in the household.

Even though I moved on to a better paying job in Frankfort, I always would stop for a short visit and would even spend the night sometimes with the family over the period of some 40 years. I still keep in touch with the children of the family as they have all grown up, are educated, married, and with children and grandchildren.

Death is an essential part in our Heavenly Father's plan. With death, our spirit leaves our bodies and goes to Spirit Paradise if we have been righteous or Spirit Prison (hell) if we have not lived the commandments of the Lord. There we will wait until we are resurrected, which is the reuniting of the spirit and the body in its immortal and perfect form. This is a blessing given to all of God's children whether wicked or righteous. We will then stand at the judgment seat of God and be judged according to our works here on Earth. We will then be placed in one of three kingdoms or degrees of glory. Only in the highest kingdom can we live in the presence of our Heavenly Father and have our families forever. In order to live in the highest kingdom, we must live all the commandments of God, it's that simple. Death is not the end. Death is really a beginning – another step forward in Heavenly Father's plans for His children. Someday, like everyone else, your physical body will die. But your spirit does not die, it goes to the spirit world, where you will continue to learn and progress and may be with loved ones who have passed on.

Death is a necessary step in your progression, just as your birth was. Sometime after your death, your spirit and your body will be reunited –

never to be separated again. This is called resurrection, and it was made possible by the death and Resurrection of Jesus Christ (see 1 Corinthians 15:20-22).

God loves all of us. He wants all of us to be with those we love, and with Him again. Life here doesn't just mean to end when we die. It goes much farther than that!

I personally know that Dot will be waiting at those pearly gates in heaven for me to arrive someday and who knows when!

BACK THEN

Checking out at the store, the young cashier suggested to the older woman, that she should bring her own grocery bags because plastic bags weren't good for the environment. The woman apologized and explained, "We didn't have this green thing back in my earlier days." The clerk responded, "That's our problem today. Your generation did not care enough to save our environment for future generations."

She was right – our generation didn't have the green thing in its day. Back then, we returned milk bottles, soda bottles and beer bottles to the store. The store sent them back to the plant to be washed and sterilized and refilled, so it could use the same bottles over and over. So, they really were recycled. But we didn't have the green thing back in our day.

Grocery stores bagged our groceries in brown paper bags that we reused for numerous things, most memorable besides household garbage bags, was the use of brown paper bags as book covers for our school books. This was to ensure that public property, (the books provided for our use by the school) were not defaced by our scribbling. Then we were able to personalize our books. But too, bad we didn't do the green thing back then.

We walked up stairs, because we didn't have an escalator in every store and office building. We walked to the grocery store and didn't climb into a 300-horsepower machine every time we had to go two blocks. But she was right. We didn't have the green thing in our day.

Back then, we washed the baby's diapers because we didn't have the throw-away kind. We dried clothes on a line, not in an energy gobbling machine burning up 220 volts – wind and solar power really did dry our clothes back in our early days. Kids got hand-me-down clothes from their brothers or sisters, not always brand-new clothing. But that young lady is right; we didn't have the green thing back in our day.

Back then, we had one TV, or radio, in the house – not a TV in every room. The TV had a small screen the size of a hankerchief (remember them?), not a screen the size of the state of Montana. In the kitchen, we blended and stirred by hand because we didn't have electric machines to do everything for us. When we packaged a fragile item to send in the mail, we used wadded up old newspapers to cushion it, not Styrofoam or plastic bubble wrap. Back then, we didn't fire up an engine and burn gasoline just to cut the lawn. We used a push mower that ran on human power. We exercised by working so we didn't need to go to a health club on treadmills that operate on electricity. But she's right; we didn't have the green thing back then.

We drank from a fountain when we were thirsty instead of using a cup or a plastic bottle every time we had a drink of water. We refilled writing pens with ink instead of buying a new pen, and we replaced the razor blades in a razor instead of throwing the whole razor just because the blade got dull. But we didn't have the green thing back then.

Back then, people took the streetcar or a bus, and kids rode their bikes to school or walked instead of turning their moms into a 24-hour taxi service. We had one electrical outlet in a room, not an entire bank of sockets to power a dozen appliances. We didn't need a computerized gadget to receive a signal beamed from satellites 2,000 miles out in space, in order to find the nearest burger joint.

But isn't it sad? The current generation laments how wasteful we old folks were just because we didn't have the green thing back then.

BICYCLE TRAINING WHEELS OFF

As I was at the age of almost three, my brother, sister, and I were in the milking barn playing hide-n-seek and it was my brother's turn to find us. My sister and I just hid in the feed barrels, where our father stored corn feed. About that time our father walked into the barn and discovered us playing in the feed barrels. Our father reminded us that we were not allowed to play in the feed barrels and for playing in them, now we were getting a whipping. Our father started whipping my brother first and I ran to the house. I'm sure my little legs were really moving. Meanwhile, my sister got her share of the whipping.

I just wonder, were children in other families disciplined with the method that we were disciplined with. Were there different methods used with other children? We were never told up front why we were about to receive the punishment or anything. We were just grabbed and punished! No following up reasoning was ever given.

I was thinking that I had gotten away with playing in the feed barrels. Wrong! About that time, in the door came my father, with a branch in hand, grabbed me by the arm and started whipping me. After a half dozen licks, he stopped. He went on to say that whipping was for playing in the feed barrels and this whipping was for running away from him.

That was the day I learned two things: not to play in the feed barrels and never run when you have punishment coming. Oh, by the way, no one ever played in the feed barrels again.

CHRISTMAS LETTER

We, Kathy and Jim, thought a Christmas follow-up letter would be good to let you know what has been going on with our lives. The last six years have been challenging for Jim as he has been in and out of the hospital and has seen many doctors. Jim has a general practitioner, kidney, heart, foot and ankle, eye doctors. Most of these doctors Jim sees two to three times a month. Jim no longer drives a car. I take him to see his doctors and then I see my doctors and that keeps us on the road all the time. In 2025 Jim will see his doctor as needed. Jim's health insurance allows him to get one pair of new shoes annually as he is a diabetic. Jim's heart doctor was suspicious that he may be over medicated. Therefore, the doctor was correct and took Jim off several mediations and told Jim he should feel better in 6 to 8 weeks. Once the meds wore off from his system, the doctor was right. Therefore, I was off the walker and decided to go out to the garden and tie up some blackberry. After a while I started feeling sick. I asked Kathy to get the car and back it up to where I was so I could sit down in the back. I got into back of the car and sat down. When I got out of the car I hurt my tailbone. The next day I had to go back on the walker for 8 more weeks and I could not walk. I was down to a duck walk or waddle. It was a very difficult time walking. In talking about our health, before it was too late for us to get around, we made the decision to sell all the cattle. The cattle sold well at the market.

Even with all that has been going on we have been very blessed, as we have one of Jim's former students, Aaron Smither, who comes out to help us as we need him.

In 2016 Jim had nose cancer on the side of his nose, very close to the left eyelid and the doctor had to conduct two surgeries to get all the cancer.

At 83 it is with the knowledge I've had just about everything worked on. With everything the doctors have done, it should allow me to live a good life from this point on.

ANIMALS

I always had a love for animals of all kinds, making pets out of as many as possible. I recall one time I collected eggs in some of the smallest chickens in the world. These chickens (Bantams) had fine fur and feathers that were much like fur.

One summer I collected these eggs and set them to hatch some babies. Well, over a hundred hatched. Therefore, I put them in the brooder house to raise them to adults. As they were grown my mother found out about the chickens. She told me that I was to save all the females and kill all the males for eating purposes. As I followed through with the orders for several Saturdays that followed to complete the order.

I learned through this experience that I would never raise Bantams again because my love of animals gave additional work to do that which was needed.

I put the females in with our laying hens with hopes in the future, they would be egg layers, too.

MY LIFE

During my life, which has been great, I have had ups and downs just as others have, but I knew everything would be fine in the long run because I had my friend, God, with me and sometimes I thought for sure I would hurt Him because of some of the major bumps in the road.

In writing this book in my way of letting stress out and finally processing the events taking place in my childhood. I hope everything was for a reason or for a season. It is over and everything is behind me. Don't get me wrong. A lot of good came out of these experiences. I have never met a person I have not liked.

GOAL

When I was in the sixth grade, I had a teacher who inspired me to set a goal to become a teacher. From that point on, anything relating to teaching, I wanted to be a part of it. In the ninth grade I joined the Future Teachers Organization and continued throughout high school and college. In college I quickly declared my major in the field of education. A few years later, I had my first teaching job. All the years I was working on my personal goal that I set in the sixth grade. If I had to I would do it all again! It is hoped for any young person reading this document that you would be encouraged to set a goal for yourself and work on that goal daily.

BUDGIE

Many years ago, when my brother was learning to talk, he had problems with saying some words. The biggest was with our dog's name. We named the dog Buddie, but my brother would call him, Budgie and that is how my brother got his nickname, Budgie. My sister and I, as adults, remain calling our brother, Budgie, even though his real name was Clifford.

CANCER

As you live your life, along the way, you will have a surprise or two. I was in my doctor's office for a checkup and after the tests were in, the doctor revealed to me that I had cancer in my bladder. This was like a bomb in my head! Questions, yes, I had many and I had decisions to make. If you are the average person, you want to live.

After some time to make the right choice, I had surgery. After surgery, I did not feel right physically or with what the first doctor was saying. Therefore, I planned and scheduled for a second opinion with another doctor. This appointment came after all tests were completed. I was told that I still had cancer! Surgery was scheduled immediately. This time the doctor told me that he got all the cancer. Nevertheless, he suggested that follow up would be with treatments of chemo and radiation. Radiation treatments took place and then some treatments took a period of twelve weeks.

I did not care for the first doctor as he had no bedside manners and on one visit I was left in the waiting room for over two hours. When he did arrive, he said, "I forgot you today." The second doctor gave back my life to me as he told me on my last visit that I would not have any more problems with bladder cancer! It has now been fifteen years since I had cancer. Yes, I'm a cancer survivor! At about the same time I had a funny looking spot on my nose. I scheduled an appointment to have it looked at. Following all tests the doctor told me it was cancer, and surgery would be performed that day. In having the surgery finished I was instructed to wait in the waiting room while they ran a test to see if they got it all. In the surgery they took another layer of skin, and it tested negative.

After fifteen minutes, a nurse came out into the waiting room and told me that I needed to come back to the surgery area as they did not get all the cancer. After the second surgery, I waited in the waiting room again. This time the nurse came out and said they got it all. Yes, I am a cancer survivor twice!

In the beginning when I made the comment for treatment the doctor told me I would lose my hair, be nauseated and would lose my appetite. Well, in the end the doctor told me I was tough as none of these happened.

My brother was in the army, and my sister was at the University of Kentucky, and I would soon be leaving for college. With all the movement taking place in the family, our father had to put the farm, livestock and equipment up for sale. Naturally, all members of the family were concerned about Romie because he was so big, strong and vicious.

Finally, Daddy found a new home with Transylvania University in Lexington, Kentucky. Romie would be walking with the night watchman on campus and would be their guard dog.

Once the puppies and the adults were sold our mother would complete registration paper work on each.

All in all, as life has been somewhat a challenge; however, I had bumps in the road of travel along the way. Some of the challenges would be surgery. I've had several surgeries and they would be: appendix, gall bladder, twisted stomach from vigorously vomiting, hernia, just to name a few.

I obtained my goal of becoming a teacher with a Master's degree and beyond. I had 44 years of employment in the field of education before retirement. In talking about our United States and every time I hear our National Anthem, I become teary-eyed. I love this country and its people.

No one knows what our United States will travel in the future from 2025. Our country is failing its people and our leadership has this country in a BIG mess. Every effort has been made to lead our country.

Knowing that God is in charge of everything. YES, He is coming back soon!

A few words of wisdom

1. Be a man of your word.
2. Always finish what you start.
3. Live one day at a time and don't worry about tomorrow, for it will bring a new set of problems.

4. Nothing ever comes to you free; you have to work hard for whatever you want.

5. All my life I loved what I did, and it made me feel like I was not working.

As for my family, we were not very expressive with love, but we had **love understood**!